T0356301

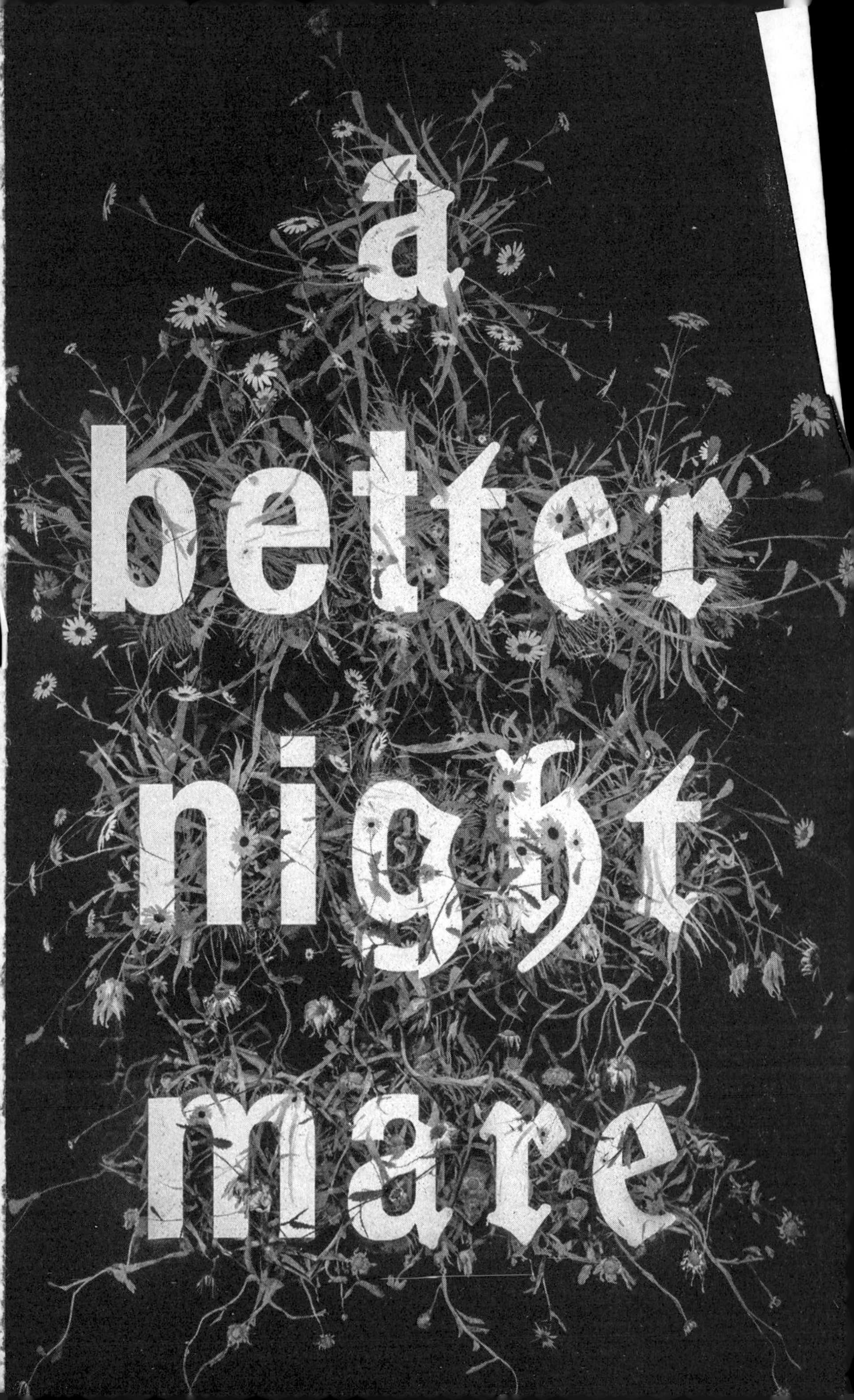
a
better
night
mare

a better nightmare

MEGAN FREEMAN

Chicken House

SCHOLASTIC INC. / NEW YORK

All rights reserved. Published by Chicken House, an imprint of Scholastic Inc., *Publishers since 1920.* SCHOLASTIC, CHICKEN HOUSE, and associated logos are trademarks and/or registered trademarks of Scholastic Inc.

Library of Congress Cataloging-in-Publication Data available
ISBN 978-1-5461-1661-5

10 9 8 7 6 5 4 3 2 1   25 26 27 28 29
Printed in Italy   183

First edition, February 2025
Book design by Maeve Norton

CHAPTER ᴏɴᴇ

I don't speak to the other girls. I don't look at them. The morning music is still being pumped through one of the speakers that line the halls and fills up what would otherwise be silence—violins and cellos and other instruments I can't name weaving together.

I follow my roommates out of our dorm and into the narrow hallway.

Single file, we trudge toward the communal bathroom and join the line of girls already waiting outside the door. Each of us carries an identical lumpy washbag in one hand and a towel in the other. The same old, brown towel I was given seven years ago when I arrived here.

I think I recognize the composer from music therapy. Bach, perhaps? I'm not completely sure, but like all the music they pump into this place, it is slow and mellow. Soft music. Soothing music. Music that's supposed to keep us calm and stop us from doing bad things.

Not that this works. Bad things happen here all the time.

The concrete floor is cold under my winter regulation socks and I am glad when it's finally my turn in the bathroom. I step through the door and blink in the sudden glare. Everything is white tiles and painted concrete. Harsh lights tint the room blue. There are stalls of toilets with no doors, a communal shower area, and a row of sinks with little mirrors hammered into the wall above.

I take my place in front of an empty sink, looking in the mirror as I fix my hair. Twenty brushes—ten times on each side just like Matron taught me to—before tying it up in a ponytail.

As a senior, I'm expected to get myself ready for the day without supervision. But Matron has trained us all well. How to wash correctly. How to brush correctly. How to tie up our hair. No looking in the mirror unnecessarily. No talking. No procrastinating. Why? *Because those are the rules,* as Matron would say.

I brush my teeth and think of nothing.

I leave the sink and another girl quietly steps forward to take my place. She starts to wash her face as I exit the room.

Back in my dorm, I deposit my washbag on my nightstand and hang my towel from my rail. I am last back and the others are already continuing with their morning routines. They fold and tuck and brush, heads down and necks bent.

I turn and make my bed. Sheets first. Each corner tucked and folded. A coarse woolen blanket draped evenly over the sides.

Next, I lay out my uniform: a white shirt and a gray skirt with pleats that falls to exactly one inch below the knee, tights that itch, and stiff black shoes. Lastly, a blazer to wear over the top. Our school crest is embroidered on one side—a bird flying above a tree. Beneath the bird, elaborate script spells out the name of our school:

WILDSMOOR FACILITY.

Three smaller words are also sewn into the crest: CARE. EDUCATION. CORRECTION.

My mind drifts as I dress myself and finish my morning chores before leaving my dorm room.

I'm outside Matron's office. I blink, registering my surroundings, surprised to find myself already here.

But time is like that at Wildsmoor Facility, bitten off in great big chunks. Whole minutes, hours, days, gone in a blink. One day it's January and the next it's June. One day I am a little kid with chubby cheeks and the next I am practically an adult, almost sixteen.

Should this make me feel something? Should it make me sad, or scared? Maybe I should care, but I don't.

Students are lining up in front of the little hatch set into the wall. I join the line, uniform in its neatness. Hands are behind backs. Girls' hair is shoulder length, tied into ponytails with a navy band. Boys' hair is short. Shirts are tucked in. No exceptions.

I fix my eyes on the hatch up ahead. I can't see who is on medication duty this morning, but I can see a pair of hands dishing out pills of all different colors and little cups of water. Mr. Peters, one of our teachers, stands on duty next to the hatch. He watches as we file past, his eyes cold and remote. Every now and again he rebukes somebody for sloppy dressing: a missed button or a loose thread or a toothpaste stain.

I step forward in time with everyone else, one place closer. By now my hands are ever so slightly shaking and my mouth salivating. Little slivers of pain shoot through my head. Doctor Sylvie says these are all symptoms of my illness coming back as the medication leaves my body. I will the kids in front of me to move quicker. I need my pills, and soon.

Finally, it's my turn.

"Emily Emerson?" A girl I know as Meera peers through the

hatch at me. Meera is almost eighteen now, the oldest girl here, but still she hasn't been cured of the same cognitive disease that affects all of us.

Grimm-Cross Syndrome. Or just "the Grimm."

We're not allowed to leave the facility until we're cured of the Grimm, but everyone has to leave at eighteen anyway. I don't know what happens to the kids who turn eighteen without being cured. I look at Meera's empty face and somewhere deep down inside feel a little prod of emotion. I don't want to end up like her. Still sick. Still here.

"Yes," I say, stepping forward. I feel Mr. Peters's sharp eyes on me. Meera turns around, rummages in a few trays, and then turns back. I hold out my hand automatically and she drops the little pills into my palm. A little white round one and a big red capsule. I take my cardboard cup of water in the other hand.

"Next," says Mr. Peters.

"No, thanks," says a voice behind me, ever so quietly.

Mr. Peters's head snaps around. "Excuse me?"

I turn to look too. A boy, younger than me by several years at least, with cropped sandy hair and wide eyes fixed on Mr. Peters. He's shaking his head and his hands are gripped in front of him, twisting into knots.

"No," he repeats, louder this time, moving his hands behind his body. "I don't need to take any more medicine. I'm better now."

Better. Better. Better—the word echoes in my head.

He turns and tries to run, pushing his way through the line. There is a series of screams. A domino effect of bodies.

A girl stumbles and lurches into me. I fall to the floor.

My cheek is pressed to the tiles. I squeeze my eyes shut and open them again, not sure what I'm seeing. The boy is running still, but his feet have somehow left the floor. He's rising into the air, as if gravity has forgotten him. He's floating. Actually floating. Like a helium balloon released from a child's fingertips.

Around me the other kids stare.

He scrabbles with his arms as he collides into the wall above the door. I can hear his fingernails scrape the concrete. He cries out, a long, keening wail that sounds more like an animal than a human. An alarm begins to clang. Doors burst open and blue-uniformed guardians rush into the room.

They grab his ankles and pull him back to the floor. One of them holds a Taser to his neck and pulls the trigger. A buzzing, crackling noise. The boy screams and arches his back. The muscles in his arms tense, pushing against and resisting the three guardians who are on him at once. A moment later he falls limp after another guardian pulls out a syringe full of clear liquid, jabbing the needle into his arm and pressing down the plunger.

The guardians lift his body between them and carry him away. His head lolls obscenely to one side and his feet drag along the floor that he was floating above only a moment ago.

I see another boy then, closer to my age, maybe a bit older. He has a head of tight-shorn curls, almost white in color. Eyes that find mine and red lips that twist so quickly and suddenly into a smile that I'm sure I've imagined it. He crouches, his hand reaching out and scooping something off the floor in front of me.

A second later and the image of this stooped, grinning figure is gone, replaced by Mr. Peters's looming face.

The alarm stops. Silence holds the air in a tight embrace for a moment before music begins to play. Mozart this time. A piano piece that rises and falls softly in the space around us. The floor is cool under my hot, thumping head. I guess it must've been mopped recently, as disinfectant stings the back of my throat.

"Miss Emerson, get off the floor immediately." Mr. Peters's thick eyebrows knit together in the middle of his forehead. His too-pale lips press together and make a thin line.

I push myself back to my feet.

"And clean up this mess," he snaps. He gestures to the floor in front of the hatch where my cup lies crumpled in a puddle of water.

"Yes, Mr. Peters," I reply. I pick up the cup and put it in the trash bin. I stare down at the floor, my eyes sweeping left and right, searching along the scuffed baseboard and between other children's feet.

"Well." Mr. Peters claps, a noise like a whip cracking, and I jump. "What are you waiting for?"

"Sorry," I say. Under Mr. Peters's gaze, I turn and walk away. There is a cupboard nearby that I know from cleaning duty has a mop and a bucket in it. I push my way through the double doors and they swing shut behind me.

I stop. I turn around and look through the window set into the door. The glass is smeared with cloth marks and it's hard to see anything clearly. Besides, I looked, and they're not there. They're gone.

My pills are gone.

For a moment I consider going back in to try to find them again, but then I see Mr. Peters yelling at someone for an untied shoelace and change my mind. He might accuse me of clumsiness or care-lessness. Or worse, lying. I've seen kids sent to isolation for less.

I walk to the cupboard. I open the door. I get out the mop.

—

I did a bad thing. That's how I ended up here.

That's how all kids like me end up at Wildsmoor Facility, by doing bad things. We stuff it down and try to hide and swallow the burning inside, but eventually it comes out.

I broke my sister's arm, that was my bad thing.

It was the year I turned eight and Amelia, my sister, turned nine. We were different in many ways. She was taller, I was shorter. She had short hair and I wore mine long. She liked soccer and running whereas I liked reading and imagination games.

But we were also similar. The same almond-shaped eyes. The same laugh. And the same fiery temper.

We argued about anything and everything, our anger flaring fast and exchanging hot and heated words. We always made up, our tempers usually burning out as quickly as they came, but for some reason this night and this argument were different. We argued without end and without resolution. Dad was furious. He yelled at us and then sent us both to bed early without anything to eat.

I fell asleep consumed by rage.

That night I dreamed of a monster that walked out of my head and came to life. It grew bigger and bigger until it filled my whole bedroom, bulging into the corners and snarling and snapping with its many jaws. Its skin was pustuled and in some parts furred and in others scaled. It glowed with its own light, as if it had eaten the moon and was now trying to burst its way back out of the monster's skin.

The monster broke out of my room with enough force that my door exploded into splinters. It stood there, casting a faint blue light across the landing, its body so large that it spilled over the banister and oozed down the stairs. A door swung open and my mother came running out of her bedroom.

"Derek," screamed my mother. "It's happening again!"

This wasn't the first time my dreams had walked. I had been hiding my strange dreams for months now, concealing my ability to set my unconscious thoughts free into the world. My parents had caught me before. Once running around the house as my dream self, chasing a puppy. And then another time when they woke up to the house covered in iridescent flowers, thick like a forest and sowed with nothing more than my unconscious thoughts.

I thought these things might make my parents smile, but instead my mother cried and my father shouted. I learned that what I could do was bad. So I stuffed it down and pretended that it wasn't there. But underneath I could feel it swelling inside me, wanting to burst out, and I knew it was only a matter of time.

When my dream monster's eyes found my sister, it lunged. Its *many* jaws snapped and globular drool oozed from its mouth. It pushed up on its hind legs and opened its chest and roared. I don't think it was ever going to hurt her, just scare her, but my sister didn't know that.

She screamed and ducked and ran. And in her panic, she fell down the stairs.

It was only then that I woke up and the monster disappeared, but it was too late. My parents had seen the monster I had made. They'd seen its drooling face and sharp teeth. They'd heard its snarls.

But worst of all, they now knew what was really hidden within me: disease and darkness. Nightmares so real that they walked the earth with flesh and bone and blood.

After that, they couldn't pretend any longer. The next night, back home from the emergency room with my sister's arm bound up tight in a pink cast, I heard them arguing in whispers. My dad's low voice rumbled through the walls and my mom's whispers crept under the crack at the bottom of my door. I knew what they were arguing about, of course. Me.

I had it. I had the Grimm. And none of us could pretend any longer that it wasn't the case.

Hours later my dad came for me. When he shook me awake, I was dozing fitfully, too distressed to sleep properly. His face was tight and unsmiling and his eyes wouldn't meet mine.

"What's happening, Dad?" I asked. "Is it Amelia? Is she okay?"

Dad shook his head. "She's fine."

I sat up and rubbed the sleep from my eyes. "What is it, then?"

"You're going on a trip," he said.

I frowned, confused. A trip? In the middle of the night? "But I don't want to go on a trip."

"You have to. You can't stay here any longer. You're—it's dangerous."

A cold, metallic taste appeared in my mouth. Dread. It began to drip down my throat, pooling like poison in my stomach. "I can't stay here?" I repeated. "What are you talking about? Where am I going?"

My dad rubbed his hand over his forehead and through his hair. "You have the Grimm, Emily. We've been denying it to ourselves for too long."

Realization hit me like a punch to the stomach and I suddenly knew without him saying where I was going: a facility.

I had heard about facilities at school from the other kids. That's what they did with kids who had the Grimm. They sent them far, far away and they never came back.

I wasn't the first one at my school, and the names of the kids who had been taken before were still whispered on the playground, rumors that passed down from the oldest to the youngest.

Ashanti, who could make the ground shake under her feet. William, who could break bones just with his thoughts. And the year before, a girl in my sister's class had been taken. Nobody knew what she'd done but it must've been bad, and after that her whole family moved away and nobody saw them ever again.

"Please," I begged my dad. "Please. It won't happen again. I can make it stop. I know I can."

But his mouth grew thinner and he pulled me from my duvet by my arm. I struggled in his grip as he dragged me out onto the landing.

My mom was standing there, watching. Her lip trembled and her eyes were glassy with unspilled tears.

"Mom!" I screamed, reaching for her. "Help me!"

She opened and closed her mouth like a fish. "You'll be okay, Emily," she said eventually. "You just need to go and get better and then you can come home again."

But I knew this was just a lie, and when I realized that my mother wasn't going to help me, I went into a frenzy. I bit and scratched and screamed. I was incoherent and unthinking. Wild.

My sister, Amelia, emerged from her bedroom. She was wide-eyed and had bed hair, peeking out from her bedroom door. "What's happening?" she cried, running forward and trying to pull me free with her one good arm. "She didn't mean it. She said she was sorry."

My father shook her off and turned to my mother. "Get me a rope."

My mother darted into the bedroom and returned with the cord from her robe. My mother had owned this robe for as long as I could remember, and even now I can still recall how she wore it in the mornings making breakfast and how it felt against my cheek when she hugged me, ever so slightly coarse from years of washing.

My father took the cord from her and used it to tie my hands behind my back. It bit into my skin and made my fingers tingle.

Amelia started to cry, her face crumpling like a piece of paper and sobs ripping through her chest.

"Get back into your room," my father said to her.

Amelia's wide, terrified eyes flickered between us. "Don't do it, Dad," she said, her words distorted by her gulping cries. "She said she was sorry. It was only this once . . ."

My father flashed my mother a look and she nodded. She pulled Amelia away, back into her bedroom, before closing the door behind her.

That was the last time I saw my sister.

Seven years have passed since that day, but it's as if the darkness that consumed me that night on my way to Wildsmoor, terrified beyond anything I'd ever felt before, has never lifted. I'm not the same person that I was.

I'm sick. I know that now.

CHAPTER two

I'm late for breakfast by the time I'm done mopping up the mess. Despite this, I do not run. Another rule I am expected to follow.

I hesitate outside the dining room doors. The slivers of pain in my head turn into little stabbing needles. My hands shake. Should I have told somebody about my missing pills? I push one of the swinging doors ever so slightly open and the clatter of cutlery and scraping of plates escapes into the corridor.

The noise sounds sharper than usual. The colors in my head dance in time. A chair squeaks and red waves wiggle. A knife clatters and I see blue spots.

I should have told somebody, I realize. Now I'm going to have to make it through the whole day without any medication at all, something I haven't done in the seven years since I arrived at the facility. I just have to hope that the medicine still in my system will be enough.

I think my dilemma through, slowly processing the day ahead. Like always, it will be drills first out in the yard, and then after that, socialization class—not ideal. But then after lunch I have art therapy and then an independent study session before dinner. Thankfully, I have no treatment sessions or work duties today. I should be able to make it to the afternoon without too many problems . . . And then after that it will be a breeze. I can go to the library, find a dark corner to take a nap.

Surely I will be all right just for one day.

I swallow the lump in my throat and push the door open completely.

The windows of the cafeteria take up nearly a whole wall and the bright light assaults my eyes. For a tiny second, a rainbow explodes in front of my vision. Blue and green spots melting to reds and oranges and purples.

Guardians stand to the left and right of the door. One of them is looking at me, his face impassive. I immediately avert my gaze. I've been at Wildsmoor for seven years now but still the guardians scare me, with their blank eyes and their polished boots and shiny weapons.

The rest of the school is already sitting down eating at the long table that stretches the entire length of the hall. Boys sit at one side of the table and girls sit on the other. They eat in silence and do not look at one another.

At the top of the hall is the teachers' table. Although they are allowed to speak, they also sit mostly in silence. Matron sits at the head, Mr. Peters to her left. After that the teachers cascade down the table in order of importance. At the very end of the table and farthest away from Matron is Miss Rabbit, the socialization teacher. Miss Rabbit is young and nervous and even we can tell that Matron doesn't like her very much.

I head for the teachers' table. As I'm late, I must excuse myself before I'm allowed to sit down.

I climb the three steps that take me up onto the raised platform where they eat. Head bent, I stop in front of the table and put my hands behind my back. I can feel their eyes on me. And although I do not dare look at them, I can also feel their scowls. I know Matron will be looking at me with her pinched expression. I imagine her voice. *Punctuality is politeness.*

"Sorry I'm late," I say. My words waver as they come out.

"Don't gnaw your lip like a rabid dog," says Matron. "Now look at me."

I look up and meet Matron's eyes. Her stare is hard and blue. "What's wrong with you, girl?" she asks.

I wait before I speak this time, swallowing hard. "Nothing, Matron. I spilled my water outside your office and I cleaned it up before I came here." Thankfully, my voice sounds more normal this time. My words are slow and measured.

"And why on earth would you do that?"

I open my mouth and close it again. Why did I do that? The morning's events are already a soft blur. The pair of floating feet comes back into my mind, and a shoe discarded on the floor. The needles in my head stab viciously and the image disappears.

"Hm," snorts Matron. "A likely story." She turns around and looks at the other teachers. "Who was on duty this morning?"

"I was," says Mr. Peters. "I can vouch for her clumsiness. One of the juniors had an episode . . . She dropped her cup in the medication line."

An episode. I conjure up the image again. A boy scrabbling in the air like a demented bird. The harsh crack of the Taser. His body floppy as a doll's as they hauled him away. I look over the teacher's heads and scout the hall, but the boy is nowhere to be seen. No doubt in isolation.

Matron turns back to me. "A Wildsmoor student is never late," she says. "Do you understand me?"

I nod my head. "Yes, Matron. A Wildsmoor student is never late. It won't happen again."

She waves a hand at me, already turning back to her breakfast. "Go and sit. But breakfast has already been served, so you won't be eating this morning. Hopefully that will make you think twice next time before being so careless."

"Yes, Matron." I turn and walk back down the steps. I make my way over to the girls' side of the table and take my seat. I pull out my chair as quietly as possible, sit down, and put my hands in my lap. On either side of me sit two girls from my dorm, Adanya and Jessica. Adanya is to my left, dark, curly hair scraped back into the Wildsmoor regulation ponytail and brown eyes fixed on her food. Jessica's eyes, green like a cat's, are fixed on nothing. Her nose twitches as she eats.

Neither seems to notice my arrival.

My gaze rests on the table in front of me. Where my tray would usually be there is only a knot in the wood that looks like a face. The face has a small eye and a big eye and a wide-open mouth, as if it is surprised, or screaming. Why have I never noticed that before?

I feel restless. Skin itching and my bones aching. My eyes flit from the face to Adanya's tray. Our breakfast is the same every morning. A small bowl of porridge, a slice of toast, and a piece of fruit. She is halfway through the slice of toast, a brown square with a red scraping of jam. No butter.

Doctor Sylvie says diet and exercise can help us control our symptoms. *A Wildsmoor student is a healthy student.* Our meals are plain but nutritious and we exercise regularly, and I know I should be glad that they look after us so well here, to help us get better. But sometimes I fantasize about the food I read about in books. The food I remember from before I came here. Fries and burgers and chocolate and slushies. Soft-serve ice cream from a truck with chocolate sauce and sprinkles. Hot dogs smothered in ketchup at family barbecues.

Next to Adanya's tray is a knife. I follow its glinting edge with my eyes. I reach out and prod it. The light wavers and gleams. Adanya looks up at me, her big eyes suddenly narrow with suspicion. She reaches out and picks up her knife, placing it back down on the other side of her tray.

"Sorry," I whisper, feeling myself blush. I look back down at the table again and knot my hands into my lap. Why did I do that?

I force myself to take slow breaths, in and out, in and out.

Within a minute the restlessness returns. I look up. Directly in front of me a boy is eating his breakfast. I focus past his head and toward the windows. Like all the windows at Wildsmoor, thick metal bars cover the glass, slicing the sunshine into fragments.

Outside, the day is yellow and glaring. In front of the window is the school garden, scraggly rows of winter vegetables basking in the sun, and beyond that is the cross-country track, a field with a muddy circle worn by traipsing feet. Behind that are the school walls. The walls are tall and lined with loops of barbed wire. Nobody can get in. But more importantly, nobody can get out.

Not that this stops kids from trying. They do try, at least one a month. I don't understand them. We are all here at Wildsmoor so we can get better. Why would anyone not want to get better?

Better. Better. Better. That word again. *Better.* It grabs hold of something in my head and twists.

For the first time in I'm not sure how long, perhaps forever, my eyes go over the wall and focus on the landscape beyond.

Wild scrubby grassland stares back at me, a pale glaring green in the late autumn sun. They don't need the walls or the wire, not really. The desolate landscape is a jailer all its own. Runners don't get very far before they're found dehydrated on a hill somewhere or come back of their own accord, tail between their legs.

I trace the sharp rise of a craggy hill, sloping up into the sky. There are rocks at the top—a cairn. For the first time ever, I wonder what it would be like to go there. To walk up that hill. To feel the cold wind on my face. To see all the world from the top.

"See anything interesting?" A voice interrupts my wandering thoughts.

I tear my gaze away from the gleaming landscape and refocus on the boy opposite me. For a moment his head is nothing but a silhouette, but then my eyes adjust and I can see the features of his face. Almost-white hair. Blue eyes. Freckles that are dotted across his nose. My stomach lurches with recognition.

It's the same face I saw this morning, peering across at me while I lay on the floor outside Matron's office. I recognize his shorn curly head and his grinning red lips. I also suddenly remember his hand, reaching out and scooping something off the floor. No. Not just something.

My pills.

I focus on the boy's eyes, blue as the sky outside. His name hangs on the tip of my tongue . . . *Gabriel*, I suddenly remember. Talking at the table is forbidden, I know that. But my head hurts and everything aches and I know I can't go much longer without my medication. I have to say something.

"Give them back," I whisper.

"Give what back?" he replies. His red lips are twisting into a smile again and his eyes light up in a way that I'm not used to, a bit like sunlight suddenly pouring out from a gap in the clouds.

I look left at Adanya and then right at Jessica. Both their heads are bent downward, still eating their toast.

I turn back to Gabriel. "I know you have them," I whisper back. Lighter than a feather, my voice is immediately drowned out by the clattering noises of the cafeteria. "Give them back or I'll tell somebody."

The boy laughs, too loud, and with the same bright edge that gleams in his eyes.

"And who will you tell?" he asks. "Matron? Go ahead." He leans back in his chair and gestures toward the teachers' table.

I feel my face grow red. I glance up at where Matron and the rest of the teachers sit. Of course I wouldn't tell Matron. I know it, and he knows it too.

"Besides, I still don't know what you're talking about."

"You do know what," I whisper back. "My pills . . ."

He tilts his head sideways and surveys me for a moment. Slowly, he reaches out and places a curled fist on the table. "What? These?" For a tiny moment his fingers uncurl and I look at the two pills nestled in his palm. A white one and a red one.

A gasp escapes my lips before I can stop it. I push my fingers to my lips and look left and right, worried that someone will have heard. *A Wildsmoor student is seen and not heard.*

"Tell me why I should give them back to you."

Why? His words confuse me. We all know why. The same reason that we are at the facility in the first place. Because we are sick. Because we need to get better. Because without them, we are dangerous.

The boy next to Gabriel has stopped eating and I can sense that he's also looking at me. I look over at him. His close-cropped hair is as dark as Gabriel's is fair and his eyes contain the same liveliness, but instead of sunshine all I can see is darkness, like the sky before a big storm. His eyebrows are drawn together and his mouth a hard flat line. For a moment his eyes lock with mine and something in my stomach twists. I am relieved when he turns to glare at Gabriel's fist. "What are you playing at?" he hisses between lips that barely move.

Gabriel turns his head a fraction and looks sideways at the other boy. He gives a bright smile. "We need to recruit more, Emir."

"Not like this."

"Why not?"

"It'll attract attention."

Emir looks up at me again. His eyes contain the same dark glare and this time his lip curls up and he shakes his head. "She's not one of us," he says. "She's just another one of Matron's mindless sheep."

They talk too fast and my brain stumbles and trips over their words, struggling to make out their meaning. But still I can see in Emir's face and feel in the sharp cadence of his words that he's insulting me.

I don't reply. I hear Matron's words in my head again, *A Wildsmoor student is seen and not heard*, and I make the decision to ignore them. Looking down, I focus as hard as I can on the knot that looks like a face in the table. I trace its whirled eyes and gaping mouth, over and over again. Definitely screaming, I think.

"See," says Emir. "Look at her."

I hear Gabriel sigh as if from a distance. "Well, how else are we going to do it."

"Perhaps not over breakfast, for one . . ."

My head gives a sudden pound and the rest of their words are lost to me. I squeeze my eyes shut. My mind is nothing but knots, pulling tighter and tighter. Seconds or minutes later, I don't know how long, the bell finally clangs. Breakfast is over.

———

After breakfast I file out into the sunlight along with everyone else. We line up in rows, forming a large square and facing back toward the facility. Wildsmoor is a big brick of a house, with huge curved windows and crumbling gray stone. Ivy covers every inch of it.

There are secluded buildings just like this all over the country, crumbling mansions, abandoned prisons, defunct factories that are one by one bought up and repurposed to house kids with the Grimm. That way society is kept safe from our dangerous symptoms.

I don't know who owned Wildsmoor before it became a facility, but I know whoever it was must've been rich. Despite the must and mold and the way everything is either creaky or cracked, there is something undeniably grand about its pillars and high ceilings and old ornate windows.

As I wait in silence for drills to begin, I can hear the ivy that covers the house rustling. Even that sounds loud today, and the sunlight isn't helping. I rub my forehead.

Matron marches out through the facility's open double doors. She sticks her hands on her hips and glares around at us all. On either side of her stand blue-clad guardians—four of them, with sunglasses and padded vests. Guns are strapped to their belts. One of them yawns.

Matron begins to lead us in our exercises. We stretch first, methodically working up through the body, toes all the way to our necks. We go into our more dynamic movements. We circle our arms and do jumping jacks and touch our toes and then reach for the sky. The whole school moves in perfect time with one another. We are windup toys, the routine so embedded it has become unconscious.

Every morning for the last seven years has started the same way. Wake up. Wash. Dress. Medicine. Breakfast. Drills. And repeat.

Today is different, however. I am clumsier than usual, my movements either too fast or a split second behind the others. Even though it's November and our breath is leaving plumes in the air, the sun feels hot on my back and my head won't stop thumping. When we stretch up on our toes, I stumble and fall into the girl in front of me.

The girl turns around, rubbing her head.

"Sorry," I say. "It was an accident."

She looks at me blankly for a moment more before turning around and continuing with the routine.

I realize Matron is staring at us and I try harder now, making sure my movements match the others'. I don't want to attract Matron's attention.

Too late, however.

She looks at me as I am filing back inside. "Emily, come here, please," she says, calling me out of line. My heart speeds up as I leave the stream of students and go to her. She takes me to one side, her hands like lumps of meat on my shoulders.

The yard is now empty of students. It's just me, Matron, and one remaining guardian who looks on from behind his black sunglasses. This one is different from the others: he's younger, firstly, clear by the baby fat that clings to his jaw. And his face is scarred white on one side, as if something burned him long ago. For once, I am curious. I trace his scars with my eyes, wondering how he got them.

Matron frowns down at me. She grips my chin and turns it this way and that. Her fingers have a grip like a vise and the pressure makes my head explode with pain. I close my eyes.

"Eyes open," she snaps.

I open them again.

"Did you take your medication this morning?" she asks.

My heart speeds up. "Of course, Matron," I say.

Liar. Liar. Liar. A Wildsmoor student always tells the truth.

"Hmm," she replies. She puts a hand on my head and pulls my left eye open as wide as it will go. She stares into it, and with no other choice, I stare back. Her eyes are a very pale blue and flecked with white, like shards of ice. My heart goes even faster, so loud in my ears I think she might hear it.

But she doesn't. With a grunt she lets go of my head, and I resist the urge to reach up and rub it. I look down at the gravel ground and put my hands behind my back. I grip them hard, to hide the fact that they are trembling.

"And you're feeling well?" she asks.

I nod my head. "Yes, I'm feeling well. I have a little headache is all."

"A headache? Nothing else? No shaking? Feeling dizzy? Sensitivity to light?"

I shake my head. "No, Matron, none of that." My answer comes out before I have time to think, and I'm surprised at how quickly I have made the decision to lie. The truth is, I'm not even sure *why* I'm lying. Perhaps it's because when I stop and think about it, there is something about Matron that makes me uneasy, afraid even. Her mean stare and red-raw hands, her rules and regulations.

But still. I'm not usually a liar. In fact, I'm not sure I've ever lied to a teacher before, and this is my second in just one day. The thought makes me anxious. Is that part of having the Grimm too? Lying? I could ask Doctor Sylvie at my next checkup.

"Well, a healthy girl like you should be able to cope with a little headache, don't you think?"

I feel a desperate urge to get away. To get inside and away from the yellow glare of the sun and, even worse, the glare of Matron's eyes. "Yes, Matron. May I go now? Miss Rabbit is expecting me for class this morning and I wouldn't want to be late again."

"You may. If your headache grows worse or you get any other symptoms, then let us know immediately. The last thing we need right now is another episode after this morning's debacle. Now off you go. A Wildsmoor student is never late, remember that."

"Of course. Thank you, Matron."

I turn, and as I walk away, I resist the urge to run.

CHAPTER three

Leaving Matron's hard stare behind, I gratefully dart through the school's front doors and quickly make my way to the classroom where I'm to have my first class of the day—socialization. Although not a typical lesson, socialization is still an imperative weekly function for our overall treatment plans. I sit down behind my desk. My partner, a girl named Clementine, is already waiting for me.

"Where have you been?" she demands, frowning at me. Clementine is not a Wildsmoor student. She goes to a girls' boarding school in the nearby village. Every other week the girls are bused over to Wildsmoor to help us with our social skills and get us ready for "assimilation back into society," as Miss Rabbit calls it. Clementine has been my partner for the past year but I'm not sure I've done much assimilating yet.

I frown, trying to remember the name of her school. My eyes drift down the front of Clementine's uniform and rest on the embroidery looped across her blazer.

"Ashbury," I say out loud.

Clementine's eyes flicker down to her blazer and back up to me. "Are you all right?" she asks.

I blush under her sharp gaze. "I was just trying to remember the name of your school . . ." I trail off.

Clementine rolls her eyes. "Christ, well, I've told you enough times. Seriously, is that part of being a grimmer? Having a memory like a fish?"

Like always, Clementine speaks too fast for me and I struggle to understand what she's just said. Something about a fish? And then she called me a grimmer. The word makes me feel dirty. I look down at my hands. I twist each finger in turn. Little finger, ring finger, index finger, and so on. And then there were Emir's words from breakfast. *A mindless sheep,* he'd said.

After a long moment, where I am focused on my fingers and Clementine is staring at me, she sighs. Her eyes flicker to the clock. "Well, what do you want to do today, then?"

Around us the other kids have begun to engage with one another, the room humming with their quiet chatter. On one side of me, a Wildsmoor boy is playing Chutes and Ladders with his Ashbury partner. On the other side, an Ashbury student is helping their partner with what looks like a math assignment. She's wearing gloves and a surgical mask, as if she's afraid we're contagious. At the front of the room, Miss Rabbit is grading papers, her red pen flicking every second or so.

While Miss Rabbit is occupied, I take a moment to put my head in my hands. Somehow my headache is growing worse, not better. It's as if the world is growing angles, sharp corners that my mind keeps grazing itself on. And the light . . . the light feels too bright.

I remember what Matron said earlier. *Sensitivity to light . . .* How did she know this would happen? My stomach lurches. What if this is a warning sign, telling me that the Grimm is coming back? I try to take a deep breath.

"Seriously," says Clementine. "Do you need me to get someone?"

I shake my head. "No. I'm okay." I look up from my hands and force myself to smile at Clementine. Her eyes blink down at me, long lashes grazing her smooth skin. Like always, Clementine looks perfect. Her green eyes are lined with gray and her lips pink and glossy. Her cheeks are the perfect amount of red.

We are not allowed makeup at Wildsmoor, but sometimes I stare at Clementine, wondering what I would look like with makeup of my own on. Red lips and lined eyes and perfect blushing cheeks. From time to time, she catches me staring and calls me a freak. She says it under her breath, as if that means I can't hear, but I do.

I know Clementine thinks I am weird, and stupid too, and maybe I am. Everything about her is so quick. Her movements are quick. Her words are quick. Her mind is quick. Being around her makes me feel like I'm in a movie stuck on fast-forward. It's overwhelming.

Or perhaps it's me. Perhaps I'm stuck in slow motion.

Clementine's eyes flick around to Miss Rabbit and then she pulls out her phone. She holds it against her chest and her thumbs move lightning fast over the screen.

This is our usual routine. I sit and do nothing, while Clementine scrolls on her phone. Sometimes pictures or videos appear on the screen and I stare, amazed at the little snapshots I see of outside life. Faces, smiling and weirdly smooth. A girl doing a dance. Dogs and cats doing cute things. Sunbathers on a white sand beach. Cities with buildings that stretch into the sky. More faces.

Clementine abruptly stops her tapping and puts the phone in her pocket. She looks up at me. "Do you want to play a game?"

I shrug.

"Let's play a game," says Clementine. She gets up and wanders over to the stack against the wall. I watch her as she considers the brightly colored boxes for a moment, before selecting one and making her way back toward me. When she sits down, she sweeps her skirt carefully underneath her legs, then crosses them in a way that nobody can see past her knees. She sits up perfectly straight. "Scrabble," she says, holding the box up.

"Oh," I reply. "I don't know how to play."

Clementine scrunches her nose up and her body collapses as she leans forward to peer closer at me. "You don't know how to play Scrabble?" I shake my head and she sighs. "Well, I guess I'll have to teach you, then." Carefully, she lifts all the different parts out of the box. She unfolds the game board, takes out a velvet bag, and tips the bag upside down. A river of plastic tiles cascades onto the desk. I stare at the pile of little beige squares. On each one is a letter.

"So the rules are simple, really."

I try to absorb as much as I can while she reviews the instructions, but all I can see is her mouth moving while a jumble of words pours out.

"Get it?"

I feel a flash of panic as I try to go over in my head what Clementine has just said. Something about making words, and then each tile being worth a different number of points . . .

Clementine rolls her eyes. "Don't worry. You can pick it up as we go along." She scrapes up the little tiles and shoves them back into the bag. She gives the bag a shake, a noise that makes my head want to explode, and then counts out seven tiles for each of us.

Following Clementine's lead, I turn my tiles over and place them into a little plastic holder.

"I'll go first," says Clementine. "That way you'll have more time to think." It seems like only a second later when a sudden smile lights up her face. "Got one," she says. Carefully, she places a row of little tiles on the game board. I notice that her nails are painted—a dark blue with tiny white flowers dotted across them.

"Nectar," she says, gesturing at the word spelled out in front of her.

I don't reply, my eyes still fixed on her nails. How did she paint the flowers so small?

"You know, like as in the stuff bees drink." She frowns and follows my gaze down to her nails. She holds up her hand, suddenly smiling again. "What? Do you like them?"

I nod my head. "Yes," I say. I look down at my own nails, neat and short and scrupulously clean, like Matron likes them. *A Wildsmoor student is clean and tidy.*

"You want me to paint yours for you? I do all the girls' nails on my dorm floor. I usually trade for it, you know, cigarettes or alcohol or whatever, but I'll do yours for free if you want?"

I shake my head. "I won't be allowed."

Clementine slumps back down in her seat. She looks annoyed for some reason, her nose scrunched up like she can smell something bad. "Are you allowed to do anything?" She waves her hand around the room. "Seems like this place is more like a prison than a school." Clementine leans forward. "And what's with those guys in the blue uniforms?"

"The guardians?"

"Whatever they're called, doesn't matter, they give me the creeps. They have *guns*. In a *school*. Do you know how weird that is?"

I shake my head, unsure of what to say.

"Well, trust me, it's weird."

I look up nervously at Miss Rabbit but she's still engrossed in her grading. "They keep us safe."

"From what?"

I think about this for a moment. *From outsiders. From each other. From ourselves.* "I don't know," I say eventually.

Clementine shakes her head. "And they're not the only weird thing. The whole school is weird. The kids barely talk and the building is just plain creepy. Have you ever seen a horror movie?"

I replay her last question, her meaning just about sinking in. I shake my head.

"Seriously?" She raises an eyebrow. "Well, this place looks like Horror Movie 101, trust me. And you lot don't help, floating around like a bunch of creepy silent ghosts, no offense."

I try to think of something to say, but clearly I'm taking too long, as Clementine smacks a hand down on the table. "Just so you know, this is what I'm talking about. You're all just so . . . starey."

I look down at the table. I feel uncomfortable under her gaze. My cheeks get hot. I don't usually think much about Clementine's visits. Like all my lessons at school, they usually pass with a soft sort of drudgery. Time becomes a river and I just lazily float along, carried by the current. But now I feel like my foot is caught on a weed and everything is bright and sharp and I can feel each second tick, tick, ticking away.

Clementine sighs. "Sorry, I shouldn't have said anything," she says. "You don't need to be embarrassed."

"Embarrassed," I repeat. Is that how I'm feeling? Perhaps. I've never really taken the time to articulate my own feelings.

"It's not your fault," she continues. "You're just sick." She reaches out and rests her hand on top of mine. For a moment neither of us says anything and her touch makes me feel better for some reason. "Wow," she says. "You feel hot, and you're shaking. Are you sure you're okay?"

I reluctantly pull my hand away. I don't bother mentioning to her that I don't feel hot at all. Instead, a bone-aching cold is slowly taking over my body. "I'm fine," I say.

"Are you—" The door swings open, interrupting whatever Clementine is going to say next.

Clementine's teacher walks into the room, a bony woman with braids and glasses. Two guardians enter the room behind her and take their positions on either side of the door.

"Okay, girls, it's time to go," their teacher says in a clipped tone. "Help your partner to clean up and say goodbye."

"Yes, Miss Reynolds," chorus the Ashbury students. They stand up eagerly and take charge of putting away the games and clearing off the desks. Only seconds later they are lining up at the door, linking arms and chattering between themselves, their Wildsmoor partners already forgotten.

Despite being subjected to visits from Clementine and the Ashbury girls for over a year now, I still can't help but be fascinated by them. The way they laugh and casually touch one another. The way they're always moving and talking. Sometimes I wonder if all other young people my age are like this. I wonder if this is another part of having the Grimm, being silent and slow.

I think about what Clementine said only minutes before . . . *you don't need to be embarrassed.* Now that she's said it out loud,

I realize I *am* embarrassed. Clementine is everything I'm not. She is lively with shiny hair and perfect nails and friends to huddle and laugh with. Next to her I am drab and dull and have nothing.

But today Clementine doesn't rush like the other girls. She puts away the game piece by piece and then she stands up. Her eyes flicker to Miss Rabbit and then to the guardians, who are still standing by the door, faces blank and silent. Clementine looks back at me. "Maybe I should let somebody know if you're not feeling well," she says in a quiet voice.

I stand up and my chair clatters backward. Luckily, the noise is drowned out by the Ashbury girls' chatter. "Please. Don't," I say, and even I can hear the desperation in my voice.

Clementine looks at the guardians again. She frowns and her lip curls up in disgust. She looks back to me, and for a moment she just looks. Then she smiles a sort of half smile. "If you say so," she says. Then she takes a step forward and wraps her arms around my shoulders. She smells like sugar and flowers and her hands press against my shoulder blades.

She's hugging me, I realize. The last time someone hugged me was over seven years ago, before I came to Wildsmoor. It's such an unfamiliar feeling that I forget that I'm supposed to wrap my own arms back around her. Before I know it, she steps away. "Well. Bye, Emily," she says.

"Bye, Clementine."

Clementine joins the line and links arms with one of the other girls. She whispers something to the girl, who then looks in my direction. Her friend has short blue hair, and thick black eyeliner rings her eyes. She looks at me quizzically for a moment, and then whispers something back to Clementine.

Their teacher, Miss Reynolds, claps her hands. I know what's coming next—every week she makes a variation of the same speech. "Girls," she says. "We're not going anywhere while you continue this gossiping. Honestly, I'm embarrassed at your behavior. Maybe you should take an example from your Wildsmoor friends; they clearly understand how to behave." She gestures toward us like she always does, and like always, we stare back blankly. The Ashbury girls also play their part, quieting down to a low hum of whispering and giggling. Their teacher turns to the front of the room. "Thank you, Miss Rabbit. Still on for our trip next week?"

Miss Rabbit smiles and nods. She half stands up behind her desk, hovering in a sort of squat position above her chair. "I . . . uh . . . yes, of course." She nods a little bit more.

"Let's go, girls," says Miss Reynolds and, after a little bit of tutting and head shaking, leads them from the room.

The classroom faces the driveway in front of the school, and I watch as Miss Reynolds crunches out onto the gravel, leading the Ashbury students across the driveway to where a bus sits waiting. The bus gleams, new and shiny with fresh paint. Across the side reads ASHBURY ACADEMY FOR YOUNG LADIES. The Ashbury students clamber up the steps and disappear, followed by Miss Reynolds.

The Ashbury kids line the windows as the bus begins to move, making a slow turn until it's facing the gates set into the barbed fence. Although I can no longer hear them, it's clear that they've already given up on being quiet. Their heads are bent toward one another, mouths moving with chatter. I can see Clementine and her friend with the blue hair again, their heads bent toward one another, so close that their hair entwines. I wonder what they're talking about. I wonder what it would be like to have that much to say.

Suddenly, the friend laughs, throwing her head back, and at the same time, something else grows alongside the embarrassment. Another feeling, which seems to go hand in hand with it but has a sharp sweet ache that makes my stomach pang.

Longing, I slowly realize, or something like it.

The feeling moves from my stomach to my heart, which suddenly feels swollen, fat and turgid and too big for my chest. It grows arms, reaching out and grasping, grasping, grasping. Because the truth is that I long to be like the Ashbury girls. I long to have their life. I long to be folded into the laughing chatter of Clementine's world and be the one she whispers secrets to.

But even if I do get better, even if I do leave Wildsmoor, I will never live a life like Clementine's. I am a *grimmer*. I am *dangerous* and *unstable*. A *sheep*. But worse than that, I am an *embarrassment* . . . Somebody to be pitied, perhaps, but not made a friend of.

This realization is almost too much to bear. I want to jump up and run or scream. I grip the corners of my desk, trying to stop the sudden flood of emotion overtaking my whole body. I am shaking and I can't stop.

What is happening to me?

I squeeze my eyes closed, blocking out the view of the bus through the window. I force myself to take deep breaths, in and out again. This is why I need my medication. If somebody like me, somebody with the Grimm, gives in to their emotions, it's dangerous. Really dangerous. I could have an episode. I could hurt somebody again . . . like when I hurt Amelia.

34

Music starts, a tinkling piano piece that fills the room—one of Beethoven's piano concertos. The other students begin to move around me, pulling out chairs and picking up their schoolbags. The silence is filled with the noises of scraping chairs and the gentle thud of footsteps. I exhale a trembling breath of relief. First lesson is over.

CHAPTER four

I sink thankfully into an armchair. The chair is soft and sagging and it envelops my body as I sit down. It smells like old things, dust and mold and something bitter. I rest my hot head against the cool cotton and take a deep breath. The smell is comforting in its familiarity.

Around me there is nothing but the gentle quiet of the library. Somewhere nearby, books thump as they are stacked up and soft footsteps tread across the old wooden floors.

But here, in my little corner, there is nothing but me and my chair. Nobody tends to come this far into the library. This is partly because the books here are old and rotting and full of uninteresting things, but it's also because the shadows and dust are thick here. Just aged chairs and peeling wallpaper, and me.

After socialization, the rest of the day was just as difficult. All through math my head thumped. During lunch, each mouthful felt like it might come back up. In art therapy I couldn't focus and my hands shook too much to hold the paintbrush. My thoughts raced backward and forward, reliving certain moments over and over . . .

My pills in Gabriel's hand and my cheek pressed against the cool tiles. The way Emir looked at me, his eyes full of thunder and lip curling. His words . . . *She's not one of us* . . . Matron's eyes boring into my own. The Ashbury girls with their bright faces and laughter.

And worse than the images are the feelings that go with them.

Fear. Embarrassment. That horrible longing for a life I cannot have.

Now, thankfully, in the cool calm of the library, the feelings finally subside. Ignoring the book on my lap, I sink deeper into the chair. I close my eyes and let my mind wander. I drift off.

A shadow falls over me and I open my eyes.

I blink, once, twice, trying to clear the haze from my eyes. A figure stands in front of me. It's one of the boys from breakfast, I realize. Emir, the one with the dark hair and glaring face.

For a moment I am still lost in the fuzzy haze of sleep, and my eyes trace over his body, taking him in in parts. Dark hair. Dark eyes. His school blazer, slightly too big for him. His shirt, untucked. I stare for a moment at the crumpled white cotton.

A Wildsmoor student is clean and tidy.

I struggle out of the depths of my chair. There is something wet on my chin. Drool. The embarrassment I felt earlier under Clementine's sharp stare returns and I feel my face flush. Quickly, I wipe my chin and hope he didn't see. "What are you doing here?" I mumble, looking down at where my book still rests in my lap.

"What?" he says, his voice harsh, with an edge I am not used to. Again I feel a flash of the same feelings from earlier. Shame and embarrassment that I am who I am, dull and stupid and sick.

But why? another, quieter part of my brain says. Emir isn't like Clementine; he is a grimmer like me. I sit further upright and force myself to meet his stare. "What are you doing here?" I repeat, trying to mimic the sharp edge that somehow weaponizes his words.

But Emir doesn't answer my question. Instead, his eyes flicker down to the open book on my lap and back up to my face. "That interesting, huh?"

His reply confuses me. "Excuse me?"

"The book. You're asleep so I just thought . . ." He trails off. "Doesn't matter." He nods at the open book on my lap. "What are you reading?"

The question hangs in the air between us. But I don't want to answer his questions, I want him to go away and leave me alone.

"Do you like to read?" Another question.

"Does it matter?" I reply.

Breaking eye contact, I close the book and look down at the front cover. *Deciduous Plants of England*. There is a picture of a tree on the front. The truth is, I don't even remember choosing this book; I had just grabbed it at random from one of the shelves.

My eyes are drawn away from the book on my lap and to Emir's hands. For some reason he is wearing gloves, but not like the gray woolen gloves we all wear in winter; instead, they are black and made from a material that shines.

I frown. "Why are you wearing gloves?" I ask. I look back up at his face and his eyes flash, the thunder from this morning briefly returning. His mouth does that curling thing again.

"Does it matter?" he responds.

It takes me a moment to realize that he has stolen my words from earlier and thrown them back at me. I grip the book in my hands, feeling the wrinkled edges imprinting into my palms. Is he mocking me? It's been so long since I've had to think about such things that I can't be sure.

The sound of a door opening and slamming shut interrupts us. I look past Emir to see Mr. Caddy, the librarian and English teacher, standing outside a door I've never noticed before. He locks the door behind him and places the key on the top shelf of a book trolley that is sitting to one side. He looks up and sees us. Suddenly, he scowls, his lined face creasing into disapproval. He emerges out of the gloom and stops. "What are you two doing back here?" he asks.

"Reading," says Emir, holding up a book that I hadn't noticed before.

For a long moment Mr. Caddy stares at us suspiciously and I look back, rearranging my features into what I hope is a blank expression.

"Well, as long as you're behaving yourselves," he says. Then he hobbles off, heading back toward the front of the library.

"You should go," I murmur as soon as Mr. Caddy is out of hearing.

"Not yet."

"It's against the rules and you know it." *A Wildsmoor student doesn't fraternize with members of the opposite sex.* Rule number five of the lengthy list I was made to memorize in my first week at Wildsmoor.

But Emir shakes his head. "Mr. Caddy? He's not going to do anything . . ."

My eyes flick back down to the book in his hand, all thoughts of his gloves suddenly forgotten. "What is that?" I ask.

"This?" He lifts up the book. "It's a book," he responds. This time the mocking in his voice is clear, even to me.

"I know it's a book . . ." I shake my head, frowning. "But what sort of book?" I can't tear my eyes away from the cover. Splashed across it is a creature that I've never seen before. It's hideous, with the head of a wolf, a furred body with skinny legs, webbed feet, and—curling from one side of the page to another—a scaled, snakelike tail. A red cloud pours from its open, snarling mouth. Whatever the creature is, it reminds me of something, although I can't think what.

"It's a collection of old stories," says Emir. "Myths, they used to call them."

"So . . . fiction, then?"

Emir nods and shrugs. "Sort of."

We have fiction books in the library, of course, but I don't like to read them. All fiction in the country has to strictly adhere to regulations, but for us with the Grimm, our list of approved literature is even more narrow. The books on our shelves are always about kids on the outside, who are healthy and free from the Grimm. They live ordinary lives where very little seems to happen. They fall in love and they fall back out. They go to school and have friends. They fight with their families and then they make up again.

But this. This book doesn't look like the other ones. "What is that?" I ask, pointing to the creature on the front cover.

Emir looks at the cover. "It's a chimera," he says slowly.

"A chimera?" I frown in confusion. I've never heard of a chimera before. "Where do they live?" I ask.

"Only in books," he says.

I am confused by his answer and I wonder if he's mocking me again. I look at his face but there is no hint of the sneer from earlier; instead, he's looking at me intently, as if to gauge my reaction. I think about his reply a moment longer . . . *only in books*. "So . . . they're made up? Imagined?" I ask.

He nods.

I take another long moment for this to sink in. Even before I came to Wildsmoor, I'd never seen or read a book like that.

"What's wrong?"

"You're not supposed to be reading that kind of . . ." I trail off and shake my head. Emir should know as well as I do that imagining things is not good for kids with the Grimm. Doctor Sylvie explained to me once that our imagination was part of the problem; we have too much. Our neurons fire too hard, making us delusional and prone to dangerous outbursts. It's even in the name of our condition. *Adolescent hyperalucinitus.* Not that anyone ever calls it that. Grimm-Cross Syndrome is what it's more commonly known as, named after Professor Grimm and Doctor Cross, the two men who discovered our condition. And even then most people just shorten it to "the Grimm."

"Would you like to read it?" Emir asks. "I could lend it to you?"

I slowly shake my head. "I don't think so." I know on instinct that there is something very wrong about this book. I know without knowing that it is forbidden. But still, I can't take my eyes off it. I think I finally know what the red cloud coming out of its mouth is: *fire.*

A creature with the head of a wolf and the tail of a snake that breathes fire.

"Where did you get it?" I ask, my palms suddenly hot and uneasiness stirring in my tummy.

"It doesn't matter," says Emir. He shoves the book inside his blazer. He takes a step toward me. And then, before I can pull away, he reaches down and takes one of my sweaty hands in his gloved one. The contact is so unexpected I just sit there like a stunned rabbit. He turns over my hand and gently opens up my fingers. Then with his other hand he presses the pills into them. My missing pills—one red and one white.

I close my fingers and snatch my hand to my chest. My heart suddenly speeds up. "You had them," I say.

Emir nods.

I shake my head. "But Gabriel said . . ."

"Gabriel is an idiot," cuts in Emir.

"But why are you giving them back to me?"

"It should be your choice if you take them or not. Not anybody else's."

CHAPTER *five*

It's past curfew, and the room is deep in shadows. For the first time in seven years, I haven't fallen asleep at lights-out. I'm awake. Wide, wide awake.

For some reason, I still haven't taken my pills. Instead, they are still tucked into the pocket of my school blazer, my dirty little secret. *A Wildsmoor student always tells the truth.* Except they don't, not always. Gabriel and Emir don't tell the truth. And nor do I, apparently.

What am I doing? I should just go and take the pills so I can fall asleep and get some rest and go back to normal. But I don't do that.

Instead, I think of Clementine's nail polish, and how I should have hugged her back.

I think of the thunder in Emir's eyes.

As the night grows deeper, so do my memories. For the first time in a long time, I start to think of my life before Wildsmoor. I think of my old school with its red, crumbling brick and disinfectant smell. I think of the playground games, hopscotch and hide-and-seek. I think of my mom. My dad. My sister, Amelia. I remember the terror on her face as she looked at the nightmare I'd created, and I wonder if she still thinks about it. I wonder if she ever forgave me.

I sit up in bed and look around the room. There are four other girls in my dormitory. Adanya, Jessica, and two other girls whose names I don't know, even though we've been roommates for at least a year now.

Adanya's bed is empty. This doesn't surprise me particularly. Sometimes we have to spend a night or two in the treatment rooms for assessments or monitoring if they are trying out a new drug.

The others, however, lie perfectly still in their sleep, just little bundles of shadows and blankets in the darkness. I can hear their breathing, soft little inhales and exhales. Other than that, the only sound is the noise of the radiators. Like everything at the facility, they are ancient. They gurgle and creak and clang all through the winter.

I swing myself out of bed and my feet land on cold wood. Despite my thermal pajamas, I shiver. I pad my way over to the window. Reaching up, I take hold of the thick curtains and gently pull. They slide open, revealing a gap through which I can look out into the night.

A bright round moon sits in the sky above. Our dorm room is at the rear of the house and backs onto nothing but tangled woodland. The moonlight rains down from the sky and turns the branches silver. Everything is still and shining and perfect.

It is so beautiful that for some reason tears come to my eyes. I've heard people talk about nature's beauty before. Pastoral poetry is considered a safe area of study for those with the Grimm, and I've studied poems in class that go on and on about it. Pathetic fallacy, metaphors, imagery . . . I know all the grammatical terms for how the poets describe the world. I've been taught to memorize and recite. I know their names and what years they lived. But I never really understood what the big deal was.

Now I think I understand.

In the moon's silver light, the world is transformed and so am I. I feel awake. Alive.

I'm not sure how long I stand like that, staring out the window. But by the time I decide to try to get some sleep, my feet are like lumps of ice and my hands stiff with cold.

I clamber back into bed, and I am glad to find that my sheets are still warm. I bury myself gratefully under the thick blankets. I tuck my hand under my pillow, and that's when I feel something.

Confused, I sit back up, lifting my pillow away and staring at the hard thing underneath it. A book. A hardback with an old torn cover. I squint through the gloom and just about make out the picture on the front. A creature with claws and teeth and plumes of fire coming out of its mouth. A chimera. Emir's book.

I throw the book back onto the sheets, my fingers burning as if the fire on the cover is real. I pull my blankets back slightly, allowing moonlight to spill across the cover. The chimera's face snarls up at me. Once again it reminds me of something, although I don't know what.

I reach out a hesitant finger and trace its body, scales and fur and cloven feet. There is something very, very wrong about this book. I know that a book like this would never be approved of, even for kids who don't have the Grimm. If this was found in my bed, I would be in serious trouble . . .

Is that why Emir put this here? To get me into trouble?

Suddenly, I feel a flash of something unfamiliar, deep in my gut. A feeling that makes me want to snatch up the book, march into the boys' dorms, and throw the book back in Emir's face. Anger, I realize, although it's been a long time since I've felt it so sharply.

I stuff the book down the crack between my mattress and the bed frame. Tomorrow I will get rid of it. Give it back to him. Or toss it out the window and let it be eaten by the tangled teeth of the woodland below.

Either way. Get rid.

I close my eyes and finally I fall asleep.

———

First, there is nothing but blackness, but then come flickers. Movement. Pictures. Faces. Colors.

I am dreaming.

I stand once again in my dormitory, but this time there are four bodies bundled under their blankets. Jessica and the two girls without names. And also, somehow, myself.

I have forgotten to close the curtains and the moon's silver light pours into the room. It bounces off the walls and lights up the shadows. I look down at my sleeping face. Unremarkable, really. Just muddy hair in a mussed-up braid. Eyes and a nose and a mouth, blank with sleep.

I drift away from where I lie, past Adanya's still-empty bed, and to the window. I look over the tangled woodland below. Somewhere deep among the trees, a light flickers. Somebody, or something, is in the woods. Curiosity tugs in my chest.

The world flickers. The dream changes.

Shadows and gloom surround me. I am deep within the woods. Above me, tangled branches try to hold out the moon, their fingers laced against its silver glow. Below me there is nothing but darkness.

Hushed voices sound from somewhere in the trees. I walk or

46

float, I'm not sure which, toward them. A fire flickers in the distance and I follow its yellow light.

Finally, I am close enough to see who the voices belong to. Figures stand around a fire, holding their hands out to its flickering flames. Masks cover their faces. There is a fox and a clown and a feathered one covered in winking jewels. The other two face away, only their backs visible.

"We need more people," says one of the ones with their backs to me.

The fox shakes their head. "No. It's already too risky."

"But . . ."

I step from between the trees. A furred face turns toward me. The fire spits and crackles. "Who are *you*?" asks the fox. Their voice strikes a little bell inside me, familiar somehow.

The two figures facing the fire also turn around. Like the others, they're wearing masks. One of them has a long, curved beak and black holes for eyes. The other is concealed by white porcelain, etched with twisting gold. Red paint dots and swirls across the china, marking out lips and frowning eyebrows.

The one with the curved beak steps forward. They reach up and grip the bottom of their mask . . .

"Don't be stupid," says the one in the white mask. He reaches out and grips the other's shoulder with gloved fingers. My eyes settle on the hand, recognition stirring through the haze of sleep.

But the figure wearing the beak mask shakes off the hand and takes another step toward me. He tugs up his mask. Underneath the mask his face looks contrastingly fragile: high, sharp cheekbones and a pointed chin. Shadows pool where his eyes should be and hang around his lips, his face no longer disguised by a mask but by shadows instead.

"Emily?" he says.

I recognize his voice. It's the boy from breakfast—not Emir, but the bright-eyed one who stole my medication. At least, I think it is, but in the shadows of the woods he looks different. There is no smile on his face; instead, his eyebrows are drawn together, holding in the shadows that obscure his eyes. His face is sharp and pointed, more animal than human.

"Gabriel," I murmur back, my voice as ghostlike as my body.

The firelight flickers and his eyes gleam. His lips part. I can't help but think there is something *hungry* about his expression. He takes another step forward and this time I take a step back. "What are you doing here?" he says.

I open my mouth to reply but no words come out. I feel insubstantial, as light as air. I look down at my body. It's flickering, like a lightbulb with a faulty connection. I hold up a hand and watch as it glimmers in and out of existence. I realize that I'm no longer breathing, the air stolen from my chest. I reach up to grip my throat, to claw at the air, but my hands fade into nothingness.

"What *is* this?" the fox says.

"Shush," says another. "I think she's going."

I look down at my body and see nothing but dirt and twigs. I'm disappearing. Heat and panic overwhelm me. I twist and turn, trying to find my solidity again.

The woods melt around me until there is nothing but darkness.

I wake with a start. My blankets are twisted tight, covering my mouth and pinning my arms to my sides. I struggle my way out of them and sit up. I am sweating so much that when I wipe my fore-head my hand comes away wet.

"Just a dream," I tell myself. "It was just a dream." I force myself to lie back down and close my eyes again. After what feels like a long time, I fall asleep. This time there is nothing but darkness, and by the time I wake up in the morning, my dreams are forgotten.

CHAPTER six

I wake up to the feeling of somebody shaking me. My eyes snap open and I sit upright. Adanya is looking at me. "You've overslept," she hisses, glaring at me with wide eyes.

I look around and realize she is right. The room is empty. Music is still being pumped into the room, however, a violin's soft crooning, another Bach number that I can't quite remember the name of.

I scramble out of bed and Adanya shoves my washbag into my hands. "Hurry up. You'll have to make your bed when you come back." I follow her from the room, tripping over my own feet.

We join the girls lining up for the bathroom. "Thank you," I whisper at the back of Adanya's head, but she ignores me.

When it's my turn at the sinks, I stare at myself in the mirror. There are deep shadows under my eyes and a crease between my eyebrows from where I must've been frowning in my sleep. My skin is pale and blotchy. I don't look like myself. I don't look well.

I am the last girl to leave the bathroom. When I get back into the dorm room, the other girls are nearly dressed. I hurry to my bed and begin to tuck and fold my sheets. Jessica, who has the bed next to mine, stops putting on her shoes and stares at me. I smile at her. "Slept late," I explain.

Her eyes widen, as if something I've said has startled her, then she turns back to her shoelaces. She ties each one with painstaking care. I make my bed in record time and am already half-dressed before Jessica has finished fastening her shoes.

Only Adanya is left in the room. She walks over to the door and pauses, as if she has forgotten something. She turns and looks at me. She is glaring at me again, as if she is cross. "Too fast."

"What?"

"You're too quick," says Adanya. Then with one last glare, she turns around and walks from the room.

I pause, briefly confused, before pushing her words from my mind. I don't want to be late again.

I hurry through the facility, joining a stream of other kids all heading to Matron's office for their medication. "Excuse me," I say, ducking in and around them.

When I arrive at the waiting room outside Matron's office, I'm surprised to find that despite my late wake-up, I am by no means near the back of the line. I twist around and watch as the other kids still file into the room. I look at their faces in turn. Some I recognize from classes, some I don't. We are a mixed bunch. Different in age. Some rich, some poor, not that it matters here. From all corners of the country. A mixture of colors and ethnicities.

Despite this, as I look at the line of children, they are somehow shockingly alike. The same hairstyle. The same uniform. The same dull eyes. The same way of standing, hands behind backs and square shoulders. We have been pruned to be the same shape.

Even though I am openly staring, nobody looks back at me. They look resolutely forward, their eyes fixed on the little hands in the hatch, dishing out pill after pill. After all, that's the one thing we have in common here. The Grimm.

I force myself to mimic their pose, to put my hands behind my back and stand up straight. But today this is a struggle. The head-ache and the shaking and the hot and cold flashes from yesterday are gone, but now my mind races. Every ten seconds or so my head spins and I get dizzy. I slip out of my skin before slamming back into it.

"Sleep well last night?" whispers someone behind me.

I turn around and my stomach lurches as Gabriel's piercing eyes stare into my own.

Suddenly, I remember my dream from last night. Him in the woods, firelight flickering at his back and his face wolflike and hungry. The other masked figures grouped around him, furred and feathered and smoothed-out faces with nothing but black holes for eyes.

I register his words. *Sleep well last night?* But that was just a dream . . . wasn't it?

A chill runs down my spine and my heart begins to thump. I open my mouth. *What do you mean?* I want to ask. But I catch myself at the last moment.

I look over at where Miss Rabbit is standing on duty. She has a dif-ferent approach from Mr. Peters, and she smiles at each student as they collect their medication. She pats the youngest children on the head and takes the time to help them with their pills.

Miss Rabbit isn't like Matron or Mr. Peters or some of the other stricter teachers, but even so, talking in line is forbidden, everyone knows that. *A Wildsmoor student is seen and not heard.*

Ignoring the pull of Gabriel's stare and the beating of my heart, I force myself to put my hands behind my back and focus on the hatch up ahead like everyone else. Remembering last night's dream has made my agitation worse, and I twist my sweaty fingers behind my back.

"It'll get easier," whispers Gabriel behind me. "You're just in withdrawal right now."

In withdrawal. I haven't heard that phrase before, but despite that I think I know what Gabriel means. My medication. My pills from yesterday are still tucked in my blazer pocket. The line moves forward again and I step in time with everyone else.

"Under your tongue," whispers Gabriel.

I frown, confused. I want to ask him what he means but I'm too close to the front of the line now. If I speak or turn around, then Miss Rabbit will notice. The line slips away and I step forward, again, and again, until it's my turn.

Meera is handing out the pills again. "Emily Emerson?" she says. I nod and she hands over my pills and my cone of water.

Time suddenly slows. I stare at the little pills in my palm. The boy whose turn it was before mine is standing to one side. I watch him. He takes his pills, slowly bringing them to his lips and then drinking his water. His eyes are dull and his face smooth, devoid of emotion. His hair is cookie-cutter neat. He puts his cone in the bin and leaves. I step forward into the now-empty space.

I look down at the bin. It is overflowing with little cups. I look back at the pills in my palm.

"Everything okay, Emily?" asks Miss Rabbit with a smile.

I nod and put my pills in my mouth. I lift the cone to my lips and drink.

CHAPTER Seven

Once I am out in the corridor, I open my mouth and spit my pills into my palm. Quickly, I shove them into my blazer pocket, where they join the other ones. My heart is racing and the medicine has left a bitter taste in my mouth.

I had been planning on taking my medication as usual. But there was something about the boy in front of me that had made me pause. *Mindless sheep . . .* It's the pills that do it to us. I could see it in the boy's dull eyes.

At the same time, I had suddenly understood what Gabriel meant. *Under your tongue.* So I did it. But this time it was *my* decision. I fight down the fluttery feeling in my stomach. The feeling that tells me I'm doing wrong. The feeling that makes me want to run away as fast as I can.

A Wildsmoor student always tells the truth.

A Wildsmoor student is always obedient.

A Wildsmoor student strives to get better.

I push through the double doors into the dining hall and join the food line stretching around one side of the room. The clear weather has passed and rain is pitter-pattering on the thin windows. It is only breakfast, but the room smells like dinner. Friday is chili night. Onion and garlicky smells float from the kitchen.

I collect my tray, go to my seat, and sit down. Adanya and Jessica are already there, eating their porridge. Across from me and one seat to the left is Emir. He does not acknowledge my arrival and instead looks resolutely down at his tray. His face is blank other than a tiny pucker between his eyebrows. In one gloved hand he holds a glass of orange juice . . .

Once again I think of my dream from last night. The figure in the white china mask was also wearing gloves. A chill strokes my spine again as I wonder what it all means.

A moment later and the chair opposite me is dragged backward. Gabriel sits down.

I ignore him and concentrate on eating my breakfast. Yesterday, I could hardly eat, but today I am starving. I get through my porridge in about ten seconds flat and move on to my toast.

"Hungry much?"

I look up at Gabriel. Amusement tugs and twists at his lips.

As I swallow the lump of chewed-up toast in my mouth, my cheeks grow hot. I feel the same sudden rush of feeling that I felt yesterday. It's much easier to recognize this time, however—*embarrassment*. But this time it's also followed by a tug of something like anger. No, not anger, *annoyance*.

Why does this boy think he has the right to mock me?

Despite this, I do not reply. Talking at the table is forbidden, and I think I've broken enough rules for one day already.

"Seriously," continues Gabriel, "you need to *slow*." He puts such a heavy emphasis on the last word that I pause for a moment. I remember that Adanya said the same thing to me back in the dorm. *Too fast.*

Suddenly, I realize. I look around. I have nearly finished my food, but everyone else has barely made a dent in it. Their arms move steadily but slowly, each bite carefully chewed and swallowed. Their eyes stare at nothing.

"Watch," says Gabriel. His eyes unfocus and stare through me. He picks up his toast and takes a little bite, then he chews for what seems like forever before he swallows and takes another one.

I nod to show that I understand what he means. I force my movements to slow down, matching the pace of everyone else around me. How have I never noticed before how slow everyone moves? So, so, so slow. Unbelievably slow. Like snails in their seats.

A moment later and I feel a horrible squeezing feeling in my chest. What if they're *not* too slow? What if I actually am too fast? Perhaps this is my neurons overfiring, like Doctor Sylvie said they would.

My mind spins and the world does a sudden lurch. My heart races. My hands and feet tingle.

What is happening to me? I feel like I'm about to pass out.

Emir is now also looking at me. He looks angry again, the pucker between his eyes deepened to a furious frown. His expression makes whatever is going on inside my body worse. I can't breathe. I try to gulp in more air but it's like my lungs have shrunk. Whatever I do, I can't get enough.

"Don't do that," says Gabriel, glancing up at the teachers' table and then back at me.

"I think I'm dying," I gasp back at him. "Or having an episode . . . I should go to Matron." I stand up.

"That's a terrible idea," says Gabriel.

A hand yanks on the back of my blazer and pulls me back into my seat. Adanya glares down at me. "Don't be ridiculous," she whispers.

Her gaze moves to Gabriel and she glares at him just as furiously. He shrugs in response. I can't help but notice the familiarity of their interaction . . . How do they all know one another so well?

I remember the dream again, the masked figures staring at me with their eyes like endless pits . . . But it was just a dream. Wasn't it?

I try to struggle out of my seat again and my chair squeaks and clatters on the floor. The other kids nearby are starting to stare. Their hands pause halfway to their mouths, eyes watching with mild interest.

"Calm down," says Adanya, still holding on to my blazer, stopping me from standing up. "You're just having a panic attack."

"A panic attack?"

"Yes, you idiot."

"Look at me," says Gabriel. "Copy my breathing." He exaggerates each breath he takes, his lips pursed and hands showing the movements of his chest.

I copy him, forcing my breathing to slow. In through my nose and out through my mouth, just like in meditation classes. I meditate at least twice a week as part of my treatment program, but I've never really understood the need for it before. Now I think I get it.

Panic is like the chimera on the front of Emir's book. It comes for you with little warning, terrifying and monstrous and breathing fire into your veins, threatening to destroy every part of you.

Except I'm not dying. And the chimera isn't real. Slowly but surely, my heart stops racing and the world stops spinning.

"Thank you," I eventually whisper. I look up at Gabriel, but he's not looking at me, he's looking between Adanya and Emir, an expression on his face that I'm not sure the meaning of. Adanya and Emir's feelings, however, are clear to read. Anger. The muscle in Emir's jaw keeps jumping as if he's clenching his teeth, and Adanya is glaring so hard at Gabriel that I'm surprised he doesn't just melt under the red-hot force of it.

Again, I'm struck by the realization that they know each other much better than the rest of us. That there's something between them all that I don't understand.

Emir turns his gaze to me and once more I'm subjected to his dark cloud look. I look away, feeling embarrassed once more.

Panic. That's what I've been feeling the past couple of days. Of course it is. Panic attacks or anxiety can trigger manifestations of the Grimm, and I've had whole classes on how to control the symptoms. The breathlessness. The sweating. Feeling like I want to run away . . . Fight or flight mode in all its glory.

I consider taking my pills again, but still something stops me.

A Wildsmoor student is a calm student.

But are we too calm? The girls from Ashbury aren't *calm* like us. I take a moment to look around the room and feel like for the first time I am properly *looking*. Mostly the kids are eating, their hands moving back and forth to their lips and their eyes focused on their food. But not all of them.

A boy a few seats down is sitting motionless, his arm suspended in midair and his spoon dripping porridge onto the table. His eyes are completely glazed over. A girl another few places down is rocking in her chair, her food untouched in front of her. Back and forth. Back and forth. Some are pulling funny faces. Somebody laughs hysterically and Matron's head ducks up from the teachers' table.

Her gaze settles on the laugher and narrows. Something about her gaze makes me shiver.

I have to face the obvious.

Since I have stopped taking my medication, I am changing. I don't know if this is for the better or for worse, but I know I am playing a dangerous game. I need to make sure I do not attract the attention of Matron. I need to make sure I don't get caught.

CHAPTER eight

I am exhausted. It's now been four days without pills. Four days of trying and pretending and faking. Trying to avoid Matron and my teachers. Pretending that the panic in my belly isn't real. Faking the slowness of the other kids.

Sometimes my hands still shake, and sometimes I still flash hot or cold, or my head will flash with sudden pain. But aside from this, I am starting to feel well again. More than well again . . . I am like a new, improved version of myself. My mind is sharper and faster. The world is more colorful and bright. I am amazed, and wonder at the smallest things.

I lie on top of my blankets and watch the ceiling, tracing the looped patterns of the plaster. It is too early to be in bed really, and the others are still scattered over the house. Most likely either in the library or the TV room. We are not allowed to watch television, but we have about thirty films and box sets that are deemed suitable watching for us, mostly little-kid movies and shows. I do not go there anymore. I've been at the facility for seven years now and I have no interest in watching the same ancient Disney movies over and over again.

I think for a moment about the little collection of pills in my blazer pocket. An urge comes over me to take them, but then I pinch myself, hard, until the urge goes away. I need a distraction.

I roll over and reach down the side of the bed until my fingers find Emir's book. It's wedged hard and it takes several tugs before I manage to free it from its hiding place. I know that the room is empty, but despite this, I look around and check each corner anyway. Satisfied that I am alone, I prop my head up on one hand and stare down at the front cover. I trace the creature's snarl with one finger.

I know that this book is wrong, but I need something to take my mind off the pills still in my blazer pocket, a little lump pressed against my heart. And besides, although I'm reluctant to admit it to myself, I am also curious.

I open the book and am surprised to see that it starts with an introduction. *Mythical creatures and their origins*, reads the title at the top. I skip the densely typed text and instead slowly begin to turn the pages. The first page, then the second, then the third. With each new page my heart accelerates. Page four, five, six, seven . . . On each one there is pictured a different creature, each one just as hideous as the last. Distorted eyes of different colors, scales and fur and red-raw dripping flesh.

I flick through, faster and faster. Teeth like knives, dripping blood. Horns. Claws. Wings. Animal parts distorted and exaggerated to the point where they are terrifying. I reach the end and slam the book shut. My breath is caught in my throat and I can feel my blood pumping furiously through my body, rushing into my arms and legs and making my head spin.

Perhaps Emir didn't put the book here to get me in trouble after all; perhaps he did it to scare me, as a warning somehow.

The door swings open and I quickly stuff the book down under the covers. Jessica and the other two girls whose names I can't remember file into the room. They don't even look at me, their eyes dull and fixed on their bunks. They begin to get changed in unison. Shoes first, then tights, then skirts . . . all the while staring at nothing.

A moment later and Adanya also comes into the room. Unlike the others, her eyes are bright and aware. They scan around the room, taking everything in, before landing on where I am sitting in my bunk. I stare back at her and her eyes narrow, as if suspicious.

I break eye contact, scramble out of bed, and start to get changed like everyone else. I am already half-undressed when I remember to go slow. I look at the other girls but, other than Adanya, they haven't noticed that anything is amiss.

Who cares, a little voice says in the back of my head. *It's not like Matron is here in the room with us.* I continue to get changed as fast as I like. I finish putting on my pajamas before the others and sit back down on the edge of my bed. I yawn, a sudden wave of tiredness making my body ache. Clearly the week's lack of sleep is catching up with me.

I watch as the other girls finish getting changed, pick up their washbags, and leave the room. Adanya pauses, holding the door open with one hand and her washbag in the other.

"Aren't you coming?" she asks.

I half stand up before sitting back down again. I stifle another yawn with my hand. I'm more than just tired, I'm exhausted. I look at Adanya, shrug, and shake my head. "Not tonight."

This seems to be the wrong response, as her eyes narrow again and her shoulders tense up. "You need to at least pretend to be normal," she says.

"Why? Nobody will know."

Adanya's fist clenches and releases around her bag. "Because you'll get us all into trouble."

Us.

I'm reminded of the way she exchanged glances with Emir and Gabriel the other morning at breakfast. I know that Emir and Gabriel aren't taking their medication, and I can only assume that Adanya isn't either. But how many more of them are there?

I think of my dream from the other night. What if my dream was trying to tell me something? Or warn me about something, I consider.

With one last glare, Adanya turns on one stockinged foot and leaves the room. The door swings softly shut behind her.

I lie back on my bed and roll over. Minutes later I hear the other girls come back in. There is the noise of washbags being placed back in their places, and then soft rustles as the other girls climb into their beds.

Silence falls. By the time the lights flicker out, I am already asleep.

———

The first part of the night is like falling into a void. It consumes me as my mind and body play catch-up to get some rest. A deep, endless darkness.

Later on in the night, I slowly become more aware. My consciousness flickers; I am asleep still, but I know I am asleep. For a while I just lie there, like a baby in a womb, safe and warm and knowing. But then my mind grows restless. I remember my dream from the other night, the masked people in the woods.

Curiosity starts like a spark somewhere deep inside me before growing, kindled by the images. I see their faces in the firelight. I hear their voices, muffled by their masks.

My mind snaps into sudden awareness. I stand beside my bed and immediately I understand that I am dreaming again. I look down at where my body sleeps beside me, just a soft mound of blankets with a face peeking out.

The night is far darker than the last time and the room is all but pitch-black. The only light is a line of green escaping from the crack at the bottom of the door. I can just about make out the other girls' beds and the shadowy lumps of their bodies. Unlike before, Adanya is also in her bed.

I look down at my body. Only a faint glow emanating from my skin gives away that this body is not real, nothing but an illusion dreamed up by my unconscious mind. Other than that, I am an identical copy of the Emily who still lies in her bed. Pajamas, messy bed hair, and stockinged feet.

I reach out, grasp the door handle, and pause. If I open the door, the others will wake up.

Yes. But you're dreaming, another part of me says. *Nobody will wake up because none of this is real. Besides, you don't have to obey silly laws like physics when you're not even awake.* This thought makes a little bubble of excitement form in my belly.

I forget the handle and merely float through the door instead.

I'm standing in the corridor. Emergency lights with figures and arrows on them cast a sickly green light over the walls and floor. I drift along, not bothering to move my legs and just directing my body where I want to go. Eventually, I emerge into the entrance chamber of the house. The wide staircase sweeps down to the doors below.

64

I float down the stairs, through the doors, and into the night.

The sky is thick with clouds, and without the moon, the night holds the world firmly in its grip. The house looms up behind me, a square, shadowed block. Not a single light gleams in the windows. The house sleeps.

For a moment, I see flickers of their dreams. A child pirouettes. Somebody flies over a cityscape. Another is having a nightmare; she's being chased by a faceless thing through a black void. Whatever it is, it's getting closer.

I shiver and move on.

I'm in the woods now. The shadows are so thick here that I think I finally understand what true darkness is. I am the only source of light. My body emits a glow like starlight, just a faint silvery sheen that lights up trees and roots as I drift past.

I reach the clearing where I saw the masked figures . . .

There is nobody there. Clues to their existence remain, however. A charred circle burned into the center of the clearing. A pile of logs and twigs resting up against a tree. The dirt and leaves scuffed with footprints.

But no masked figures. Disappointment settles in my stomach, heavy like I've just swallowed a handful of rocks.

Twigs crack behind me and leaves rustle. I turn around just in time to see somebody emerge from the shadows of the night and into the clearing. I expected to see the masked figures again, but instead a lone bare-faced figure stands in front of me. Emir.

He freezes, body suddenly tense. He stares at me wide-eyed across the charred remains of the firepit and I stare back.

There is something about Emir, with his dark stare and

permanently angry expression, that makes me uncomfortable. Nervous, even. But not tonight. This is *my* dream, after all. "What are you doing here?" I ask, breaking the soft silence of the woods.

"I think I should be asking you that question."

"This is *my* dream," I reply.

Emir raises an eyebrow. "Well, what am I doing here, then?"

I frown. I look again at the sooty remains of the firepit and the logs set around it, and then down at my body, still emitting its starshine glow. "I don't know," I reply eventually, looking back at Emir. "What *are* you doing here?"

"Couldn't sleep," he replies, reaching up with one gloved hand and rubbing his fingers over his dark hair. I remember how the figure in the white mask last night also wore gloves. "Emily, have you considered that this might be more than a normal dream?"

I shake my head. "What else would it be?"

"Have you ever had a dream so vivid before? So like real life?"

I try to recall a single dream from the last seven years. But I can't think of even one. I drift around the clearing. I trace the rough bark of the trees and pick up a brown-edged leaf from the ground. I squeeze it and it crumbles under my fingertips.

I get closer to Emir, and I notice how mud is splattered like a constellation up one of his pajama legs and how a thread is loose on his school coat. I notice how his eyes are dark as the night, other than a tiny gleam that is the reflected light from my own body. Suddenly, I feel uneasy.

Because of course, I have had dreams this vivid before. Back before I came to Wildsmoor, back when I still had symptoms of the Grimm.

The world grows sharper, clearer. My feet find solidity on the ground. I can feel the twigs and bark and dirt under my feet. I look down at my body. Other than a faint silvery glow, I am a perfect replica of me. I look up again at the trees and the night sky and the charred firepit, too detailed to be a regular dream.

I shake my head slowly, unwilling to face up to the possibility. But of course it makes sense: I have stopped taking my medication, and now my dreams are coming back. The Grimm is coming back.

I spin around and walk out of the clearing.

Footsteps crunch behind me. "Wait. Where are you going?"

"Back to bed." Panic moves my feet, clumsy in their haste and stumbling over roots and rocks. "This is bad. This is *really* bad."

"Nothing bad is happening, Emily."

I spin on one heel and glare at Emir, suddenly angry. "Of course something bad is happening. This is my illness coming back. That's how the Grimm manifests in me, through dreams . . . *dangerous* dreams."

"The Grimm is nothing to be afraid of . . ."

I think of Amelia then. I hear her scream. I feel the sharp pull of my mother's bathrobe, tightened around my wrists.

"Of course it is," I say.

He folds his arms. Under the trees, the gloom is too thick to see the features of his face, but I can feel in the rigid stance of his shoulders that he's glaring at me again. "Go on, then. Run back to bed like the scared little sheep you are."

I register the insult in his words, but the panic in my stomach stops me from caring. Emir doesn't understand . . . he couldn't understand. The monster that came from my dreams. My sister's cry as her arm broke.

With Emir in front of me, I am reminded of the book he left in my bed, and suddenly I understand why the creatures in the book felt so familiar to me. Suddenly, I know why they made me feel so afraid. They are monsters too, just like the nightmares that live in my head, ready to be dreamed into existence.

The panic in my stomach rears, growing claws that tear at my insides, and at the same time, a rumbling sounds deep in the woods. A loud crack shatters the peaceful stillness of the night, followed by a roar.

Emir turns. "What is that?" he asks.

Far in the distance, something huge and shining moves between the trees, coming closer with every second. It stamps and grunts and crashes through the branches. I know what it is. I try to subdue it, but I can't. As my panic grows, the beast grows closer.

"It's my monster," I say. "It's back."

"Are you doing this?"

"Yes, I am. I'm dangerous, Emir. I tried to tell you."

"Can't you stop it?" he asks.

I shake my head. "I don't know . . . I don't think so." My heart is racing. I feel frozen. My legs numb. I twist my fingers in my palms.

"You need to calm down," Emir says. "Learn some control."

"I can't." Somehow, I feel resigned to my fate. "It's coming for us."

"You need to wake up, then," he says. "Before you wake up the whole school."

I nod my head. The monster is getting closer. The monster that hurt my sister didn't have a tail, but this one does, just like the chimera on the cover of Emir's book. It waves and flicks above the treetops. It roars again.

Emir reaches out. He shakes me by the shoulders. "Wake up *now*, Emily."

—

I bolt upright, gasping. I hold my hands in front of my face. No longer glowing. No monsters. I am not floating. I am in bed, safe. The soft breathing of the other girls tells me that they are still asleep.

Across the room, somebody stirs. They sit up. "Are you all right?" asks a voice—Adanya, I realize, her voice thick with sleep and without her usual sharpness.

I nod my head and then realize she wouldn't be able to see. "I'm fine," I whisper. "Just a bad dream is all."

She scoffs, a soft huffing out of air. I hear her lie back down and then silence.

I also lie back down, left alone with my thoughts again. I feel calmer. But I can still feel it, the panic still lurking somewhere inside. It's curled up tight in my stomach, a monster in its lair. It pretends to sleep, but its eyes are open, and I know somehow that it's just waiting. Waiting for a moment to emerge, and when it finally does, chaos.

CHAPTER nine

A bus waits for us by the tall entrance gates, the engine chugging as it turns over and the exhaust emits puffs of smoke. Miss Rabbit leads us in single file out the front doors and onto the gravel. The ground crunches beneath our feet, a mixture of pebbles and fallen leaves, edges browning to gold. "One at a time, please," she says. Not that there is any reason for her to say this, as we are as sedate and silent as always.

I follow my classmates up the steps.

"Get a move on," grunts a guardian, standing to one side in the front row of seats.

I nod and begin to move through the bus, my feet sticking ever so slightly to the floor. I choose a pair of seats with nobody in them yet and take the seat closest to the window. A moment later and somebody slides into the free seat next to me. An elbow nudges mine and I look up to see Gabriel.

I look back toward the front of the bus, where Miss Rabbit and the guardians are ushering the final few kids on board. I look back at Gabriel. "You can't sit here," I hiss under my breath.

"Why not?" asks Gabriel.

I look at him as if to say, *You know why not.* There is no explicit rule about talking to boys on buses, but Gabriel knows as well as I do that we wouldn't be allowed to sit next to each other.

But Miss Rabbit and the guardians don't seem to notice Gabriel's choice of seat. A moment later everyone is sitting down and the bus doors swing shut. The brakes hiss and the engine groans and grumbles as we begin to inch toward the metal gates set into the fence. The gates are high and looped with barbed wire at the top. On either side of the gates stand two guardians. One of them keys a code into a little pad and the gates slowly swing open, letting us through.

Suddenly, we are outside Wildsmoor.

Leaving Wildsmoor is a rare occurrence for us at the facility, and as we wind and bump down the twisting track, I forget all about Gabriel next to me and just stare out the window. All of us do, noses glued to the glass. There is nothing much to look at. Just wide expanses of grass, rocky hills, and the odd tree bent sideways from the relentless wind that sweeps across the exposed landscape, but for us, it's like a cold glass of water on a hot day. We press our noses against the glass and drink it in greedily.

Miss Rabbit stands up and turns to face us, holding on to the seats on either side. "When we arrive in town, we will be meeting up with our Ashbury partners, ready for today's learning activity," she calls out over the noise of the engine. "Who can remember what this is?"

Silence, until eventually a lone hand floats into the air.

"Yes," smiles Miss Rabbit encouragingly.

"Shopping?"

"Exactly," says Miss Rabbit. "Ashbury village is the perfect place for our field trip today, where we will be practicing how to buy goods in a shop. Now, who can remember our three Cs for interacting with others? How about we say them all together."

"Cordiality. Courtesy. Communication," the other kids drone in reply, as if we're all in daycare. I do not join in with their response. Nor does Gabriel, I notice.

"Well done," says Miss Rabbit, nodding. She holds up one finger. "Cordiality: Say hello, and remember a smile goes a long way." She holds up a second finger. "Courtesy: Always be polite and say please and thank you. Make way for other people on the street." She unfurls a third finger. "And finally, communication: Explain what you need and don't be afraid of a little conversation."

Some of the kids nod, but most are still looking out the windows. We drive down a smooth double-laned road that takes us up and down over the desolate hilltops. Cars pass on the other side of the road, making a thwump noise as they go past.

"I heard about your little adventure last night."

I tear my eyes away from the window and glance at Gabriel. His keen eyes stare back at me. I slowly process his words, feeling uneasy when I realize that he's talking about my dream walking. Emir must've told him. My eyes flicker down the bus to where I can just about see Emir's dark head poking out above his seat. I glare at the back of his head.

"Still not taking your pills, then?" Gabriel continues, unfazed by my lack of response.

"Shush," I mutter under my breath. But my already-hot cheeks feel like suddenly they're on fire, because he's right, I still haven't taken my medication.

I reach up and brush the little lump of pills hidden in my top blazer pocket, a growing bulge that reminds me constantly of the rules I am breaking. I was going to take my pills again, after what happened last night. I was going to stop being so foolish and focus on getting better. But this morning, when it came down to it, I just couldn't bring myself to do it. Everything feels sharper and clearer. The world is more detailed. My life before Wildsmoor is slowly resurfacing, memories popping up like fish coming to the surface to feed: people and places and things that have happened. Emotions and feelings that are coloring over the gray dullness of my mind.

I'm not ready to lose it all just yet.

I glance sideways at Gabriel, remembering how he looked in the woods with the other masked figures. Now that I know that it wasn't just a dream, I can't help but run it over and over in my mind. Who are they? What were they doing there?

"I'm not the only one who likes nighttime adventures though, am I?" I say.

A slow grin spreads across Gabriel's face and his eyes sparkle, bright blue. "I've got no idea what you could possibly mean," he says.

I open my mouth to accuse him of lying, but then I close it again as I register the humor in his voice. He's being sarcastic.

I look up at the front of the bus, but Miss Rabbit and the guardians are sitting looking forward in their seats. "What were you doing in the woods the other night?" I ask. "I know that wasn't just a dream. You were there . . ." I think about the white-masked figure in the gloves. "And Emir. And others too."

Gabriel's head tilts sideways ever so slightly. His expression takes on that strange, hungry look that I remember from my dream in the woods. "Why?" he asks. "Do you want to come along next time?"

I recoil slightly. "What? No, of course not."

I am curious about Gabriel and his masked companions, but there is something about them that also makes me feel uneasy, afraid, even. The masks. The nighttime meeting in the woods. The secrecy. Whatever they're up to, I know that it can't be anything good. They could be dangerous, for all I know.

"If you don't want to join us, then why would I tell you anything at all?"

I frown. "You would get in big trouble if someone were to find out."

Gabriel gives a soft chuckle that's immediately drowned out by the rumbling of the bus. "Is that a threat?"

My forehead puckers, confused for a moment. "No."

"We could help you, you know, if you did want to join us."

"Help me with what?"

"With understanding yourself and the world you live in. With finding the truth."

I shake my head. "I don't need help."

Gabriel's blue gaze pierces mine for a moment, then he nods. "Let me know when you change your mind," he says. Then he shifts his body slightly and looks in the other direction, across the seats on the other side and out the window, making it clear that the conversation is over.

When.

I could say more, but I don't. Instead, I turn to look in the opposite direction, out my own window. I am surprised to see that we are already arriving in town, the desolate grassland replaced by houses. I stare along with everyone else at the glimpses of civilization that roll past us. Streets, narrow and cobbled. People, tending gardens and out walking. Houses, crooked and funny looking, with black beams and windows with wooden shutters and flowers haphazardly growing up the outside. Nothing at all like the house I lived in as a child, which was a gray concrete block, neatly set into a perfect row of other gray concrete houses.

We swing around a corner and suddenly we are in the center of town, the bus choking to a sudden stop. Miss Rabbit stands up. "Follow me, everyone," she says.

She leads us off the bus and out onto the pavement. We stand, huddled in a tight group and looking around wide-eyed. There are four guardians accompanying us and they wave us to one side, out of the way of passersby. We watch as shoppers make their way down the cobbled street, moving in and out of boutiques and cafés. Some of them have dogs in tow or push strollers that bump over the uneven pavement.

A woman walks past and she stops and openly stares at us. Her eyes travel over our pale faces and school coats with our logo embossed on the front. Her eyes widen until they're cartoon big before she spins on one heel and marches across the street, shaking her head.

On the other side of the street, she stops to talk to somebody else. Another woman, younger this time. She points in our direction, her voice raised. The younger woman also looks at us. Her eyes widen too and her nose wrinkles. I consider her expression . . .

Not fear. Not hate. Disgust, perhaps?

Disgust with a tinge of shock, I decide.

I inwardly smile to myself, feeling satisfied at my analysis. I am getting better at reading people's expressions, at understanding their emotions. Even if they are not very nice ones.

Two more people join their group, an older man and woman, both with walking sticks. The first woman has turned to them now. She's pointing at us again, her voice shrill. They both stare. The man shakes his head.

This is our third trip out of Wildsmoor this year. A new thing for the older kids, led by Miss Rabbit with the aim of getting us ready for assimilation back into society. In the spring we visited a farm where we were shown how food is grown, and in the summer we visited a nature park where we trailed along behind Miss Rabbit while she pointed out the "natural fauna and flora."

But this is our first trip into somewhere more civilized, and as I watch the gathering knot of onlookers, I start to get a bad feeling. It's clear we're not welcome here.

"Now, where are our Ashbury friends . . ." Miss Rabbit looks around, her head twisting this way and that. I notice how her eyes also keep glancing toward the bystanders gathering across the street, her cheeks growing pinker every second.

The guardians have also noticed the attention we are attracting. They move until they're standing in front of us, hands suddenly resting on their weapons. I wonder briefly if they're thinking that they might need to protect us from them, or protect them from us . . . maybe both, I decide.

At that moment I hear a buzz of voices from down the street. We all turn around to watch as the Ashbury students round the corner. They're walking two by two, arms linked, chattering and laughing with one another.

"Ah, finally," says Miss Rabbit, her features collapsing with relief. She strides down the street and stops to shake hands with Miss

Reynolds. The two women exchange some words that I can't hear. Miss Reynolds turns and looks at the knot of onlookers that are still watching us from across the street. She rolls her eyes and turns back to Miss Rabbit. "Ridiculous," I see her mouth.

"Find your partners, everyone," Miss Rabbit calls. Suddenly, we are enveloped by the chatter and laughter of the Ashbury students. I can smell perfume and all their different shampoos and products, strawberries and watermelon and sweet flowery smells.

Clementine appears in front of me. Her thick hair bounces around her face and her glossy lips stretch into a wide smile. "Hi, Emily."

I return her smile automatically. "Hi, Clementine."

"So they finally let you all out, then?"

I shrug. "For now."

She looks me up and down. "You look better."

I remember the last time we met, five days ago now, and the first morning not taking my medication. It feels like a lifetime ago. I remember how she hugged me, how she seemed concerned that I wasn't well. I nod my head. "I feel better," I say.

"That's good," says Clementine.

Miss Rabbit and Miss Reynolds make their way to the front of the group. "In your pairs, in a single line, please," calls Miss Reynolds over our heads.

We shift and move until we are in a single line, each of us with our socialization partners. My and Clementine's arms and shoulders are touching.

"Now follow us," says Miss Rabbit. Dutifully, we all begin to snake after them down the street. The guardians take up their positions. One at the front, one at the back, and two on either side of the line.

"Look," Clementine says, elbowing me and holding out her hand. She wiggles her fingers and I notice that her nails are painted with tiny pumpkins and red and orange leaves.

"For autumn," I reply.

"Exactly. Next time we meet, I'm doing your nails, I don't care what *they* say." She nods her head toward Miss Rabbit and the guardians.

"It's not Miss Rabbit. And the guardians wouldn't notice something like nails. It's Matron."

"Matron?" Clementine raises an eyebrow.

I open my mouth, about to respond, but then I close it again. How would I describe somebody like Matron? With her bitter antiseptic smell and heavy hands and eyes that somehow see everything.

"Isn't that old-fashioned, to have a matron in a school?"

I shrug. "I don't know. Is it?"

Clementine snorts. "Yes. We have a nurse. But she doesn't do anything, we just go to her room when we want to get out of class and then she'll give us an ice pack for our headache or whatever else we say is wrong."

"Don't you get in trouble?"

"Why would we?"

"For lying?" *A Wildsmoor student does not tell lies.*

Clementine shakes her head. "We don't get in trouble for stuff like that at Ashbury."

I consider this. "Do you not have rules?"

Clementine gives me a sideways smile, and an expression comes over her face that I recognize as something secretive, yet somehow bad and somehow amused too. It's a look that I used to share with my sister when we were doing something that we knew would get us into trouble. Mischievous is the only way I can think to describe it. She elbows me and says, "Rules are made to be broken, you know."

Rules are made to be broken. Are they?

I feel a little stab of something like fear mixed with excitement and also, strangely, pride. Because I am breaking rules too, which means I am more like Clementine than I thought.

"You know," says Clementine as we pause at a road, waiting for the light to turn green. She peers into my face. "There is something different about you today."

"Is there? Like what?" I am curious to know how I have changed since I have stopped taking my medication.

She nods. "You're not as slow, for one. No offense, but usually trying to have a conversation with you is like playing tennis with a lamppost. Again, no offense. But it's not just that, you look different too. Your eyes are brighter." Her lips purse and she tilts her head to one side. "Prettier, somehow. Like you've found a glow or something."

Her approval gives me a warm buzz in my stomach. "Uh, thanks."

The traffic lights turn red and the crossing signal begins to beep. "Quickly," calls Miss Rabbit, striding across the road. We all follow until we're standing on the other side of the street.

We are standing in front of a food shop.

Clementine stifles a laugh with one hand. "We're going to the supermarket? This is your version of a school trip? You know, the last school trip I went on, we flew to the Alps. Two weeks skiing."

I give a tiny nod. She's right, it is ridiculous. But probably necessary, I also think to myself, looking around at the Wildsmoor kids. They are eyeing the shop front warily, taking in the floor-to-ceiling glass and bright posters. The doors suddenly slide open by themselves and one of the students startles backward, tripping over their own feet.

We have all spent too long at Wildsmoor.

"Now," says Miss Rabbit. "Everyone will be given a small amount of money to buy one item of their choosing. Ashbury students, allow your Wildsmoor friends to take the lead on this. They can be in charge of the money, selecting the item, and going to the checkout to pay for it . . ."

"No sweets, ice cream, cigarettes, alcohol, or any other type of contraband," cuts in Miss Reynolds, her eyes flickering over the Ashbury students. "Pick a piece of fruit or similar."

Miss Rabbit looks flustered for a moment. "Well, yes," she says. "I'm sure they know not to—"

Miss Reynolds snorts. "You don't know these girls like I do. Now. In you go. Meet back here in fifteen minutes."

"And remember your three C's," calls Miss Rabbit. "Cordiality, courtesy, and communication."

Miss Reynolds's nose ever so slightly wrinkles and next to me Clementine suppresses another laugh.

We make our way into the shop, those who are reluctant swept along by their Ashbury partners. As we pass Miss Rabbit, she gives each of us a coin from a plastic bag. I hold mine in my fist, feeling the cold press of it in my palm. This is the first time I've held or seen money since my life before Wildsmoor.

The noise and smells of the supermarket hit me like a slap in the face. First the cool brush and whirr of air-conditioning. Then the slightly sweet smell of ripening fruit mixed with floor cleaner. Carts squeaking. The beep of the checkout.

Memories flood back to me. Trips to the shops with my mom and sister, trailing behind the cart, squabbling and begging for treats.

Again I think of Amelia. I can see her face so clearly, freckles dashed across an upturned nose, her eyes alight with laughter. I wonder how I could have forgotten about her for so long. I try to imagine her as a teenager and feel a sudden pang of loss. So many years have passed with my barely realizing.

"Are you okay?" asks Clementine, peering at me.

I nod. "Fine," I say, although my voice comes out slightly more high-pitched than usual. "What shall we get?" I ask, changing the subject.

Clementine rolls her eyes. "Whatever you want, I guess. It's not like you can buy anything good with that amount of money. Come on." Clementine pulls me further into the store and we aimlessly wander around the aisles.

Most of the shoppers just ignore us but some people stare at us as we pass, and I see similar expressions on their faces that I saw earlier: fear, shock, disgust. One woman pulls her children behind her. Another mutters under her breath. "Unbelievable," I hear her say. Followed by, "Disgusting."

"Well, that's horrible," says Clementine, surprise clear in her voice. "I mean, you lot are a weird bunch, but you're not *that* bad."

I nod. I am surprised too by the vitriol in the woman's stare and her words. I know that having the Grimm is a bad thing, that it can be dangerous, and that we are put into institutions like Wildsmoor for a reason. But I don't think I ever realized how much everyone else hates us . . .

Because that's what it feels like when I'm absorbing their stares and mutters. It feels like they hate us. What I don't really understand is *why*.

Clementine links arms with me, and I recognize that she's trying to make me feel better. She glares at the muttering woman until she has the decency to look away.

We move onward. We're now in an aisle where everything is silver and brightly packaged. Chocolate and sweets and bags of chips. My mouth waters when I look at the shiny packages, all lined up in their neat little rows.

Clementine notices my expression. "Don't tell me you're not allowed chocolate at your school?"

I shake my head. "Processed sugar is bad for us," I say. "Our diets have to be strictly monitored. It's part of our treatment program."

"That is the most depressing thing I've ever heard." She nods her head toward the shiny rows. "Pick one, go on, and then we'll stuff it down before Miss Rabbit or Miss Reynolds even notices."

I remember what Clementine said earlier. *Rules are made to be broken.* And besides, this is only a little rule. I drift past the rows of sweets, eventually reaching out and taking a packet that is familiar to me. A chocolate bar, blue with red writing, one of my favorites from when I was a kid.

"Great," says Clementine brightly. "And now we pay before anyone can stop us." She pulls at my arm and marches us through the store. We pass the muttering woman again and Clementine walks purposefully close to her, pulling me along beside her. As we pass, she and Clementine make eye contact. Clementine looks her up and down before wrinkling her nose, as if to say, *You're the disgusting one.*

We reach the checkout before any of the other Wildsmoor and Ashbury pairs and join the line. There are several people in front of us and only one shop assistant behind a lonely checkout.

Behind us, other Ashbury and Wildsmoor kids slowly start to emerge from the aisles and line up. The Ashbury kids giggle and jostle their friends. The Wildsmoor kids look shell-shocked, gripping on to bits of fruit and cans of food that will never be eaten.

Finally, it's our turn to pay. I place the chocolate bar on the little conveyor belt and watch as it slides its way up to the shop assistant. The shop assistant pauses. She looks at Clementine, then she looks at me. Her eyes flicker between our uniforms, before settling on the crest embroidered into my school coat.

Her eyes widen. She looks at the line gathering behind us, more Ashbury and Wildsmoor kids waiting to pay. She stands up. "Is this a joke?"

Clementine looks confused for a moment, then she looks the woman up and down and gives her a look that is somewhere between amused and annoyed. "A joke? We just want to pay for the chocolate."

The shop assistant shakes her head, the curls on her head bouncing like little gray snakes. Her cheeks grow pink spots. She leans over, presses a button, and speaks into a microphone. "Manager to the till, please. Manager to the till."

"Is there a problem?" asks Clementine.

The shop assistant pushes back her wheely chair and stands as far away from us as possible. She looks at Clementine. "There's no problem with *you* . . ." She nods her head at me. "It's your . . . *friend* that is the problem. We don't accept her sort in here."

"Why not? Because she has the Grimm?"

The woman nods.

"It's not like she's contagious or anything. You can't actually catch the Grimm."

"Well, how do I know that?"

"Hmm, how about basic science? It's a condition you're born with, not a virus."

"And I should trust the word of a teenager, I suppose . . ." She shakes her head. "And that's not the real issue besides. It just isn't safe. I don't know what your teachers are thinking, bringing such a large group out in public."

At that moment a man that I suppose to be the woman's manager arrives. He's young-looking, with pimply skin and long hair in a ponytail. "Uh, what's the problem?" he asks, looking between us and the shop assistant.

She points a finger at me, then jabs the air in the direction of the rest of the kids lining up behind us. "Look at them," she says, her voice wavering. "The shop is full of them."

The manager nods. "I don't see . . ." His eyes drift down the line and understanding suddenly dawns in his eyes. "Right . . ."

The shop assistant puffs up. "Well, aren't you going to do something?"

"Uh. Like what?" replies the manager.

"Like tell them to leave."

"And why should we leave?" asks Clementine. "We're paying customers like anyone else and we have a right to be here."

The manager looks awkward. "Well. I don't know . . ." By now the Ashbury kids have stopped their laughing and jostling and are looking on as silently as their Wildsmoor partners. His eyes move over them before turning back to the shop assistant. "They're not causing any trouble, Annie," he says. "Can't we just serve them? I mean, they're here now."

The woman stands up, shaking her head. "No, I will not serve them."

"And nor should you have to," a voice sounds behind us.

I turn to see the woman from earlier, the one who called me disgusting. Her sharp, pointed chin is lifted like a weapon and her fingers grip the handles of her basket so tightly that they've turned white. "I've been watching these troublemakers run around the whole shop, terrifying the other customers. Probably shoplifting too and god knows what else. I nearly called the police."

I stare at the woman. "That's a lie," I say before I can stop myself. "We're not doing anything."

The woman turns to me and I want to recoil. I don't have to try to figure out how this woman is feeling; there is nothing but pure hate in her eyes.

"I know firsthand the trouble your kind can cause," she says. "It was a grimmer like you that hurt my Terry. The whole lot of you should be locked up and the key thrown away." Then she purses her lips and spits on me. Her saliva flies through the air and lands on my cheek. I can feel it, wet and warm on my skin.

Glares and insults are one thing, but I am unprepared for what it feels like to be spat at. Shock, first. Then a burning feeling that starts somewhere in my chest and floods my veins with heat. I can see nothing but red, red, red.

I am not in control of my body. I lunge at the woman, gripping the collar of her shirt in my fists before pushing her to the floor. The basket flies across the linoleum, scattering cans and packets and pieces of fruit. She falls down, lying there for a moment, before scrambling back to her feet. Her skirt is rumpled up and hair has come loose around her face. "See," she screeches. "She just pushed me! Somebody help! She's trying to kill me!"

"You're a liar! A liar!" I yell back, although I'm hardly aware of what I'm shouting. All I know is this red feeling that's overtaken my whole body. I lunge at her again but this time an arm reaches out from nowhere and pulls me back.

"Stop," says a voice in my ear. "The guardians . . ."

I look up. Emir is looking down at me, his hands firmly gripping my shoulders. I follow his eyeline to see blue figures jogging toward us from the other side of the shop.

"Your emotions are just a bit heightened right now because of the withdrawal," murmurs Emir. "You're angry, but you need to try to control it."

I struggle out of his grip, furious. I turn my glare on him. "And why do you care," I hiss.

He gives a soft shake of his head and straightens up. He gently steers me around, until his body is slightly angled in front of my own.

The guardians stop in front of us, looking from me to Emir to the woman. One of them is pointing a Taser in my direction. The other holds a gun angled at the floor, fingers tense around the handle.

"Sorry," says Emir. "Just a tiny misunderstanding."

"Step back," one of the guardians commands the woman.

The woman shakes her head. "I will not step back. It's them that should leave, not me."

"What's going on?" Miss Reynolds says, pushing through a group of onlookers and followed by Miss Rabbit.

"She tried to kill me," says the woman again, pointing in my direction. "You should take them back to wherever it is you keep them and lock them up."

Clementine snorts. "She did *not* try to kill you."

Miss Rabbit's face grows red. "Now, I'm sure this is just . . ."

"Are you in charge?" demands the woman, rounding on her. "I've just been assaulted by one of your students. And I *will* be pressing charges."

"Well . . . I'm terribly sorry . . . I'm sure it wasn't meant . . ." Miss Rabbit shakes her head and opens and closes her mouth.

Clementine steps forward and addresses Miss Reynolds. "That's just not true," she says. "This woman spat at Emily. She was the aggressor, not Emily."

"Is that true, Emily?" Miss Reynolds turns to me. I nod my head.

"It is true," says the manager. I turn and look at him in

surprise. "And we don't tolerate spitting or aggressive behavior here in store." He turns to the woman. "So I'm going to have to ask you to leave . . ." He frowns. "Now," he adds, his voice surprisingly authoritative.

The woman grows so red I think she might explode. She looks at Miss Rabbit and Miss Reynolds and jabs a shaking finger in their direction. "Don't think this is the end of this. My lawyer will be in touch."

We all watch silently as she leaves the store, her heels clip-clopping across the polished floor. The automatic doors slide open and shut behind her.

The manager turns to the shop assistant. "I think it's time for your break, Annie," he says.

Annie opens her mouth as if to say something, then thinks better of it and closes it again. She nods once, and then turns to leave.

"Now," says the manager, sliding behind the checkout and into the now-empty seat. "Who's next?" He looks up at me and offers a smile.

I stumble forward and wait silently as he scans my chocolate bar. Behind me I can feel the eyes of everyone else watching. I half expect Miss Rabbit or Miss Reynolds to say something about the chocolate, but they don't.

Clementine pulls at my arm and I stumble alongside her as we leave the store. I stand, breathing in the cold air. A guardian has followed us and is standing to one side. His hand is still on his revolver, but it is tucked back into the holster that hangs from his belt. He watches us warily, as if expecting another outburst at any moment.

"Are you okay?" asks Clementine.

I nod.

"I think that woman might be the worst person I've ever met."

Behind us, the door opens and shuts as more Wildsmoor students and their partners come to join us on the pavement. My anger is still churning in my body with nowhere to go. Why does that woman hate us so much?

I turn around and seek Gabriel out of the crowd. I remember what he said. How he could help me understand the world, help me see the truth. He's standing with Emir and Adanya, talking softly. All three of them are looking at me. Emir looks furious, his eyes shooting daggers in my direction, and Adanya doesn't look much happier, her mouth a thin, unimpressed line.

I know they're talking about me, but I don't care.

Clementine raises an eyebrow at me. She looks back at the three of them and then at me again. "Do they have a problem with you or something? The tall, hot one looks like he wants to kill you." She suddenly giggles. "Although he did stop you from battering that lady in the shop, which is probably doing you a favor, although she would've deserved it."

"Wait here," I say to Clementine.

I go over to them, ignoring Emir's and Adanya's angry stares and instead focusing on Gabriel.

"I've changed my mind. I want to come to your next meeting," I say.

"After what just happened? Absolutely not," says Emir, glaring at Gabriel.

Adanya also shakes her head.

But Gabriel just looks at me and grins. His eyes light up with that hungry look again. He nods his head. "Tonight. Midnight. Same place."

I nod, and head back over to Clementine, feeling the cold air in my lungs and adrenaline cascading around my body.

Excitement.

Fear.

Guilt.

I know whatever Gabriel and the rest are up to is bad, but maybe I've had enough of being good all the time.

"Here," says Clementine. She reaches out and pushes the chocolate bar into my hands. I pull off the wrapper and take a bite. The rich creaminess explodes across my tongue, and at the same time, Clementine's words from earlier pop into my head.

Rules are made to be broken, you know.

CHAPTER ten

The seconds tick past painfully slow as I wait for midnight. I know that I'm being stupid. I know that I could get into trouble. I know that what I should be doing is focusing on getting better, trying my hardest to overcome the Grimm. But after what happened today, I've realized that if that's what the outside world is like, then I can't afford to be walking around like a *mindless sheep.*

I want the truth, I want to know more, and I have a feeling that Gabriel and the others could be the answer to this.

I listen for the strikes of the old clock as I wait. First it strikes eleven, and then quarter past. Half past. Quarter to. Finally, midnight is here. I count the gongs as they pass. One, two, three . . .

"Twelve," I murmur to myself. I sit upright and slide my way out of bed. I have left my coat and shoes nearby and fumble for them in the dark. I lace up my shoes, shrug my coat over my pajamas, and creep out of the room.

"What are you doing?" hisses a voice behind me. I jump and spin around.

Adanya is behind me, shaking her head. She slides through the doorway and closes the dormitory door. "You're making so much noise you're going to wake the whole house."

I open my mouth to reply but she holds up a hand, blocking my words. From her coat pocket she pulls out a mask, orange and softly furred.

The fox.

I watch as she pulls it over her face. The only light in the corridor comes from the emergency exit signs set over the doorways, and the green glow falls eerily over her now-transformed face, lips a snarling snout and eyes wolflike.

"Be quiet and follow me," she whispers.

I watch as she walks ahead of me, her face furred and fierce. I hesitate for a moment, eyeing the way she slinks like a predator, completely silent. I force my legs to move, trying to mimic her way of creeping, but in comparison, I am a lumbering bear. My footsteps thud and floorboards creak underneath me. I stumble and clatter into a wall.

Adanya stops to turn and glare at me.

"Sorry," I mutter.

We slip through the final door and onto the landing of the entrance hall. Together, we tiptoe down the curved staircase and to the gilded double doors. Next to the double doors is a floor-to-ceiling poster of our school rules, all fifty of them, framed ornately by gold. I read the rule at the top. *A Wildsmoor student is always obedient.*

Adanya turns the handle and the door creaks open.

"It's not locked?" I whisper in surprise.

Adanya puts a finger to her lips again before slipping through the gap.

The night is brighter than last night and there is a breeze.

"This way," Adanya whispers, beckoning me into the shadows of the house. Up against the wall of the house, there is nothing but a deep gloom and the damp smell of old stone. I follow Adanya around to the back, where the woodland crowds up against the garden walls. I stare apprehensively at the top: the wall is double my height and lined with loops of barbed wire. But turns out this is not a problem.

Adanya leads me through a patch of overgrown bushes, and there, hardly hidden at all, is a gate. She lifts the latch and it swings open. I stare, dumbfounded. "A gate. You're joking," I whisper. I frown up at the walls again. What is the point of the walls and wire and guardians if there is just an open gate that leads out of the school for anybody to find?

"Not joking," says Adanya. "Now come on."

We duck through the gate and once again I am walking in the woods. However, this time I am not asleep, I am awake. The woods are much more menacing to my waking mind. Branches like twisted skeletons scratch and creak. Rustles and snaps make me jump. Every shadow is hiding a monster that will jump out at us at any second.

Even though we are no longer in the school, Adanya still doesn't speak. But despite this, I am glad to have someone guiding me. My sleeping mind knows instinctively where to go, but my waking mind is a nervous mess, and the woods look all the same to me.

Finally, we arrive at the clearing. There is the same ring of dense trees, charred firepit, and logs, but other than that it's empty. "Sit," says Adanya to me, pointing to a log.

I sit and watch as Adanya flits around the clearing, collecting twigs and logs that she stacks into an upside-down ice-cream-cone shape on top of the blackened remains of the last fire. She leans down and I hear the swish of a match. A tiny ember glows somewhere deep within the stack of twigs. She blows softly and sparks jump, before flickering into flame. She blows more and adds more twigs. They catch and now the fire crackles and spits. She adds several thicker branches, until finally the flames are licking up toward the sky.

"A Wildsmoor student follows the rules," hisses a voice. A figure, beak nosed and wearing a long black cloak, jumps out from the shadows and grabs Adanya's shoulders. She yelps and twists, dropping an armful of sticks.

I jump up, my heart in my mouth.

"Gabriel, you great big shit," says Adanya. She thumps him in the arm. "You sounded just like Matron, and look what you made me do." She gestures to the scattered sticks on the ground.

"Sorry, Addie. I just couldn't resist. You're not usually so jumpy."

"It's her," said Adanya. She nods at me. "I had to show her the way. It was like dragging a corpse through the house, all the noise she was making. I don't know why you've made me bring her. Emir is going to lose his shit."

"She could be useful. Her ability isn't like anything I've ever seen . . ." He turns to me and cocks his head. Underneath his mask, I imagine his hungry expression.

Cloak dragging on the ground, Gabriel makes his way toward me across the clearing. His mask is particularly menacing, a long beak like a crow with round eyes covered with glass. I don't know why, but it makes me think of death.

In his hand he's holding a hat with a flat top and wide brim. He pauses in front of me and places the hat on his head, perched slightly to the side. "You came, then . . ."

He trails off and his head turns toward the trees. I follow his eyeline and watch as more masked figures steal into the clearing, ducking under branches and sliding out from behind tree trunks.

The clown is first. Whoever it is walks with a gaiting limp and leans heavily on a walking stick. Right behind him is the brightly colored one. A bird like Gabriel, but their mask speaks of life instead of death, brightly colored feathers fanning out from eye-holes ringed with gleaming stones. Their stature and movements remind me of a bird too, slightly smaller and quick, flitting out from the undergrowth.

Gabriel nods at them both and tips his hat. "Good evening," he says.

The final masked figure appears in the clearing and we all turn to look. Tall, in a white mask. Black gloves. His shoulders are rigid and hair dark. Emir. His face turns toward me and I notice that his mask is intricate and graceful in a way that the others aren't. The porcelain gleams; white and gold wire twists among the black paintwork, defining his lips and eyes.

They are silent, waiting for something, although I don't know what. Gabriel turns and walks even closer to me. I stand up, heart suddenly racing again. "You must have questions," he says.

The rest of the masked figures drift toward us: fox, clown, feathers, and Emir. They stand behind Gabriel, peering at me with black holes instead of eyes. Firelight flickers at their backs and shrouds their faces in shadow. Alone, each masked figure is unnerving. Together, they are terrifying.

Suddenly, I am struck by a thought . . .

What if this is a trap? Something thought up by Gabriel and the others to protect their identities and stop me from squealing on them to Matron. What if they're planning on hurting me? *Or worse*, a little voice says from somewhere deep in my mind.

"Yes," I finally reply. I lift my chin and plant my legs farther apart. I don't want them to know I am afraid. "I do have questions, like first of all, who are you?"

Gabriel cocks his head. Behind him, somebody laughs. Gabriel gestures around to everyone, a dramatic one-armed sweep that makes his cloak ripple in the air. "We are the Cure. Welcome."

Adanya snorts from behind her mask.

"What?" snaps Gabriel.

"You're so dramatic."

"We are the Cure," imitates the feathered mask figure. They all laugh and Gabriel gives a sweeping bow, pulling up his cloak.

"The Cure?" I ask.

Gabriel turns back to me and nods. "It's a joke, of a sort. Among other things."

"And what do you do?"

"Let's go and sit by the fire," says Gabriel. "I'll try to explain."

Feathered mask sighs. "But don't make the explanation *too* long, will you? I want to get some good practice in tonight."

"How about a demonstration?" asks Gabriel.

Feathered mask does a little pirouette and dances over to one of the logs. "I could be persuaded," she says, sitting down and hugging her knees to her chest.

We settle in a circle around the fire. Adanya and Emir sit next to each other and begin to have a whispered conversation. Clown mask sits next to me. He lays down his walking stick, pulls off his mask, and smiles. "Hi," he says. Judging from his smooth cheeks and height, I guess that he might be a year or so younger than me.

"Hi," I reply.

"I'm Isaiah," he continues.

"Emily."

"This is Margie," says Isaiah, gesturing to the feathered girl who is sitting nearby.

I look over just in time to see something jump up on her lap. Something furry and with eyes that gleam in the darkness. I catch a glimpse of a tail and black and white patches. A badger?

Margie looks up at me. "Hello," she says. With one hand she pets the animal on her lap but with the other she lifts up her mask and winks at me. She has a round, cheerful sort of face.

Both of them I don't know, although I do recognize their faces from meals and classes and being around the facility. I relax a little bit under their friendly gazes, smiling back at them in turn.

Gabriel stands up. "Shall we start?" he asks everyone else.

Isaiah pulls his mask back on. Next to him, Margie does the same, obscuring her face once more. Adanya and Emir stop their whispered conversation and look up. For a moment, everyone is still, waiting.

I look around. There is something so surreal about the scene in front of me. The dark woods. The masked figures. The fire flickering and spitting into the night. No wonder I wrote it off as a dream.

"Does anyone else want to explain? Or shall I?" Gabriel asks.

"You brought her here," says Adanya. "She's all yours."

"Suits me." He turns to me. "So what do you know about the Grimm?"

I shrug. "Same as everyone else. It only really affects children and young adults. All children have the brain defect to some extent, but usually it causes only very mild symptoms. When the symptoms get bad, that's when it becomes the Grimm. I mean, Grimm-Cross Syndrome."

Gabriel nods. "Pretty much. And what are the symptoms?"

"Delusions, paranoia, headaches, angry outbursts . . ." I trail off and shrug. "It's different in everybody, right?"

"And do you feel sick right now?"

I think about this for a moment. I shake my head no. "But . . ." I continue, thinking about my dreams.

"But strange things have been happening?"

I nod. "My dreams are coming back." *Which means that the Grimm is coming back*, I add in my head.

Gabriel nods. "What if I were to tell you that the medication you've taken all your life isn't to help you, or make you better. They're actually tranquilizers to make you dull and stupid, to stop you from asking questions."

I frown at this. "Ask questions about what?"

"We're different, Emily. We have . . . special abilities that we've never been able to properly explore."

"Properly explore?"

Gabriel nods. "And I think you know what I'm talking about. In fact, I know you do."

"My dreams," I say, frowning. I shake my head, remembering the monster I'd conjured up only a few nights ago. "But if my dreams are coming back, that's not good. They're *dangerous*. And I wasn't having them until I stopped taking my pills."

"Those pills don't just make us dull and stupid," cuts in Emir. "They stop our abilities too. The kids at Wildsmoor are different from everyone else, but we are *not sick*." He all but spits the last two words.

"We don't believe our symptoms are dangerous or should be repressed," says Gabriel. "Instead, we train to control our abilities . . ."

I stare, shocked, processing his words. *Train to control our abilities* . . . "That doesn't make any sense. The Grimm is a disease. How can you control a sickness?"

I hear a snort that I think comes from Emir. I look over at where he watches from the other side of the fire. His arms are folded and his shoulders tense.

"We *can* control it," says Gabriel. He cocks his head at me and I can see that under his long crow's beak a smile has spread across his face. "Let me show you."

Emir stands up, his limbs snapping upright. "Wait," he cuts in. "Are you sure that's a good idea? Then she'll know what we can do."

Gabriel shrugs. "What does it matter? She already knows that we're here."

"And that's bad enough," says Emir, his voice tight and words clipped. "We shouldn't be sharing all our secrets like this."

Gabriel's grin spreads wider and he laughs. He turns back to me. "Watch," he says. Flames dance at his back. The outline of his body blurs, becoming soft, and for a moment I'm not sure that what I'm seeing isn't an illusion caused by the glimmering firelight. A moment later, bodies flicker into existence around the clearing, translucent and ghostly at first before becoming solid.

Where there was one Gabriel, there are now many—at least ten identical Gabriels dotted around the fire and under the trees. All of them wear the same cloak and have the same grin, just about visible under their identical masks.

Another Gabriel appears on the log next to me, so close we are almost touching "Is this not control?" he asks.

I pull away. My heart is racing. I stand up and look around. There are more Gabriels now, at least twenty, maybe more. They fill the space, obscuring the others from view, all of them looking at me with black, glassy eyes. "Up here," I hear a voice. I look up and see another Gabriel perched in a tree above my head. He waves at me.

"Stop!" I shout.

Immediately, all the Gabriels fade around me, until there is only one left. The real Gabriel pulls off his mask and smiles. "Sorry, didn't mean to scare you," he says. "But as you can see, I am more than in control."

I sit back down heavily on my log. Isaiah reaches out and pats my arm.

Adanya snorts. "Who wouldn't be scared? One of you is more than enough Gabriel." She stands up and claps her hands together. "My turn," she says.

Next to me, Isaiah shakes his head. "That's not a good idea," he says.

Adanya puts her hand on her hip. "What? Why?"

"You know why."

"I'm not going to *hurt* her. I was just going to give her a few pins and needles. That's not even pain really. You don't mind, do you?" Adanya turns to me, and the black holes of her fox head mask peer over the flickering flames. "If I give you a little bit of a vibrating foot?"

I think I do mind, but instead I nod my head.

"What's the harm?" Gabriel shrugs. "She can handle it."

Isaiah sighs and shakes his head. He looks at me. "You don't have to agree to this, you know."

"I'm not afraid," I say, although my voice wavers ever so slightly as it comes out. I turn to Adanya. "Do what you want."

Adanya nods. She reaches up and takes off her mask. Her eyes close and she opens her mouth, baring her teeth and tongue. A wail emits from somewhere deep in her throat. It grows louder, until she is all but screaming. The sound makes every hair on my body stand up on end. Then she opens her eyes; they bulge in her head. Her gaze finds mine. Our eyes lock.

Pain. A feeling like a knife being jammed into the bottom of my foot. I can't help it; I scream and keel over onto the ground. I tear off my shoe. I am still screaming. The pain is unbearable. There is nothing else.

"Adanya!" somebody shouts.

Adanya's wail stops and the pain disappears. My screams turn to sobs as I cradle my foot in both hands. "Are you all right?" Isaiah asks. He kneels next to me and puts a hand on my shoulder.

My sobs dry up. As quickly as it came, the pain has gone again. With shaking hands I feel my foot, but there is nothing wrong with it. I am fine. Whatever pain I had been feeling was just in my head.

Everyone else is standing up too. Emir's hands are clenched by his sides. He's several steps toward me with one foot in front of the other, as if frozen midstep.

"What?" Adanya says, looking around at everyone.

"Not cool," says Gabriel, pointing at Adanya.

Adanya pulls a face. "It's not my fault I don't get much chance to practice." She turns and shrugs at me. "As you can imagine, it's hard to find a willing victim."

Gabriel snorts. "That's so messed up, Adanya."

"We don't hurt one another," says Emir.

"Honestly, I barely gave her even one percent, and it was only in her foot." She turns to Emir. "And why do you care anyway? You think the same as I do about her."

"That might be true, but we don't hurt one another," repeats Emir as he sits back down.

"Well, it shouldn't have hurt her. She's obviously got a low pain threshold. Besides, it was a mistake, like I said."

I scramble back to my feet and stand for a moment, trying to control the shaking that has taken over my body.

"Apologize, then," says Gabriel. I can see his lips twist into a smile under the long beak of his mask, as if he knows that she will find it difficult.

"Why should I apologize? I've already said that it was an accident."

"I know it was an accident," says Isaiah.

There is something about his soft voice that pulls. We all turn and look at him.

Isaiah lifts off his mask and looks at Adanya. His gaze is as soft as his voice. "I know you would never intentionally hurt someone, Adanya. That isn't who you are."

For a long moment, Isaiah and Adanya lock eyes. To my

surprise, her eyes grow glassy, as if she is about to cry. She turns to me. "Sorry," she says. She doesn't sound particularly sorry at all, but I don't make a fuss.

Instead, I just shrug and say, "That's okay." Then she pulls her mask back on and sits down.

"Shall I go?" asks Margie.

I look at her. I'm no longer sure if I want to find out what she can do, after Adanya's pain.

"Don't worry. It doesn't involve you at all."

I sit down and gesture for her to go ahead.

Margie picks up the badger on her lap and gently puts it on the ground. She crouches down next to it. A moment later, her arms go slack by her sides. Her head drops and her mask wedges against her chest. She starts listing to the side as if she's going to fall and Isaiah puts out a hand to steady her. She goes still.

The badger, however, is not still. It stands up on its hind legs and walks toward the fire. The fire's glow lights up its black-and-white face as it looks around at us all. It makes a strange sound as if it is talking, and then it *waves*. I stare . . . surely not. But no, it is waving. It spins, a pirouette like a ballerina, and then it bows.

The others laugh and clap. I do not laugh. I do not clap. I have no idea what is happening.

The badger goes back to where Margie is slumped on the ground and snuffles her leg with its snout. Margie's head snaps upright. She pulls in a sharp breath, gasping. "Sorry," she breathes. "It's always a shock to go from one body to another."

"Margie can inhabit the bodies of animals," explains Gabriel. "Among other things."

"What was it like?" I ask Margie, who has now settled back on her tree stump.

Margie cocks her head at me. "What is what like?"

"Being in there." I nod at the badger, which is back in her lap but curled up, as if asleep.

"Loud. And smelly," she says.

The others laugh.

"Badgers have excellent hearing and sense of smell," she explains. "It can be overwhelming."

I nod my head. I am trying to process everything I am seeing and hearing, but I'm struggling. She turned into a badger. *She turned into a badger.*

Gabriel points at Emir. "Your turn," he says.

Emir shakes his head. "No," he replies stiffly.

"Why not?"

"You know what I think about . . ." He pauses and looks at me, then looks back at Gabriel. "All of this."

Gabriel shrugs. "We've talked about this. We need more people . . ."

"And I've said already that I disagree," replies Emir. "More people will just be a danger to us."

"And what if it comes to a fight?"

Emir snorts. "You would love that."

Gabriel grins. "Maybe. And don't pretend that you wouldn't. Imagine letting loose everything we've been practicing on the guardians and Mr. Peters and Matron . . . Wouldn't that feel good?"

"No. It wouldn't."

"You're no fun."

"I agree with Emir," cuts in Adanya. "If it does come to a fight, she won't be any use to us anyway. What is she going to do? Dream them all to death?"

Gabriel turns to me and cocks his head. "I don't know, but I'm sure she would be useful somehow. Besides, while she's not taking her medication, she's a risk to us all. Better she's here and learns some control rather than trying to pulverize strangers out on the street."

Emir stands up. He pulls his mask off. Underneath, his face is tight with suppressed anger. "I disagree. Her inability to control her emotions is exactly why she *shouldn't* be here."

Up until that point I'd been following their conversation as if in a daze, still reeling from everything I had just seen. But Emir's words pierce the daze like a sudden needle jabbing into my skin.

But it's not just his dismissive tone, or the way he glares just at the idea of me joining them. It's the truth behind his words . . . I'm not able to control the Grimm. That's why I was sent to Wildsmoor in the first place. To keep others safe. I think of Amelia, screaming in pain with a broken arm. I didn't mean to do that, but still, it was my fault. And it could have been far worse.

I stand up. I don't say goodbye; instead, I just spin on one heel and leave. Stumbling in the dark, I shove branches and tangled undergrowth out of the way, forcing my way through.

"That's the wrong way," somebody says.

I ignore them and continue to push my way into the woods. Thorny brambles grab hold of my clothing, snaring me in and making me stumble.

"Somebody needs to go after her," I hear one of them say. "She'll just get lost otherwise."

A moment later I feel a hand tug on my elbow. "This way."

I shake the hand off.

"Seriously, this way." The hand is more insistent this time, pulling me firmly to one side. A moment later we fall out of the trees and onto the path. The sky's gray light glances off white porcelain. Emir.

I shake off his hand and glare at him. "Don't touch me." I stride away. I'm hot. Too hot. Everything is racing. Memories flicker. I think of my sister again. Amelia. But who even is Amelia? What does she even look like now? I realize that the little girl in my memories no longer exists. Because of the Grimm, there is a void where my life should've been.

Emir strides after me. "You need to calm down," he says stiffly. "Panicking will only make it worse."

"Don't tell me to calm down," I hiss. I think about everything I've seen tonight. Adanya's and Gabriel's and Margie's abilities . . . but they're not *abilities*, they're a symptom of the Grimm.

"What you're all doing," I say to Emir. "It's dangerous. You could hurt somebody, or kill somebody, but you don't even care." In fact, it's the opposite. They're not suppressing the Grimm at all. They're turning it into weapons.

"I do care," Emir replies. "And I'm not arguing that it's dangerous. But some things are more important."

"Like what?"

"Like the lies we've been told. Like how they keep us all locked up and tell us we're sick, when we're not. Like the truth." His words are hard and angry.

"This isn't the truth." I speed up, too fast, and I trip and stumble through the darkness. Everything I'd felt earlier, the desire to know more, understand the outside world, has dissipated. Suddenly, all I want is not to be told how to think or feel. "You need to speak to someone. Doctor Sylvie maybe, she's nice. She can help you all."

Emir suddenly grabs my sleeve, forcing me to stop. "Don't be a fool. Just because she's nice to *you* doesn't mean what she's doing is right. Our parents, doctors, the government even, they're all in on it. They're not on your side."

I shake his hands off. Frustration is boiling inside me. "Get off me!" I yell, overspilling.

Emir releases his grip and lifts up his hands as if he's surrendering. "I'm sorry. I didn't mean . . ." He trails off.

The boiling feeling is getting worse, just like in the shop earlier today. I want to scream. I want Emir to stop talking. "I don't feel right," I say.

"You're just angry, Emily," says Emir.

Just angry. The word *angry* couldn't possibly sum up the activity coursing through my body, the thoughts cycling through my brain.

"It's the withdrawal from the medication," Emir continues. "Everything can feel . . . intense for a little while."

I shake my head. "Angry outbursts are a symptom of the Grimm." I put my head in my hands.

"Don't be ridiculous. It's not a symptom of the Grimm. It's normal to have emotions and to feel frustrated. And you can feel more than one thing at once. We have more than most to feel frustrated about."

I shake my head. But this might be the first thing he's said tonight that actually makes sense.

"Emily, you can't trust Doctor Sylvie, or Miss Rabbit. You can't trust any of them. You don't trust us either? You don't believe me? That's fine. But maybe take this as an opportunity to figure out what you actually believe."

"Just leave me alone."

Emir looks at me for a long moment before laughing softly, low and dark. "With pleasure." He turns and begins to walk back the way we just came, back toward the others.

It takes me a long time to find my way back through the woods, and by the time I do emerge, my skin is scratched and bruised, my clothing torn from stumbling off the path so often.

Exhausted and barely making an effort to be quiet, I stumble back around the house and into the facility, then up to the girls' dorm and finally back into my room.

I let my exhaustion pull me into the escape of sleep. I'm too tired to have proper dreams, but they're still there, flickering at the back of my subconscious. Images kaleidoscope through my mind. Snarling faces, feline one moment and human the next. Eyes turning to black holes. Flicking tails. Growls and roars that fill my head.

CHAPTER eleven

I stand outside in the cold winter light. The weekend is reserved for chores, and today, along with ten or so others, I am assigned to garden duty. I shove my spade into the ground, pushing down with a big heave. The blade catches on a rock and I wiggle it until it is buried into the earth. I pull backward and dirt spews outward. Kneeling down, I search amid the earth, pulling out two potatoes, pink skins just about showing through the thick layer of dirt.

Despite the cold air, I am sweating from the physical exertion. For once I am glad of the chore and to be doing something physical, as it gives me something to focus on other than last night. I throw the potatoes into my half-full bucket.

Somebody comes close to me, placing their bucket of potatoes on the ground. "Hi," says Margie, looking up at me over the handle of her spade.

I look up and down the row of other kids digging, but of course they don't notice us. Even the two guardians in charge of watching us are barely paying attention. I recognize one of them as the young one with the scar. He's half-turned away from us and surreptitiously looking down at his phone. The other is older, with a round belly. He claps his hands together and moves from foot to foot, clearly trying to keep warm in the frigid air.

I sigh. This is the third time today that Margie has tried to speak to me. Once in the bathroom, and then again in the line for lunch. "What is it?" I ask.

"I just want to check that you're all right after last night," she says. She digs her spade into the dirt with a surprising amount of strength for somebody so small and unearths a pile of soil and potatoes. She crouches down and begins to pull them out, throwing them into her bucket.

I follow her lead and continue with my task. Dig, crouch, sort. "I'm fine," I say.

"I thought perhaps we scared you off."

I shake my head. "I'm not afraid," I say. And it's true, I'm not. "But what you're doing isn't right. You could hurt somebody."

Margie shakes her head. "Trust me, no matter what Gabriel says, that isn't our intention."

"And do you believe what he says? That we aren't sick?"

Margie nods slowly. "I don't believe we're sick. Do you feel like you're sick?"

I don't say anything for a long moment. Dig, crouch, sort. I inspect a potato, brushing off the dirt before putting it in my bucket. "No," I eventually admit in a voice so quiet that I know I'm admitting this more to myself than to Margie. The truth is that I feel better than I've done in years. How did Clementine put it? *You've found a glow.* And she's right, I feel brighter, freer.

Straightening up again, my eyes rove down the line of other kids. They dig slowly, eyes focused on nothing but their shovels. They don't look up. They don't speak. They're . . . I struggle to find the words to describe it. Empty?

I think about the Ashbury girls and even the Cure members too. None of them are empty; they're full of life.

I shovel my way into the dirt again, a sudden anger making

my blade sink in hard and fast. "It's not fair," I mutter.

"What isn't?"

"If I don't take my medication, the Grimm comes back. But if I take it again, I'll just end up like them again." I nod my head at the others, slowly digging and rooting through the earth.

Margie nods. "Which is why we try to learn to control our abilities naturally, rather than rely on medication to do it for us."

I shake my head and repeat my words from last night. "You can't control a disease." I jab my shovel into the dirt again, feeling another flash of anger. But my anger isn't aimed at Margie, its aimed at myself. Despite everything I had seen last night, this morning I couldn't bring myself to take my pills again. Apparently, I can't even listen to my own good sense.

With every stroke of the blade I chastise myself. I am weak. I am irresponsible. I am a stupid fool. Just like the others.

"Come again tonight," says Margie. "Just give them another chance, and I think you might change your mind."

I throw my spade down onto the earth and frown at where it lies. "Why did you join the Cure, Margie?"

"I have a sister," she says.

Her words make me look up.

"A twin. She goes to Ashbury, actually."

"She goes to Ashbury?" I repeat.

Margie nods. "I grew up nearby and our parents didn't want to send us too far away. I went to Ashbury as well, before . . . you know."

"Do your parents come see you still?"

Margie nods. A faint smile appears on her face. "Yes. They

come as often as they can, which, as you know, isn't very often at all."

"Do you like them visiting?" I know that I am asking lots of questions, but I am curious. I have my own story about how I ended up at Wildsmoor, but I've never really stopped to think that the others would have their own stories too, but of course they do.

Margie shrugs. "It's good and bad. I miss them. They never wanted to send me to Wildsmoor, you know. They took me out of school when they realized that my gift with animals was something more than just that, but eventually a neighbor saw me, and he was the one who called the police."

I nod, processing what Margie has just told me. An unfamiliar and murky feeling turns my thoughts dark. Jealousy, I recognize. Margie at least knows that her parents still loved her and never wanted to send her to Wildsmoor, unlike my own parents.

Like all the other emotions I'm slowly coming to understand as my medication wears off, the jealousy feels almost overpowering. I grip my shovel and tell myself to stop being so ridiculous. Margie is just another grimmer like me and there is nothing there to be jealous of. "You were saying about your sister?" I ask, forcing myself to look up and give her a weak smile.

Margie nods. "She was the one who suggested that perhaps the Grimm wasn't such a bad thing after all. I stopped taking the pills they were giving me and started sneaking out to see her in disguise."

"Disguise?"

"Sometimes a passing cat or mouse. I would inhabit their bodies and we would go for walks. We couldn't talk but it was better than nothing."

"Weren't you afraid you would hurt her?"

Margie gives me a strange look. "No, of course not."

I look down at my spade, thinking about Amelia again.

"One night I saw Gabriel sneaking out," continues Margie. "I followed them and saw what they were doing in the woods. I went back every night after that and I would hide in the woods by the meeting place. At first I just listened to what they were saying, until eventually I found myself agreeing with them. Finally, I went to them in person. I asked to join."

"And you never regretted it?"

Margie shook her head. "The opposite. The Cure have given me something I didn't even realize I was missing."

I frown. "Like what?"

"It's just nice, you know, speaking to other people. How long has it been since you had that?" She gestures between us, as if tracing an invisible line. "How long has it been since you had a conversation like this, even?"

Her words make me pause. I realize that she's right. Sometimes days can pass where I don't exchange so much as a word with another human being. Maybe even weeks. I've spoken more in the last week or so than I have in an entire year at Wildsmoor.

"Humans need connection," says Margie. She picks up a potato and brushes off the dirt. "And now I have that again, I know I don't want to live without it."

I stare at her, the puzzle pieces of my mind slowly clicking into place. I've been lying to myself, I realize. Saying that I want to know the truth. Saying that I'm *curious*. Telling myself that I'm not taking my medication because I'm enjoying a clear head for once, being able to think and feel and seeing the complexities of the world around me.

And all these things are true.

But underneath it all, the answer is more simple than that.

What's really pulling me to the Cure is the same thing I feel that makes me want Clementine to like me. The same thing that makes me feel so much longing when I see her laugh and joke with her friends. And it's the same reason why I've been avoiding my medication.

And the answer is so simple it stuns me, and also makes me feel incredibly sad.

Connection. Human connection. I don't know what I believe, but I know I don't want to be alone.

"Aren't you just lonely?" asks Margie. "I know I was."

Something inside me recoils from the word, like pulling my hand away from something gross I don't want to touch. *Lonely.* I feel the word brand itself into my skin. *Lonely, lonely, lonely.* And another word that goes right alongside it. *Pathetic.*

Margie crouches down. She holds out a hand and a worm wiggles its way out of her pile of dirt and onto her palm. She strokes its pink and squirming body. "You know when you're a kid and you're told that if you cut a worm in two it'll create two worms?"

I nod.

"Well, it's just a myth. That doesn't happen at all. The head part can sometimes grow a new tail, but the other part will just die."

"Right," I say.

"Sometimes I think about all those poor worms, chopped in two and left for dead, and all because of some rumor that was started somewhere."

"Let me guess, we're the worms?" I say, a faint smile creeping onto my lips.

"Hey, you two," shouts a voice.

We both turn. The guardian with the pudgy belly is glaring at us, his hands now tucked up into his armpits. "Quit it with the chit-chat," he yells over. He pulls his hands out of his armpits and makes a parting motion. "I want to see space between you."

Both of us nod, pick up our baskets, and move several steps apart.

"Now get digging." He shakes his head and turns away from us, spitting on the ground and tucking his hands back up into his armpits.

I immediately lift up my spade and start to dig, but Margie crouches down and buries her hand in the dirt. Her lips purse up.

A moment later and the guardian hops and stumbles sideways. "What the . . ." he says, slapping at his leg. He starts to do a funny dance, swiping at random parts of his body and hopping from leg to leg.

"What is it?" asks the other guardian, running over.

"Spiders! They're everywhere!" He continues to strike at different parts of his body and jump from foot to foot. "Well, help me, then!"

The young guardian steps forward and also begins to slap at the other's uniform, both of them now jumping as if they're doing a strange dance. All the kids are now staring, their spades and potatoes forgotten.

Next to me I hear a tiny giggle. I glance over at Margie. She looks at me and winks.

—

That night I try to force myself to go to sleep, but sleep doesn't come. I toss and turn all the way until midnight, the gongs striking through the house. I watch as Adanya leaves the room.

For some reason I get out of bed. I stand there, looking at the door. My mind is hovering on a knifepoint, tipping one way and then another. I don't want to go, but I do. I don't agree with what they're doing, but also, a part of me can recognize a kernel of truth in some of what they're saying.

And now that I'm standing here, in my sagging school socks, feeling the cool breeze that sneaks through the old windowpanes, I know that there was never any question of it anyway. The Cure is offering me something that I didn't even realize I was craving. Something that Margie put a name to earlier—connection. I've been alone for so long and didn't even realize it.

I steal my way through the house, out the door, and into the woods. The wind is strong and cold and whistles through the trees, a reminder of the winter that's about to set in. Below me the ground is muddy from recent rain and above me the sky is revealed in segments through the tangled branches, the odd star peeking through the patchy clouds.

I thought that I would find sneaking through the school and the woods by myself scary, but there is a comfort in the darkness I never realized before. I don't need to fear sneaking, threatening things, because I am one of those things. I am a creature of the night, and the shadows aren't a threat, but a place to hide.

I follow the path until I start to see the glow of firelight in the distance and hear the sound of their laughter. Slowly, I walk closer, intrigued by their chatter.

The last time I went to them it seemed like they did very little but argue and jab at one another, but now I can hear the unmistakably good-natured layering of voices that reminds me of Clementine and her Ashbury friends.

I step out from behind the trees and the clearing falls silent.

"You came," crows Margie, jumping up and hopping over to greet me. "I wasn't sure you would."

"Good to have you back," says Gabriel, nodding in my direction.

Isaiah waves from where he is sitting. Adanya and Emir say nothing.

"Come sit with me," says Margie, tugging on my arm. I follow her around the fire and sit down between her and Isaiah. Margie's arm is still linked through mine and Isaiah lifts his mask to smile at me. I feel a warm glow inside that has nothing to do with the blaze and crackle of the fire.

But tonight, there is a sixth figure. He sits next to Isaiah. Unlike the others, his face is bare and maskless.

"We have another newcomer tonight," says Gabriel. "This is Arthur."

Arthur looks at me warily. I can tell by the roundness of his face and his small frame that he's younger than the rest of us by several years. I also realize almost immediately that I recognize him—he's the boy who had the episode the morning when Gabriel stole my pills. The one who floated up from the ground before being Tasered and dragged away by the guardians. I remember he wasn't at breakfast that day, and now that I think about it, I haven't seen him since.

"Fresh from isolation," says Gabriel.

I raise my eyebrows. "You've been in isolation all this time?" I ask. I've only been to isolation once, back when I first arrived, and I only spent one day there. But it was horrible. Permanent lockup without anything to do other than bounce off the walls and count the seconds as they pass.

Arthur nods.

"That's . . ."

"Barbaric," offers up Gabriel. "But no harm done, as Arthur is here now, and he's one of us, aren't you?"

Arthur nods, although he doesn't look sure. He's looking around nervously, and I don't blame him. The masks, the woods, the fire—I remember how I felt when I first saw them too.

"We were just about to do our demonstration," grins Gabriel at me. "Lucky you, you get a repeat of last night."

I nod and don't reply. I may have given in and come tonight, but that doesn't mean that I agree with what they are doing.

I watch as first Gabriel, then Margie demonstrate their Grimm abilities. Gabriel sticks to the same show as last night, right down to the perching in the tree above Arthur's head at the end. But Margie does something different.

Closing her eyes, she begins to hum. A moment later, the woods around us come alive. Animals scamper and crawl from the undergrowth: mice and badgers and hedgehogs. Snakes and insects too, slithering and scuttling on their bellies. Bats swish through the trees and hang from branches above our heads. Owls hoot and jostle for position, their great eyes turned in Margie's direction.

The animals crowd closer. A snake slithers over my foot and I jump up and move away, not wanting to be swarmed by Margie's animal menagerie. She opens her eyes and holds out a hand. A toad jumps into her palm and she smiles.

"Christ, Margie," says Adanya. "You didn't need to call the whole forest." She has also risen up and is standing right at the edge of the clearing, looking around with an expression that reminds me of our trip to the village—disgust.

Margie laughs. She whispers something to a bird on her shoulder and it flaps into the air, then swoops over to Adanya, fluttering around her head. Shrieking, Adanya bats furiously at the bird. As it flies away, everyone laughs.

"So the fearsome Adanya is afraid of animals?" laughs Gabriel.

"I'm not afraid," replies Adanya. "I just don't want to be close to them. All that flapping and scuttling . . . ugh. Margie, in the name of all that's holy, please can you make them go away now."

Margie nods and begins to hum again, a slightly different cadence to her voice. A moment later the animals turn and disappear back into the woods, until finally there is only the toad left on her palm. "Off you go," murmurs Margie, holding her hand to the ground. The toad hops off and waddles back into the night.

I sit back next to Margie, stunned. "That was . . ."

"Revolting?" offers Adanya. She marches back toward the fire and takes a seat. "Warn me next time before you pull a stunt like that, won't you?"

"Well, I enjoyed it," says Gabriel. "Our very own Disney princess"—he grins—"only she has the Grimm and a penchant for revenge. Could you control them? Get them to attack if you wanted?"

Margie nods thoughtfully. "I could," she says. "But I wouldn't unless there was no other way."

Gabriel's grin spreads wider. "I'll take that as a yes." He turns to Emir. "Are you in the mood to show us your skills tonight?"

Emir shakes his head. "Absolutely not."

Gabriel sighs. "You're no fun at the moment," he says. "Don't you get tired of being so serious all the time? Besides, if you don't practice, how are you going to learn to control it?"

"I'm in perfect control, thank you," counters Emir. "But I'm not going to sit here and pretend everything is all right when there are people here who shouldn't even be here."

Gabriel sighs again. "How many times do we have to go over this? We need new people."

"Yes, but . . ."

I draw my attention elsewhere while they continue their repetitive argument. The others have also started talking now, and the low hum of their voices joins the spitting and crackling noise of the fire.

"Isaiah," I say eventually.

"Yes?"

"What can you do?" I look over at him uncomfortably. "I mean, everyone here seems to have some kind of obvious marker of the Grimm, but I haven't seen you demonstrate yours . . ." I trail off.

Isaiah shrugs. "It's not a secret. It's only that I struggle to control it. It's too big for me, that's why I still take my medication."

I stare in surprise. "You still take the pills they give you?"

Isaiah nods. "I have to. I tried to come off them, and, well . . . it wasn't good. Even with the pills, I can feel that they're barely containing it. If I wanted to use my abilities, it would be easy. Too easy."

"What is it you can do?" I stare at Isaiah, full of curiosity. What kind of power is, in his words, *too big*?

"Explosions, mostly," he replies.

I burst out laughing. Some of the others turn and stare and I cover my mouth. "Sorry. Explosions?"

"Like dynamite," he says. "But lots of it."

"Wait, are you being serious?"

He nods his head.

"Wow. That's some talent, I guess. Can you show me?" I ask. "Just something small."

Isaiah shakes his head. "No." There is a hard edge to his voice now that I've never heard before. "And please don't ask me again. Sometimes it feels so tempting to give in to it, it's all I can do to keep it below the surface."

I blush and nod. "Sorry. I shouldn't have asked . . ."

Isaiah puts his hand on my arm and turns to me. "I blew up my house. There was nobody in the house, but still."

"You blew up your house," I repeat, part in wonder and part in disbelief. "Sorry," I say, looking sideways at Isaiah. "It's just hard to believe."

Isaiah nods. "I couldn't believe it either. After that, I think my parents were glad to get rid of me. I was never the son they wanted anyway." He holds up his walking stick meaningfully. "And I was painfully shy and quiet. And then my brother was born and he was everything I wasn't. Healthy, bright, lively . . . *normal.* And then when my abilities started to show and I was diagnosed with the Grimm, on top of cerebral palsy . . . Let's just say they were glad to see the back of me."

"That's awful," I say.

Isaiah shrugs. "It's not their fault, not really."

I wrinkle my nose and frown. I've not really thought about our parents' roles before in all of this. But Isaiah's story is so similar to my own, and probably similar to a lot of other kids' stories too. Our parents dump us off here, and in some respects who can blame them? It's illegal to conceal a child with the Grimm, not to mention dangerous. But we're also just kids.

I think about my own dad, tying me up and handing me over to the guardians. After that he never came to see me ever again, not once. Did I really deserve that?

Isaiah seems to sense my thought trajectory and he nudges me with his elbow and smiles. "It's not their fault that they're taught to be afraid of us. Besides . . ." Isaiah frowns and his mouth thins into a tight line. "They're not the ones who are really to blame."

"Who, then?" I ask. "If not the people who've sent us here."

Isaiah snorts softly. "That's the million-dollar question, isn't it."

Margie suddenly stands up and holds out both her hands to keep Gabriel and Emir from their bickering. "Before you two start at it again, I have something which might be of interest."

Everyone turns to look at her. "Like what?" asks Adanya.

Margie reaches inside her school coat and tugs out a bundle of creased-up paper.

"Is that a newspaper?" asks Gabriel. "Where did you get it?"

"My sister gave it to me. But look . . ." Margie kneels down on the ground and smooths the newspaper out in front of her. We do not have access to things like newspapers at Wildsmoor, and we all draw closer, curiosity pulling us in. I kneel down next to Margie, my eyes on the bold text splashed across the front page.

"'Facility riots lead to mass escape,'" I murmur. My eyes trace the text again and I frown, trying to process the meaning of the words.

"'After three days of rioting at Hertford Facility for Grimm-Cross patients, the violence reached a crisis point on Friday night, resulting in several dead and a mass escape of students,'" reads Adanya from behind my shoulder. "'The whereabouts of the missing students is still unknown, although there are believed to be at least thirty escapees in total. The prime minister gave an address this morning, warning that these fugitives are highly dangerous and unpredictable, and they are considered to be a significant threat to the population at large' . . ."

"Yes!" crows Gabriel. "Finally, some action. This is great news."

"Hardly," says Emir. "All this is going to do is make it harder for us."

"And why's that?"

"They'll tighten up security. You just see if they don't. This"— Emir waves his hand around the clearing—"We can only do this as the guardians and everyone else have become completely complacent, almost bordering on reckless, really. But if they realize that we really are a threat, then they'll clamp down. Hard."

Gabriel rolls his head around in a circle. "Why does everything have to be so negative with you? What about the good side of this?

That there are others like us, who think the same that we do?"

Emir folds his arms and mutters, "Somebody has to be the voice of sense around here."

"So is that what you're planning, then?" I ask. "Running away?"

Everyone falls quiet.

"What? It's obvious, isn't it? Although I'm not sure the running away would be the hard part, more the where would you go and how would you get there part . . ." I trail off, thinking about the kids in the newspaper article. Where would thirty kids with the Grimm possibly run to . . . ?

"Don't you get it?" says Margie. "Somebody must be helping them."

Everyone looks at Margie. Adanya laughs. "Who would help grimmers like us?"

"Somebody must have given them a place to stay, food to eat, a way out."

"Or nobody is helping them," says Adanya. "And they'll be found starved to death in the middle of the woods somewhere in a month's time."

Inwardly, I think that Adanya's words make sense. I know what happens to kids who run away at Wildsmoor. They're rounded up, sick and hungry a few days later. Or they starve or freeze to death on a hilltop somewhere. There's never a happy ending.

Despite this, for the next hour or so the rest of the Cure reads and dissects every inch of the article, searching for clues. But it seems the reporter who wrote it was nearly as much in the dark as us. Other than the basic facts, most of the article seemed to be quotes from random members of the public.

We're terrified ... The idea that our lives, that our children's lives could be at risk ... none of us are sleeping ...

And so on.

The only thing that is clear is that somewhere in the country, thirty kids are hiding from the guardians and the police and even the military. But *how?*

It's an hour or more until we start to make our way back through the woods and to the facility. Emir lags behind, slightly apart from the rest of the group. I hang back.

"Wait," I say as he goes to walk past me. He stops, a look of surprise on his face.

"Aren't you two coming?" asks Adanya, also stopping and turning back.

"One moment," says Emir, still looking at me.

Adanya scowls and stands there for a moment longer, looking at us both. Her eyes linger for a moment on Emir. "Fine," she snaps, walking off again.

"What is it?" asks Emir, turning to me.

"Here," I say, pulling the book he left for me out of my blazer pocket and shoving it at him.

"Oh," he says, his hands closing around the book.

I look in distaste at the front cover, where the chimera is still snarling up at me. "I don't know if you were trying to get me into trouble or scare me, but that is a horrible book. I can't even imagine how you got your hands on it."

"Why? Because you thought they got rid of all the books like these? All books about magic and myths and anything that might remind anyone of the Grimm?"

I turn to walk off, uninterested in continuing a pointless conversation with someone who clearly doesn't even want me here. The rest of the group has already gone.

"They were storybooks mostly," he says in a quiet voice. "Kids loved them, but they burned them all."

I pause, half-turned toward Emir and half-turned toward where I can still hear the others, murmuring as they weave their way through the woods. "They burned them?" I repeat, interested despite myself.

"In some places, yes; in others they just disposed of them. Recycled them. Binned them or buried them in landfills."

"How do you have this one, then?"

"I found it in the library in the history section," says Emir. "It must've escaped the cull somehow."

"You should get rid of it, then," I reply. "Before someone finds it and you get into trouble."

"There goes Matron's sheep again. Baaa."

I round on him fully and cross my arms. I've had enough of Emir's insults and comments and the way he seems to think he's better than me. "Why do you have such a problem with me?"

Emir's head tilts sideways. "What?"

"Because I'm pretty sure you hate me, although I can't figure out why."

"What makes you think I hate you?"

"You're always mean. You've made it clear to everyone that you don't want me around. And I don't understand. What have I ever done to you?"

"Nothing . . . yet."

"What's that supposed to mean?"

"You said yourself that you think what we're doing is wrong and against the rules. What if you go to one of the teachers, or Matron?" Emir shakes his head. "You can't be trusted. Not to mention the fact that you seem to have no control over your emotions or abilities whatsoever."

Irritation boils in my belly and rises in my throat. I want to slap his self-righteous expression right off his face, but I know I have to swallow the feeling back down. It's exactly what he wants me to do. I take a deep breath. "You know nothing about me. But if you must know, I can say firsthand that we *are* dangerous and that the Grimm *can't* be controlled. I nearly killed my sister before I came here and it was one of my dreams that did it. So yes, I do think that what you're all doing, practicing your 'abilities,' as you call them, is wrong. In fact, I think it's reckless and dangerous and completely selfish."

By the time I finish my rant I am breathing heavily. I think these are the most words I've spoken since before coming to the facility, not to mention that speaking out loud about my sister is painful in a way I wasn't anticipating. Suddenly, I feel embarrassed.

Emir stares for a long moment and when he finally speaks, his voice is suddenly soft. "Well, why are you even here, then?" he asks.

I grow even redder because he's right, of course. Despite everything, I do want to know more. I'm a hypocrite. I know it, and Emir knows it too.

I don't reply and turn to walk off, but Emir scoots around me until he's standing in front of me.

"And selfish?" he says, his words coming out in a rush. He points toward Wildsmoor, where the rooftop has just about emerged from the tree line. "They're the selfish ones. Taking children from their families and controlling them with drugs just because they're scared of us."

I glare at him, not wanting to listen to the sense in his words. "Have you finished?" I try to duck around him.

"No," he says, stepping into my pathway again.

"Move." I step to the side but he steps too, mirroring my movements.

He rips his mask off and our eyes meet. I pause, taking in his face. I was expecting his usual glare or thunderstorm expression, but instead there is an expression on his face that I'm not familiar with. He's biting his lip and a softness shapes his eyes. "I'm sorry about your sister," he says. "You must think about that a lot . . ." I see him take a deep breath, his chest rising and falling. "And I also wanted to say that I understand how you must feel in a way that most of the others can't."

It takes me a moment to register the meaning behind his words. "How?"

Emir's face grows taut. His eyes stare off into the trees, as if there's something or somebody there that only he can see. "I hurt someone too."

"Who?"

"Does it matter? Somebody close to me. But for a long time, I was like you. I blamed myself. But it's only now that I'm beginning to realize that it wasn't entirely my fault. Maybe you should think about what happened with your sister. Was it really your fault? Or was there something else that triggered what happened?"

"I don't understand. It was my dream. A monster that somebody had told a story about in the playground at school. I made the monster real and it attacked her."

Emir shrugs. "Maybe. But it might be worth thinking about what else happened that night. Why did you react like you did?"

I shake my head, frowning. "I can't remember," I say. "We had an argument, I think. But does it really matter? It was my monster. It was my illness that hurt her. I tried to control and hide what I could do, but eventually it came out anyway."

"Perhaps if somebody had taught you how to manage your abilities, instead of hiding them, then it would never have happened."

"Do you really believe that? Do you really believe that you have control?"

Emir pauses for a long moment. "Yes," he says eventually, although I can hear the hesitation in his voice.

"Show me, then," I say. "Show me how you have control."

Emir hesitates again. A muscle jumps in his jaw, before finally he nods, a short, sharp duck of his head. He takes several steps away from me, away from the path and into the trees. There is a gap in the canopy where he stands and a tiny bit of starlight filters down to light up his face. His forehead is cut deep with a frown. His mouth is a thin line. "You need to stay back," he warns. He reaches down and pulls off his gloves. I realize that I have never seen his hands before.

He puts his gloves in his pocket and holds his hands out to me, palms facing up toward the sky. I hear it before I see it. A crackling sound that reminds me of television static, followed by a heavy feeling in the air. His hands start to glow. Bolts of light flicker and dance between his fingers, like storms held in the palms of his hands.

"Oh my god," I mutter.

His eyes also begin to glow. The bolts in his palms spread over his arms and down his torso, crackling. Around him, trees dance and judder and flicker in the sudden light. He is blinding. Brilliant. Terrifying.

CHAPTER twelve

That night, it takes me a long time to fall back asleep. My mind is racing. Memories of my early life at Wildsmoor crop up like saplings in the spring. Isolation and screaming for my mother. Doctor Sylvie explaining to me that I am sick. The sting of Matron's slaps and being reprimanded for every little misdemeanor.

For some reason I can't shake Emir's words out of my head. *What else happened that night?* And so I try to remember.

For the first time in years, I sift through my past.

I remember good things. My father taking me and Amelia swimming every Saturday. We would play a game, making shapes in the air with our bodies as we jumped in. My favorite toy, Mr. Bear, who I'd loved since I was a baby. My mother reading to me, her words soft and lilting as they spun a story from the page.

The memories slice deep into the depths of my heart, and for the first time in a very long time, I cry. Silent tears stream down my cheeks and I stuff my blankets into my mouth to silence my sobs. After not really feeling anything for so long, the flood of emotion is overwhelming: a tap that I can't turn off.

But then I remember the not-so-good things. My father's temper, the stomping and shouting. His words like fists. My mother crying. Silvery apparitions that would haunt the house at night.

When I finally fall asleep, I relive the night when my monster came.

I remember the argument with my sister, about whose turn it was playing with a particular toy that I can no longer even remember. Then my father coming home, his footsteps stamping up the stairs. The way he looks between us and tells Amelia to go down to dinner, patting her head as she skips down the stairs. Then the way he rounds on me, a sudden fury in his eyes. He grabs me by the arm and ushers me into my room, locking the door behind me. "You're old enough. You should know better," he says. I hammer and scream at the door but nobody comes. If my mother is home, she pretends she doesn't hear me, as she often does when my father makes up his mind about things. I cry myself to sleep, hungry and alone.

I dream of monsters and bad things. Screams surround me. I become aware that I'm standing on the landing, my body glowing with the faint milky light that means I'm dreaming. My mom and dad and Amelia are all there. And so is my monster . . .

Sharp teeth, furred limbs, and oozing pustules. The monster towers far above us, crowding the little space in the landing.

The monster's limbs collapse and bend until its face is level with my own. I'm struck with recognition, like a hammer falling down on my heart. Where I always remembered black soulless eyes, I can see now that the monster has my father's eyes.

It lunges at me, grasping fingers stretched outward. I hear screams. Amelia comes from nowhere. She shields my dream body with her own very real one. She stumbles backward and trips and falls, her body tumbling down the stairs. The last thing I hear is her scream of pain.

———

I sit up sharply, gasping for air. The sobs overtake my body. I am gasping and sobbing, and I can't stop. Panic. Hot, pure panic rushes over my whole body, like it's set on fire.

Something growls. I hear a deep snapping sound. Light flashes behind the curtains.

I stumble from my bed and to the window. Around me, the other girls are waking up. They sit up in bed, staring at me. "What's going on?" whimpers Jessica. "You're *glowing*."

Suddenly, Adanya is by my side. "You need to wake up," she says to me. "Wake up now!"

I wrench back the curtains and look out the window. A huge silvery shape rises up from the woodland. My monster is back, but it has changed. It's morphed, taking on characteristics from the creatures in Emir's book: a humped and furred back, horns coming from its head, and wings that are nothing but bones and stretched skin. The air thrums as the beast flies upward. Its head snakes back and forth and then it looks straight at us. My father's eyes stare into mine. His mouth twists and he snarls at me.

The beast flaps its wings. It swoops and flies straight for us.

Behind me the other girls are screaming.

"You need to wake up!" shouts Adanya. "Now!"

Suddenly, I understand. I look down at my body and realize I am glowing silver. Then I look back at my bed and see my sleeping body. I'm not awake at all. I'm dreaming.

I'm dimly aware of Adanya running over to my sleeping body and trying to shake it awake.

But it's no use. I am frozen. Paralyzed with fear.

The beast beats its wings and comes closer to the window. It opens its mouth, and I somehow know what's coming next. "Duck!" I scream. I throw myself down behind the window.

Light engulfs the room. A silver cloud of fury that burns cold instead of hot. Fire.

Alarms begin to wail and the lights come on. The door bursts open. Guardians rush into the room. Their guns are drawn, pointing at each of us in turn. The other girls scream and cower in their bunks, pressing themselves up against the wall. Matron barges in behind them. "Quiet," she snaps. Instantly, the other girls stop their wailing.

The guardians settle their guns on me—dream me, that is. One of them recoils, whether in disgust or fear I can't tell. They start toward me, but Matron stops them. "Don't be stupid. There, on the bed," she says. She points at my sleeping body.

I watch as the blue guardians tear away my blankets and jab a needle into my neck. I reach up as I feel the stab of pain. Then, darkness.

—

When I wake up, it feels like I'm crawling out of a deep black hole. The first thing I notice is a rhythmic beeping, coming from the right side of my head. I tear open my eyes. The ceiling above me is a white nothingness.

Something is in my hand. My body feels heavy all over but I just about manage to raise my arm an inch or so off the bed. A tube leads from the back of my hand to a clear bag of liquid hanging from a metal frame. I wonder briefly what they are pumping into my body, but then my head slumps back down as I realize I don't really care. I don't have the energy.

A strange floating sense of happiness holds me in its grip. It's like being wrapped in cotton wool, or a cloud. I imagine myself floating through the sky with all the other clouds, and I giggle.

I am not sure how long I lie there, grinning to myself, but at some point the door opens. Matron walks into the room, followed by Doctor Sylvie and two guardians. The guardians position themselves at either side of the door. Their guns are drawn, but pointing toward the floor this time, rather than at me.

Doctor Sylvie smiles as she comes toward me. Like always her lips are perfect and red. Her hair a sheen of silk pulled back into a ponytail. "Hi, honey," she says. She stops by the side of my bed and reaches out to stroke my head. Her touch is feather soft. "You poor thing. Matron explained everything that happened, but don't worry, you're safe now."

I smile back at her. I try to speak but my words come out as a nonsensical mumble. I sound so stupid that it makes me giggle.

"What's wrong with her," snaps Matron, looming up behind Doctor Sylvie.

"We've had to sedate her before starting her on a stronger medication. This way she won't have another nasty episode in the meantime. However, there are some side effects, as you can see, euphoria being one," replies Doctor Sylvie. She smiles down at me again. "Do you understand what I'm saying, Emily?"

I shake my head.

"You've had an episode, Emily, and a serious one at that by all accounts, but don't worry, once you're all better, we can have a good chat about it. But just so you know, you're in the best possible hands. No doubt you'll be back on your feet in no time at all."

My mind replays her words until they mean something through the fuzziness. *Better.* That word again. It strikes something in my head. *Better . . . because I'm sick.* "I want to get up," I say.

"Not yet, honey. As soon as you're better you can get up."

Better. There it is again.

"But I'm not sick," I say. I force my body to move, clawing myself into an upright position.

"Here," says Doctor Sylvie, helping me upright. She reaches for something on a metal cart and then holds out her hand. In it is a collection of pills. "We've increased your dose for the time being—that should keep any little episodes at bay until we can properly figure out what's happening."

I don't reach out to take them. "I'm not sick," I repeat, louder this time. I try to get out of the bed and Doctor Sylvie reaches out to me, gently holding me in place. The guardians at the door raise their guns. They point them in my direction.

Doctor Sylvie looks at them and then at Matron. "Are they really necessary?" she asks.

Matron snorts. "You wouldn't be asking that if you saw what she did. We used to lock them up and throw away the key when they got out of hand like this." Matron looks down at me, her lip curled as if she's looking at something particularly disgusting.

"Well, that sounds entirely unethical," says Doctor Sylvie.

Matron snorts and shakes her head. "You're new here but you'll soon learn. Coddling them only makes the behavior worse." She turns to me. "You heard the doctor. Take your meds."

I look again at the collection of pills in Doctor Sylvie's hand. I imagine picking them up, putting them in my mouth, swallowing them down. How the little lumps would stick in my throat . . . "I'll take them later," I say.

"You'll take them now," says Matron, her eyes narrowing.

I shake my head. "I can't," I say, desperation leaking into my voice. "I won't." I can feel the stirring of a panic attack in my stomach. That monster again, its eyes fixed on mine. Suddenly, I'm struggling to breathe. My breaths are short. My head spins.

"You need to calm down, honey," says Doctor Sylvie.

But I do not calm down. Instead, I rip the tube from my arm and pull my arm from Doctor Sylvie's grip. I roll out of the bed, landing on the floor, before scrambling to my feet and making a run for the door.

The guardians step forward and block my way. I try to push through them, but I am so weak and feeble it's pathetic, my attempts like a pebble glancing off a brick wall.

A hand grabs my hair and yanks me backward. Matron leers down at me, her hand knotted into my hair at the back of my scalp. She slaps me, a hard smack that should hurt more than it does.

Doctor Sylvie steps forward. Her eyes are wide, her perfect red lips parted. "We don't . . ." she trails off. "I mean. Corporal punishment isn't . . ."

"Are you questioning my methods?" asks Matron.

"I find communication to be just as effective . . ."

Matron snorts with laughter, cutting her off. "Communication? What these little wretches need is a firm hand, not some modern, namby-pamby rubbish." She shakes me like a dog, as if to prove her point. I feel her hand loosen on my hair slightly and I turn my head and bite, my teeth sinking into flesh. Salt coats my tongue.

Matron yells and throws me to the floor. She examines her hand where red teeth marks now dent her skin. "See? She's out of control, just like the others. We tried it your way, now"—she looks from Doctor Sylvie to the guardians—"take her to isolation."

———

The room is bare, just four white walls and a glaring white light overhead. The only other thing in the room is my pills and a small paper beaker of water. I still can't bring myself to take them. Partly because I don't want to feel lifeless again, but also partly because I am angry. Angry enough to not care what happens to me.

The room is tiny, but I curl up on the hard concrete floor anyway. I close my eyes for a moment. I think I must drift off, as the next thing I know the door is opening. Matron stands there, flanked by guardians. Her body is a wide silhouette but I can still make out her eyes, pale blue and glaring. They flicker to where my meds still lie on the floor and she smiles softly. "You want to play?" she asks, in a voice as soft as her smile. "Fine, we can play, Emily Emerson. But trust me, I always win."

I don't reply.

"One last chance?" she says, nodding toward the pills.

I don't move or speak, and for a long moment I just absorb her ice-blue stare and try not to let the chill of it invade my bones. I cling to the anger instead, letting it warm me, giving me strength. I don't know what she sees in my face, but the smile fades and hardens into a thin line. Finally, she turns to the guardians. "No food, water, or bathroom privileges until she takes them," she says. Then she steps backward and slams the door shut.

I manage to sleep awhile, but all too soon I am awake again. Time passes. Hours. A whole day? Perhaps even longer. I can't be sure. Thirst sets in, my throat dry and my head aching. Then hunger. At intervals the guardians check on me, their eyes flickering from me to my medication before leaving again. I need to go to the toilet and eventually I give up and wet myself, my pee burning and the urine soaking into my clothes.

But the thirst and hunger and humiliation aren't the worst things about isolation. It's the blank four walls. The nothingness. The way that time becomes meaningless. It's somehow worse than what I imagined.

It's torture.

My thoughts get stuck in a loop. Again and again I see the beast out the window. The other girls screaming and cowering in their beds. The heat as it breathed fire in our direction. The feeling of being paralyzed. The panic.

I remember Dad's punishments. I remember him locking me in my bedroom the night of the accident. How I'd screamed and cried until I'd fallen asleep. How Mom didn't do anything to stop him. And then I picture the monster's eyes, my father's eyes. Its mouth. The image that my eight-year-old self conjured up.

Finally, I recognize that I had dreamed of my father that night. He was the nightmare that tortured us day after day with his moods, whether he understood it or not.

The monster didn't attack Amelia that night. I was always Dad's target. It attacked *me*.

Amelia had stepped into its path.

She was only trying to protect me, and we both paid the price for Dad's rage.

I sleep again. I wake. I sleep again. The dryness in my throat has infected my whole body. My chest rasps and my skin itches. My mind glances off the four walls. I play a game, counting the flecks I can see in the concrete floor. I think about the kids who've been sent here before me and wonder if they did the same.

But still I don't take my medication.

I am sleeping when the door opens and somebody clip-clops into the room. I open my eyes and see a pair of black high heels. I struggle into a sitting position.

Doctor Sylvie looks down at me. She reaches out a hand, and after a long moment, I accept it. She helps me to my feet. "Come with me," she says.

"But . . ."

Doctor Sylvie puts a finger to her lips, then points backward. I look behind her, where two guardians are lurking in the corridor. "Matron has requested a medical checkup," says Doctor Sylvie. I hesitate, before just giving a simple nod. Anything to get out of here.

I follow her through the school, my legs stumbling and weak at first before finding their momentum. After the blank four walls of isolation, everything is overstimulating. Bright lights. Colors. A gust of fresh air blows from a nearby window that's been left ajar, cold and fresh and promising winter. I greedily breathe it in as it briefly dances across my face.

We reach Doctor Sylvie's office and she ushers me inside. She smiles at the guardians who are still trailing us and says a bright "Thank you" before closing the door in their faces.

Her office is serene compared with the rest of the facility. Plants and polished wood and the smell of perfume. Doctor Sylvie gestures toward the reclined couch and I reluctantly take a seat, perching on the end of the soft leather. I eye Doctor Sylvie warily. "Why am I here?" I ask, my voice rasping the words.

But Doctor Sylvie ignores my question and instead walks over to where a water fountain sits in one corner of the room. She presses a button and I stare as water glugs in its plastic tank before sploshing into a paper cup. "Here," says Doctor Sylvie, bringing the cup over to me.

I don't hesitate. I take the cup and drink the water. Its cool earthiness banishes the dryness from my mouth and I gulp it down, water dribbling down my chin. "More," I manage to say.

"Not yet," says Doctor Sylvie. "Let us have our chat first and then you can drink all the water you like."

I grit my teeth but nod anyway.

I watch as Doctor Sylvie takes a seat opposite me, sinking back into a cushioned chair. We watch each other for a moment.

"I thought it might be best if you and I could have a discussion. An adult discussion, just between us ladies."

"Does Matron know?"

Doctor Sylvie shifts in her seat and for a moment I see a look flicker across her face that could just be uneasiness, but also could be fear. I wonder if she's afraid of Matron too. But a moment later she's smiling at me again. "How about this chat remains our little secret, just between us. What do you say?"

I shrug. "Suits me."

"So I want you to tell me, and you can be completely honest, how are you feeling? And don't worry, anything you say won't get back to Matron or anyone else, this is just between you and me."

I say nothing for a long while. I am exhausted and everything hurts, but still I cling to that burning coal of anger on the inside. I can still feel where Matron grabbed my hair, where she slapped me. And Doctor Sylvie, she didn't do anything, not really. She let them take me to isolation. She let them lock me up and try to starve me.

But more than anything I am angry about my lack of choices. Surely it should be my choice what goes into my body. Only apparently, it isn't.

"Emily?" prompts Doctor Sylvie. Her eyebrows are crumpled in what appears to be genuine concern.

"What?"

"I was just asking how you're feeling?"

I sigh and finally lean back into the chair, letting the soft leather overwhelm me. "Confused," I say. And it's not a lie; there is a part of me that feels confused. Since meeting Gabriel and Emir and the rest of the Cure, my whole life has turned upside down. I don't know who to trust or what to believe.

Doctor Sylvie nods sympathetically. "Of course you are. It can be a very confusing thing, being unwell."

"I just don't understand what happened," I say. Another half-truth.

"Well, that I can help with," says Doctor Sylvie. "As you already know, Grimm-Cross Syndrome can be a tricky thing and manifests itself differently in every child." She pulls a faded yellow folder from the top of her desk and begins to flick through it. I see on the front of the folder that it says my name—*Emily Emerson*. "We've worked very hard to make you better, Emily, but it's quite normal to have a little lapse. What happened last week was really nothing more than a psychotic episode. I believe that you've developed resistance to your medication, quite normal in somebody of your age, and this caused your hallucinations and emotional dysregulation."

I think about the monster out the window. Was that only a hallucination? I remember the other girls screaming. I frown and shake my head. "But surely if it's my own hallucinations then only I would be able to see them?"

"Aha!" says Doctor Sylvie. "You're a very observant girl. I like it. You see, that's what makes Grimm-Cross different from other mental illnesses. The hallucinations and delusions are so powerful that they take on a physical form. Even we don't completely understand how it's possible, but the brain is a very powerful and mysterious thing."

I think about this, trying to sort out my thoughts. I think about my dreams and I think about Emir and the rest of the Cure and their special "abilities," as they call them. Are all of these just manifestations of their psychosis? The imagination gone wrong, and the mental somehow turned physical? There is a sense to this.

"That's what Professor Grimm and Doctor Cross are working on right now, solving these little mysteries behind the disease. It's fascinating really. One moment . . ."

She turns and lifts something up from the top of her desk. A newspaper, slightly rumpled. She opens it up and flicks from page to page. "Aha, this is what I was looking for." She begins to read out loud, an article about Doctor Cross and his most recent research. But I'm hardly listening.

Instead, my eyes are fixed on the front page.

There is a picture of a tall building, gray and blocklike. Some of the windows are smashed and in front of the building there is a burned van, black and still smoking. Police tape rings the building and guardians and officers survey the scene, hands on hips.

A headline is printed in bold above the picture: **Grimmer Breakouts Continue . . .**

My heart gives a sudden lurch. My eyes skim the rest of the page, trying to absorb as much information as I can.

Belle Vue latest facility struck . . . violent unrest . . . mysterious disappearances.

"What do you think, Emily?"

I say nothing, eyes darting farther down the page.

Escape . . . riots . . . high alert.

Doctor Sylvie lowers the newspaper and frowns at me. "Did you hear me?"

"Yes," I say hurriedly. I even smile, trying to put her at ease. But it's too late. She looks at the front page and goes bright red. She shoves the newspaper back on the desk.

"Well, anyway," she says, clearly flustered. "All I'm trying to say is that there is light at the end of the tunnel, Emily. All you need to do is keep trying, keep taking your medication, and you'll be out of here in no time. I know it might not feel like it sometimes, but we're all on your side. All of us. Even Matron in her own way, although I know she can be a bit of a battle-ax."

I know her words are supposed to be comforting but instead they make me pause. There is something familiar about her words. I hear a voice in my head. Emir.

They're not on your side.

"And really I don't think there is too much to worry about in regard to your little episode." She opens up my folder again and

144

flicks to the beginning. "You've been here seven years now and have been on the same medication since you arrived. We do gradually increase the dose but in your case, it appears this isn't enough."

She walks over to the water fountain and refills my paper cup. She holds it out to me, and in the other hand, she holds out my medication. I stare down at her outstretched hands, one holding water and one cupping pills. Two white. Two red. And a blue.

"Isn't there another way?" I ask. "A way where I can remain myself."

Doctor Sylvie smiles. "But you are still yourself, silly, you're just a better, calmer version of yourself." She smiles. "Take them now, honey. You'll be feeling right as rain in no time, then we can get back on track with you working toward your release."

"And then I'll be sent home?"

"Yup," smiles Doctor Sylvie. "Wouldn't that be wonderful?"

I think about this, again conjuring up the images of my father's pinched face, and for the first time, I entertain the thought that perhaps home isn't a place I would even want to go back to.

"And what if I still have another episode? What if I never get better or if I'm never cured? What will happen to me then?"

Doctor Sylvie looks uncomfortable for a moment. "Well. You have three more years to get better before you have to think about that."

I frown. "But what does happen to the kids who don't get cured?"

Doctor Sylvie's eyes shift left and right. "In all honesty, I don't really know. But best not to think about it, hon."

There is something about her shifting eyes that makes me know that she is lying. And whatever happens to the kids who don't get better, I'm guessing isn't good.

I look down at the pills again. *They're not on your side.*

Something gives in my mind, like a light suddenly being switched on, allowing me to finally see clearly. I tally up in my head all the injustices and cruelties I've seen over the years. The children like ghosts, sucked dry of their wants, dreams, wishes. Left without any choices. The people who keep us here: our teachers, doctors, and Matron, all of them allowing the cruelties that govern our lives. Our parents giving in to fear and sending us here in the first place.

I think about what I've just read on the front of Doctor Sylvie's newspaper and recognize there are other kids across the country waking up to this same realization.

My thoughts are razor-sharp and dark and I could let them feed the anger inside me, but instead I push the rage down. Anger gives me strength, but it's not strength I need right now. What I need is to be cold and calculating. I need to be one step ahead.

"Do you want to get better?"

I look at Doctor Sylvie and absorb her half smile and wide eyes, and I realize that perhaps she does genuinely think she's doing what's best for us. Perhaps, like all of us, she's been led to believe that this is the only way: locking kids up and turning them into brainless sheep in the name of *treatment*. But that doesn't mean that she's not completely *deluded*.

I slump my shoulders and look down at the ground. I let tears fill up my eyes. "Of course," I say. Then I reach out for the pills and the water. I swallow the water but the pills I let settle under my tongue. Doctor Sylvie smiles at me and I smile back. I can see my reflection in the window behind her head, and my smile is a work of art. It's a small, wavering sort of smile. A smile that says—I'm tired and confused, but I'm also sorry and I trust you, and yes, of course I want to get better.

But the smile is a lie. There is no confusion left in my mind. If they won't give me choices, then I guess I'll just have to make them for myself.

CHAPTER thirteen

I'm standing in my room. Everything is dark apart from a silvery soft sort of light that reflects off the white walls and sheets. There are no windows and I look around for the light source stupidly for a moment before catching a glimpse of my own hands. They glow softly like the moon. "Goddamn it. Not again," I mutter.

It's me. I am the light source, which means that I'm dreaming.

After meeting with Doctor Sylvie, they allowed me out of isolation and put me back in the treatment room to allow me time to adjust to my new dose. I've mastered the blank expression of someone who is taking their medication but I keep each day's pills under my tongue before spitting them into the hole I managed to tear in my mattress.

I think about Matron's words—*you want to play?* I'm determined to beat her at this game. Determined that she believes my lies. But as much as I want to be in control, I have to face up to the truth that it was only a few days ago that my subconscious summoned a fire-breathing chimera. I have to somehow make sure this doesn't happen again and get my symptoms of the Grimm under control.

I look down at my sleeping body and sigh. Control. That is apparently something I still need to work on.

A noise interrupts my thoughts. The fumbling of a hand as it tries to find a handle, then the almost imperceptible swish as the door swings open. The corridor's green emergency lights shine into the room.

My heart leaps and I crouch down by my bed, trying to make myself as small as possible. I look toward the doorway, expecting to see the silhouette of guardians, or even Matron. But I don't. Instead, a lone figure sidles into the room and shuts the door behind them. They shine a flashlight in my direction, the light glancing off my sleeping body.

I straighten up. "Who are you?" I ask.

"Shhh," hisses the figure. "It's just me."

They turn the flashlight and hold it under their chin. The harsh light turns their face into a skeleton, all bones and shadows and dark holes where their eyes should be.

It takes me a moment to realize that it's Emir. And then it takes me another moment for the confusion to set in. *Why? Why is Emir here?*

He shuffles toward me. He places the flashlight on one end so it points toward the ceiling, diffusing light around the room. His face is no longer a skeleton and I take in his rumpled bed hair and too-small pajamas, ankles poking from beneath his trousers. His stockings sag around his feet. He looks far younger than when I met him in the woods, all adult and scary in his mask and buttoned-up coat. Now he just looks like little more than a child, which I suppose he is.

He looks from my real body, still unconscious in bed, then back to my dream body. He looks as if he's about to say something but I get in there first. "You shouldn't be here. You'll get us both in trouble."

Emir shrugs. His eyes flicker between my dream body and the hump of blankets that is my real body again. For some reason I feel protective of the real me and I move to sit at the end of the bed, blocking my sleeping body from view. "Seriously, why are you here?" I ask.

"I don't know," says Emir. He shifts from foot to foot, as if uncomfortable. I frown, considering his expression. He looks unusually vulnerable, unsure of himself. Somehow I have the upper hand, even though I'm not sure why.

I raise my eyebrows at him, as if to say, *Go on.*

"I was just checking that . . ." He pauses and runs a hand through his hair. His eyes flicker around the room. "I was just making sure that . . ." He pauses again and swallows. There is a pained expression on his face now. "That you're all right," he says.

I stare at him, surprised, shocked, even. "You're checking up on me?"

He nods, a tiny bob of his head.

I wrinkle my nose, suddenly suspicious. Emir has never shown any concern for my well-being before. "You mean you wanted to check that I haven't told Matron about you?"

Now it's Emir's turn to be surprised. "What? No. Of course not."

"Only that you've never cared about how I'm doing, other than how it relates to you, so forgive me if I don't quite believe you're only here for my benefit."

Emir gives me a funny look. "Well . . . have you?"

"Have I what?"

"Have you told anyone about us."

I roll my eyes. "I knew it. I knew that you weren't here just to check how I am. I'm not stupid, Emir."

He shrugs and shakes his head. "Believe what you want," he says, before adding under his breath, "I should've known coming here would be a waste of time." He turns and walks back toward the door.

I move without hardly realizing it, a step toward him as something twists in my chest. I don't want him to leave, I realize. He's the first person besides the guardians and Doctor Sylvie who I've seen in five days. "Wait," I say.

He turns back around. "What?"

"Maybe I *should* tell somebody about you all," I say.

Emir's vulnerable expression is suddenly gone. Heat radiates from his body. I hear a tiny crackle and see a flicker of electricity race around his shoulders. "You wouldn't dare," he hisses.

"I'm not afraid of you," I say.

"Not yet," he says.

I register the threat in his words, but instead of fear, I feel a little thrill. I've gotten under his skin, and for some reason the knowledge of this makes me feel powerful.

"Besides, we're not the only ones with secrets." He looks meaningfully toward my physical body that's still lying in bed and then back to my dream body. "I'm sure Matron and Doctor Sylvie would love to know that you're still not taking your meds."

I fold my arms and glare at him. He's right, of course. "So you're going to rat *me* out?"

Emir shakes his head. "Don't be stupid. Of course not. But I won't need to; it's only a matter of time if you don't learn some self-control."

"And I suppose you think you could help me?"

I wait for Emir to say something, or leave, but still he doesn't go. "I know that we haven't always got on that well," he finally says.

I nod my head. That is the truth, if nothing else.

"But if you need help, Emily, then you just have to ask."

"Help? From you?"

He nods.

I fold my arms and say nothing. Is Emir seriously offering to help me? I peer harder at his face, but he just looks back, open-eyed and, as far as I can tell, with nothing but sincerity. Confusion dulls the edges of my anger. His personality changes are like riding a seesaw. One moment he's telling everyone not to trust me and glaring at me with such force that I feel like he is trying to burn me with his eyes, and the next moment he's risking his own skin to come and offer to help me.

I don't understand him. I look away, realizing that it doesn't matter. I don't have the time or energy to figure out the inner workings of Emir's mind right now. "I don't need help," I say.

"Clearly, you do," he says.

I feel a tug of embarrassment. And suddenly I feel sick of it. Sick of other people's judgments and being told what I need or what to do. Emir doesn't trust me to manage my own symptoms or to keep their secrets. That's why he's here, I remind myself, to check that I haven't given them away.

I swallow my feelings and fold my arms. I lift my chin and look down my nose. "Emir. If I did need help, then trust me, you would be the last person I would ask."

We stare at each other for a long moment, then he throws back his head and laughs. His face turns hard and smooth, covering up any trace of vulnerability. He looks down at me.

"Don't look at me like that," I say.

But he carries on glaring and then his lip curls, giving me that look that makes me feel so small.

I stand up. I don't want to feel small any longer. I don't want to feel like I am less than somebody, or foolish, or weak, or powerless. The feeling swells and somehow I grow, my chest puffing outward and my arms and legs gaining length.

I tower above Emir, so tall my head is nearly touching the ceiling. I look down at my body, glowing and powerful and strong in a way that my real one isn't. Up until that moment I'd almost forgotten that I was dreaming, but now I am glad of it. I look down at Emir and twist my features, trying to make myself as fierce as possible. I feel my teeth sharpen against my tongue and my lips. I bare them at him and hiss.

And now its Emir's turn to cower under my gaze. Again I feel that same thrill from earlier but even more so.

"Get out," I say, and my voice comes out like a growl.

"So this is you controlling your abilities, then?" he bites back.

"Actually, it is," I retort.

He laughs again, derision turning each chuckle into a weapon. Then he grabs his flashlight, pulls open the door, and shuts it behind him, leaving nothing behind but darkness and silence.

My mind is swimming. The power is overwhelming, filling my body. I hear the swish and beat of wings.

No.

I force myself to take a deep breath, then another. This is my body. These are my emotions. I am in control. I do not need medication to control the Grimm, because the Grimm is me. My body deflates, going back to its usual size. I perch back on the edge of my bed and breathe a sigh of relief. I feel a little bubble of excitement as I realize that I've managed to somehow stay in control.

I turn to my sleeping body. I close my eyes and concentrate hard. I can feel both versions of myself—dream me and real me. I follow the thread to real me's body, and with a great wrench, pull my eyelids open.

I blink in the pitch darkness, in bed again. The only light filters through the tiny frosted window set into the door, and I hold my hands up into the light. I check each of my hands in turn, squinting through the gloom at my fingers. But no. I am definitely not glowing. I'm awake. I smile to myself, and this time when I fall asleep, I do not dream.

CHAPTER fourteen

The next night when I fall asleep, I find myself above my sleeping body once more. I feel the instinct to panic, fearful of the memories that continue to creep back into my consciousness. But then I force those thoughts away. I can choose to breathe. I can choose how to react.

I look down at myself, just a bundle of blankets lit by the silvery glow from my own skin. I am fifteen and think of myself as a child no longer, but in the peacefulness of sleep, my face looks terribly young, not as far removed from that eight-year-old who was originally sent to Wildsmoor as I thought. I suddenly feel a sharp stab of sympathy for the girl hidden under those sheets, which is a strange and disorienting thing to feel about yourself. That girl is helpless. That girl was afraid. That girl was abandoned.

I feel an urge to get away.

I don't think about the how or why of what I'm doing, and instead I just imagine myself somewhere else.

Thick darkness surrounds me. The woods.

I stand in the grove where the Cure meets. It is empty tonight, just the shadowed sentinels of trees standing guard in a circle, and in the middle, a charred spot where a fire once burned.

Wind blows and branches creak around me, as if the trees are talking to one another. I wonder what they could be saying. Tree things, most likely, I decide. Things that I couldn't possibly understand with my stupid human brain.

I go to one and put my hand against its trunk. I can feel and smell it as if I am in my waking body. Rough bark with knots and grooves. A deep and earthy smell that speaks of many years in this dark and ancient forest. I rest my head against the trunk and close my eyes.

With my eyes shut, the thread that tethers my dream body to my physical form becomes more apparent. It feels stretched, taut, as if it's pulling me back. I could wake myself up, if I wanted to, but I don't. Instead, I let my mind wander and realize that I can also feel all the others too. They are flickering lights in the corners of my mind. Dreamers in their beds, children and adults, guardians and doctors alike. All of them. I have a strange feeling that their sleeping minds are flowers in a field, ready for me to pluck.

Sometimes I recognize the dreamers. Adanya and Jessica and the other girls in my dorm being some of them. Jessica's and the other girls' dreams are nothing more than dull flickers, but Adanya is different. Her sleeping mind is alive with colors and shapes. I expected her thoughts to be sharp, but they're not; everything has a surprising softness to it. Her dreams morph and swirl from one thing to another. Masked figures. Moonlight cascading through tree branches. Her lips pressing against someone else's . . .

She's kissing somebody. Part of me is curious and wants to know more. Who is this person that she dreams about? But a split second later I pull away from her. That is a private thing, and I am intruding where I shouldn't.

I seek out the other members of the Cure, shuffling through Wildsmoor's slumbering minds. Gabriel's unconsciousness immediately jumps out at me. He dreams he's on a boat on the ocean. His fingers trail in the water and salt spray buffets his cheeks. The sensation of the cold water and wind and fresh air is so vivid that I know this is more of a memory than a dream. Something from his before life.

Isaiah and Margie I can't sense, and I come to the conclusion they must be awake, or so deeply asleep that no dreams can touch them.

Finally, I seek out Emir. His dreams glimmer in my mind, an image of starlight and ink-blue sky. There is a girl there with him. A girl with long dark hair and big eyes and parted lips. She glows softly like moonlight on the edge of a vaguely shadowed landscape, like a cliff top. She is strange and mysterious and beautiful.

He laughs at something she says and the sound of it takes me by surprise. I've only ever heard Emir laugh in derision, but this laugh is unfettered by pain or anger and is full of joy. I am curious. Who is this girl? Who is this dream girl who can make Emir laugh like that?

I fall further into the dream. The lines of the cliff grow clearer until I stand next to them, perched on the edge. The girl's features grow sharper, and then the surprise hits me like a slap in the face. I realize that I know her, sort of.

Me.

Emir is dreaming of me.

But this is a twisted, beautiful version of myself. My hair is longer and thicker, my eyes bigger and brighter, my lips pinker.

I don't know whether to feel flattered or annoyed.

His dream grows clearer, filling in around the edges until I feel like I'm actually there. I watch as Emir steps forward and reaches out to hold the dream girl's hand. He smiles at her and she smiles back.

I can't help myself. "Is that supposed to be me?" I say. "Because I don't look like that."

Emir's head lurches back. His dream version of me disappears. So does the cliff top and the star-studded sky above us. We float in a void. He turns and frowns and for a tiny second looks straight at me. His eyes, which up until that point had been vaguely unfocused, suddenly grow sharp. "Emily?" he says.

I feel a flash of panic when I realize that somehow he can hear me, that he's looking at me. I yank myself out of his dream. But I must've done something wrong, as when I open my eyes, Emir is now standing next to me. I take my hand off the trunk and turn to him.

We stand in the woods, the real woods this time, but now both our bodies are glowing. He looks down at his body, his feet, his arms, and finally his hands. He turns them this way and that. "Is this real?" he asks.

"I don't know," I say slowly, trying to figure it out. "I think I somehow pulled you here, out of your head."

"But this is real," he says, gesturing around the clearing, touching the tree trunk again.

"Yes. This is real. It's only us that aren't."

"But how?"

I shake my head, feeling suddenly mortified. If I answer his question, he'll know that I was prying in his head. And then he might wonder *why*. The answer to which I don't really know. Why did I seek out Emir's dreams?

He frowns and his gaze sharpens. "You were in my dream," he says, his tone vaguely accusatory.

"Sorry . . ." I trail off and wave my hand at him, trying to convey a wordless apology. *I didn't mean to pry in your head. I didn't mean to watch your dreams. I didn't mean to drag your unconscious mind around according to my will.*

"You were dreaming of me," I say, trying to justify myself.

"I . . . was I?"

I nod.

Now it's Emir's turn to be self-conscious. "Sorry," he mutters.

"Why were you dreaming of me?"

Emir looks anywhere but back at me. He touches both of his arms in turn, then he touches the tree trunk next to him, one finger tracing over the bark. "Does there have to be a reason why? Dreams are meaningless."

Are they? I think about this, and decide that, no, dreams aren't meaningless. Dreams are a window to the soul and what resides there. I think about what I just saw in the other Cure members' heads. The sea spray freedom of Gabriel's dream, the surprising softness and romance in Adanya's.

"It was just a dream," he says eventually, looking up from the tree trunk. "Nothing more . . ." Emir trails off when his eyes meet mine.

But I think about my own dreams, haunted by the foulest parts of me, my worst memories come to life. The understanding hits me like a train. I can't run from it. I can't run from myself.

Panic.

The world swims in and out of focus and the air solidifies in my lungs.

Snap. Thump. Noises sound from deep within the trees. Our

necks twist and both of us stare in the direction the clamor is coming from. A chittering noise fills the air, followed by a bone-chilling screech. Whatever it is comes closer, and closer still, snaps and screeches and branches shaking. Emir peers into the darkness of the woods, head twisting and turning, trying desperately to catch sight of whatever is coming for us. But I don't need to see it to know what it is.

My monster is back.

I push my hands to my throat. I know that this body isn't real, just a figment of my unconscious, but still I get the overwhelming feeling that I can't breathe. I gasp and my chest heaves in and out.

Emir turns back to me. "Emily, you need to calm down."

But my memories have me in a vise. I'm a child again, hammering my fists against a locked door, firstly in my bedroom, and later on in the back of the van that took me away. I fall to my knees.

The monster screeches again, followed by a noise like wind gusting against a sheet, but louder, and I know it has taken flight. I look up through the clearing. It soars into view. It looks different this time, more meshed-together images from Emir's book. A looped tail and cloven hooves, a head that is ape shaped but with twisted, curling horns. Its wings are bird wings, feathered and black. Its neck is oddly elongated, weaving left and right, eyes searching the forest. I know what it's looking for. Me.

Next to me Emir is staring too. "What is that?"

"My monster. A childhood nightmare."

"You have to stop it," he says. "You have to learn some control."

I realize that there's desperation in his voice. Or worse, doubt. He doesn't think that I can control it. And the worst part is that

I agree with him. "I . . . I . . ." I watch as the beast circles once more in the sky, then it looks down. Its eyes stare into mine. I see my father again, and again I feel paralyzed. "I can't," I eventually get out.

"You have to. Emily, you're in control. That thing is just part of you."

"I don't know how," I whisper.

The monster folds back its wings and dives, descending on us headfirst.

"Stand up," says Emir. He pulls me up but my legs feel funny and I collapse back to the ground.

And then it's too late anyway. The monster pulls up sharply and lands with a thump on the forest floor. It's huge, two, three times the size of us. It rears upward, going from all fours to standing on two legs.

"I can wake us up," I say to Emir. "That's the only way."

But Emir frowns and shakes his head. "No," he bursts out. "If you run from it now, you'll always be running. The only way to deal with your fears is to face them."

Clawed feet stamping, the beast begins to circle. Its neck weaves left and right again, still looking, still searching for us.

"How can I fight that?" I ask. "And what if we die here? How do we know that we won't also die for real?"

Emir shakes his head. "I don't know."

Still the monster is circling, struggling in the small space, but it won't be long until it finds us. I have to make a decision, and I have to make it now. Either I follow the thread back to my body and wake up, or I stay and face the monster of my own making.

I want to run. My body is screaming at me to get out of there. But also, I know Emir is right. If I let the monster win tonight, it will always be there; it will always be trying to get me. And what then? Am I just never going to sleep again? Never dream again?

No.

I have to stay. I have to try, at least.

Even though my legs are shaking, I force myself to stand up.

Finally, the monster is facing us. Its face turns wolflike, elongating and growing bristly fur and a long snout. Its eyes finally catch sight of me. They flash bright, like white-hot suns. Then it pulls back its lips and snarls. Teeth stare back at me, rows of knives that gleam.

"Emily, do something!" Emir shouts.

But I can't. My legs are numb and rooted to the ground. My arms are heavy and hang uselessly at my sides. I remember all the times that I was punished for my dreams. Locked in my room for the entire night, sent to bed hungry so that I would eventually be too exhausted to linger in a dream state. And through it all, my father's furious expression, but behind that, something like fear too.

I think of my years at Wildsmoor. Dragged here screaming and petrified, Matron's punishing looks and cruel words, all the rules I'm expected to follow. *A Wildsmoor student is obedient. A Wildsmoor student strives to get better. A Wildsmoor student never complains.*

Emir steps in front of me. He holds out his hands and sparks fly from his palms, crackling and spitting. But the wolflike monster doesn't so much as flinch, sparks glancing off its skin. It steps closer. A growl rumbles from its throat.

Emir tries again. The air grows close and warm. He raises his

162

arms to the sky and yanks them back down. A bolt of blinding light shoots down from the sky. *Crack*—it hits the beast, spidering over its skin, so bright I can't look. The monster throws back its head and howls, loud and long.

It's not doing anything, I realize. I blink stupidly for a moment before understanding suddenly creeps in. Of course Emir's electricity isn't working. The beast and Emir are both part of my own subconscious, and that means there's only one person who can stop the monster. Me.

I push Emir out of the way and step farther into the clearing.

The beast huffs when it sees me. Its eyes burn again. But this time, I don't run.

Up close I realize the monster doesn't just have my father's eyes after all. He's there, but so is Matron, and Doctor Cross, and Doctor Sylvie, and even myself. I see a thousand endless faces flickering. The monster is all of us and it is also none of us. It is fear and hate and all the terrible thoughts in the world that make people do bad things. It is evil made flesh.

For years I've taken responsibility for this monster, taken responsibility for what happened to my sister. But the reality is that I was only a child, and I was only manifesting what I could see in the world around me. I've tried to be a perfect student, to put up with whatever is dished out in the name of getting "better," in the name of getting "cured," in the name of doing what's "right."

I let myself be controlled. But that is coming to an end.

I have the Grimm. And nothing will ever change that.

"You won't hurt me," I say. "You're mine, I know that now." The monster pauses, pawing at the earth and watching me. For a moment the fire in its eyes dims . . .

But I'm wrong.

The beast opens its mouth and before I can so much as blink, let alone run, fire roars around me.

My skin prickles with a strange cold heat, and then it is over.

The fire burns out and it's just me and my monster again. It bends its neck until its head is level with mine. Eyes still burning, it snarls into my face. The sudden gust of breath blows my hair.

My heart speeds up and for a moment the fear takes over again. I force myself to take a deep breath. *It can't hurt me*, I tell myself. *It's my dream. And it can't hurt me.*

My heart slows back down again and the beast loses some of the brightness in its eyes. "You're all right now," I say. "There's nothing to be afraid of."

The beast gives a little huff this time and moves from foot to foot.

Taking a deep breath, I reach out a hand and touch its head, feeling the softness of its fur between its horns. It huffs again and weaves its head slightly before falling still.

"Hello," I finally say. "I'm Emily, and I think you must be my monster."

The beast's eyes suddenly dim, losing any trace of my father and the others, and leaving only something animal-like in its place. It huffs again, sending my hair blowing, strands tickling my face.

"I think you're a bit big for this place, don't you?"

As soon as I've spoken, the beast shrinks in size, smaller and smaller. Its head grows canine and elegant. It falls back onto all fours. It grows paws and a long, looping tail. It glows silver, fur bristling. A she-wolf.

Reaching out a tentative hand, I stroke her thick fur. The beast purrs under my palm.

"Is it . . . is it purring?" Emir asks, stepping up beside me.

The huge silver wolf fixes her eyes on Emir and snarls, showing a glimpse of her still-razor-sharp teeth. I smirk as he recoils slightly.

"You did it," says Emir.

I nod my head. "I did, didn't I."

"I helped," says Emir.

I glare at him, suddenly annoyed, but then I see his smirk. "Is that a joke?" I ask.

Emir shrugs and one corner of his lips tilts upward. "Maybe."

I snort in disbelief. I didn't know Emir was even capable of joking.

The wolf yawns and begins to pace around the clearing. I realize that I could easily evaporate her entirely if I wanted to, but I don't.

A feeling of control that I haven't had in years floods through me. I remember all my dream walking as a kid, when I would be a little mistress of my own world, creating castles and beaches and ponies for my own amusement.

I wave a hand, and in between the trees of the clearing, new ones grow. Silver trunks shoot into the night, higher and higher until it seems as if they are touching the sky. Branches sprout and grow leaves and fruit. I make the fruit glow brighter and they light the clearing up like a hundred miniature moons. We are bathed in dream light.

More, I think.

I turn the clearing into a lake, turning the forest floor into water just by the will of my mind. The surface shimmers like liquid starlight, and above the surface, dragonflies. They hover and dart with wings of lace.

Still not enough.

I think of Gabriel's dream, the boat and the silky water running between his fingers. As soon as I've thought it, a boat appears, tethered to a little jetty. The sound of wood gently knocking joins the thick rustling of leaves.

"There," I say. "That's better."

My wolf slinks up to me and snuffles my hand. I reach up and pluck one of the moon fruits and hold it out.

Emir watches as she eats the fruit from my hand. "You're powerful, Emily," he says. He looks around the now-transformed clearing and waves a hand. "This is like nothing any of us can do."

I turn to him. His words light something up inside me. Right then and there, I feel powerful. The girl I am right now feels a million miles away from the other version of myself, baby-faced and powerless, trapped in her room.

For a moment both of us just look at each other, but for once, neither of us is glaring, neither of us is angry or defensive or suspicious. Emir is not wearing his mask, figuratively or literally, and I do not know how to interact with Emir in a way that isn't any of these things.

Despite his helping to overcome my monster, he is still Emir, after all. He is not my friend, or even my ally. I'm about to suggest that we wake up now, and I'm already reaching for the invisible tether that connects me to my real body, when suddenly he speaks. "Shall we?" he asks, gesturing toward the boat.

It takes me a moment to understand his meaning. I stare at the boat and then out across my dream lake. I'm tempted. I feel a pang of sadness for the little girl locked in her room, thinking that what she could do was bad. I want to explore and have fun, just like I did when I first discovered my dreams, before my parents found out, before I knew I had the Grimm.

I nod and follow him onto the jetty. He clambers into the boat and turns and holds his hand out.

"You're not wearing your gloves," I say, staring.

Emir nods. "Benefits of being a figment of someone else's dream, I suppose."

CHAPTER fifteen

Several days pass and still I'm not let back into the main school. The treatment room is better than isolation, but barely. During the day, I pace around my room and try to not let the torturous tedium take grip, but at night, when the school succumbs to sleep, I escape.

Dreaming, I return to the woods and turn the forest into a different world. A beach with silver palms. An endless ocean where we fish for stars. A cityscape, where we fly like birds among the tops of skyscrapers. Emir joins me during these nighttime adventures, our original truce growing and morphing into something else. Something exciting and fragile, a secret between us that exists in the twist of his smile and the flashes of excitement I see in his eyes.

I am getting good at controlling the Grimm. It's like playtime, almost, and there are times where I feel like a child again, the world and my imagination at my fingertips. An escape.

But tonight sleep evades me, and besides, I don't feel like playing. Instead, I can't stop thinking about the article in the paper Doctor Sylvie brought. *Grimmer Breakouts Continue . . .*

Questions occupy my mind. Where are they going? Who's helping them?

My goal at Wildsmoor has always been to get "better" and to go back home. But now that I don't believe the Grimm is something I need to get better from, and with the memory of what home is actually like fresh in my mind, that leaves the gaping, obvious problem of, what next? My mind turns to Amelia, my sister. A pang of long-ing to see her again, but also worry. What has her life been like since I left? It was always me that Dad was the hardest on, but when I left, did he come down on her instead? The thought makes me want to weep.

It's much later in the night when finally my exhausted body pulls me into the land of sleep, and it's not until much later that my dream self flickers into existence. I stand for a moment, staring at my sleeping face, then I turn and walk through the window, bars and glass and all. I float softly to the ground.

I don't head for the forest and instead leave Wildsmoor through the nearest fence, heading toward the bluff that's visible through the cafeteria window. I drift up and up through scrubby grass, waving blue in the evening light, interrupted by shadowed lumps of granite and black patches of gorse. The night is bright and clear, and I crane my neck upward, searching for the moon. But she's nowhere to be seen. Instead, stars splatter across the night. I look at the different constel-lations and wish I could remember which was which.

I stop by the pile of stones that marks the top of the hill. Snuffling sounds from behind the stones and my beast, still in wolf form, sidles into view. She growls and stalks closer to me. I reach out and let her lick my palm.

I hop from rock to rock, ascending to the top of the cairn and perching on the highest slab of stone. A cold breeze tickles my face, and the stone is frigid under my bum. My legs swing beneath me. My wolf follows, silently padding over the rocks and coming to sit next to me. She yawns, showing off her impressive teeth, before lying down and settling her head against her massive paws.

The hill slopes downward, uninterrupted until it suddenly becomes woodland. Between the two sits the facility. From up here the house looks tiny amid the landscape: a little square blob, entirely dark other than the odd window where light shines. Inside the house, I can feel minds drifting into sleep. I skirt over them, searching for Emir, but he must still be awake, as I can't feel him.

Behind me I can also feel dreamers. I crane my neck and look in the other direction. Far in the distance, I can see Ashbury village. The village is still speckled with lights from houses. Smoke drifts from chimneys into the indigo sky.

My sister is still fresh in my mind. I wonder if she's also out there somewhere, dreaming. I'm struck by the idea that if I can find Emir in his dreams, then I might be able to find her too. I close my eyes and reach outward, past the village. I feel other dreamers, dotted and clumped, stretching on and on and on. It's overwhelming, too many minds and colors and shapes. Gasping, I wrench my eyes open.

Disappointed, I turn back toward Wildsmoor and wait. The sky darkens and becomes black. The few remaining lit windows go dark. And finally, I feel Emir's mind as it drifts into unconsciousness. Faint at first but becoming stronger as sleep takes its grip. I pull him to me and he appears. He stands on the hillside beneath the cairn where I sit. For a moment he can't see me, and I watch him. I take him in in parts, just like I had that day in the library. Dark hair. Dark eyes. His shirt, untucked. He is dressed in standard Wildsmoor nightwear, the same for boys as it is for girls. Winter thermal leggings and a long-sleeved top, thick socks with holes that sag. His hands are bare. He is ridiculously good-looking, "hot," as

Clementine called him, and I'm mad at myself for acknowledging it even in thought.

He blinks, disoriented for a moment. He looks up. "Emily," he says. He looks sleepy and sad.

I push my beast's head from my lap and clamber down to the grass below. "You couldn't sleep?" I ask him.

He shakes his head. "Gabriel is trying to convince the Cure to run," he says. "Sooner rather than later. There's been more breakouts."

Grimmer Breakouts Continue . . .

"Belle Vue," I say, remembering the article I saw in Doctor Sylvie's newspaper.

Emir's head snaps to look at me. "How do you know about that?"

"I snuck a look at Doctor Sylvie's newspaper," I admit.

"Apparently it was done silently this time, and nobody knows how or where they've gone." Emir's face grows grim. "It's only a matter of time before they tighten up security here at Wildsmoor. Gabriel thinks we have to act fast. And I think this is the first time I actually agree with him."

"Where would you even go?" I ask.

"Gabriel thinks he knows somewhere we can get to by boat, where we can hide out for a bit, a stretch of coast that nobody goes—"

"So still no plan, then," I say, cutting him off.

It is almost winter, too cold already for sleeping outside, and eventually somebody would discover them, or they'd have to come out for food or supplies.

"We would need help," I say. "Outside help."

"No," he says forcefully. "We can't trust anyone."

I sigh, expecting his answer, and also understanding the

sentiment. Since everything that's happened, I'm not sure I'll trust another person ever again. But that doesn't detract from the fact that we are just a bunch of penniless and friendless grimmer kids with nowhere to go.

I turn around, away from Wildsmoor and back toward where the village sits in the distance. The chimneys have stopped their smoking and most of the lights are out now, but it's still visible, a few windows still winking in the darkness. I can feel their sleeping minds, vivid and full of life.

An idea slowly buzzes to life in my brain. Clementine's voice rings through my head unbidden. *Rules are made to be broken, you know.*

—

We fly there. The land falls away beneath us and the sky opens up. Cold air buffets my cheeks and whips at my medical gown. Emir floats silently next to me, his eyes dancing.

I smile, remembering how I morphed my body the night Emir found me in the medical room. I imagine wings—bird wings, feathered and soft and snowy like an owl's. Before I was flying, but now I am soaring. I am graceful and swooping and suddenly fast. A shriek escapes my lips as I fly ahead. I give Emir wings of his own. Bat wings, black and spiked and thin as silk. He javelins past me, wings folded back and shooting through the night.

I race after him, impossibly fast. We compete, taking turns to draw ahead of each other.

We arrive at the village all too quickly. I am not used to flying with wings and I misjudge the landing. I hit the ground hard and fall flat on my face. I pull myself up just in time to watch him step smoothly from the air and onto the ground, so graceful it's like he's done this a million times before.

He looks at me on the ground. He frowns. A strange expression takes over his face, and he laughs. Like before, the sound takes me by surprise.

I push myself to my feet. "What's so funny?" I snap.

But instead of one of his usual retorts, Emir continues to laugh, and eventually I smile too. I can't not; his laugh is unexpectedly silly, soft chuckles that shake his whole body.

I do not know what's happening with me and Emir. We dance around each other, navigating our new ceasefire, sometimes friendly and sometimes awkward and sometimes defensive.

Emir folds his wings behind him. The black spiked look of them suits him somehow. He looks like a mythical creature, almost like something from the book he gave me. *Or the devil*, some part of me whispers.

"Where are we going, then?" he asks, looking around.

We've landed on a narrow, cobbled street. Cottages crowd the streets, small and wonky with tiny windows set into old stone walls. The night is thick around us but up ahead I can see the lamplight from the main village and around me the odd window still shines yellow in the darkness.

I reach out and sense the dreamers nearby—I drift over them until I find what I'm looking for. Somewhere nearby there is a hive of sleeping minds, vivid and bright and calling to me.

I lead him through the night, weaving our way in and out of cobbled streets. As we pass each house, the dreams of the people inside flicker in my mind. A woman dreams of a vast, empty beach. A man dreams of work, his computer screen flashing.

Eventually, a tall brick wall stops our path. There is a metal gate with spikes, and beyond that, a wide driveway lined with trees that leads into darkness.

"Ashbury Academy for Young Ladies," reads Emir from a sign next to the gates. He frowns. "Why are we here, Emily?"

"We're breaking in," I tell him.

He looks at me and shakes his head. "No, we're not."

"Yes, we are."

"Why?"

"I want to speak to Clementine."

Emir raises an eyebrow.

"My socialization partner," I clarify. "She's not like the others. She's a friend."

Emir shakes his head. "All the Ashbury girls are stuck-up snobs. They live trivial, privileged lives and some of them might be nice to our faces but there's not a chance they would lift a finger to help us if it came down to it."

The vehemence in his voice makes me pause. "Do you like or trust anyone?"

"No one's ever given me any reason to."

I sigh, but wonder whether I might feel the same way. Suddenly, I am full of doubt, but what other choices do we have?

"Sooner or later we're going to need to find someone to trust," I say eventually. "We don't have any other options, and like you said earlier, we're running out of time."

"And you think those Ashbury snobs are going to be those people?"

"It's a start, and I *do* trust Clementine." *Maybe*, I add in my head, but I don't express my doubts out loud. I flap my wings and rise into the air before landing on the other side. "Coming?"

He glares at me before stretching his wings. Two swoops and he's rising into the air. He hovers above the gate. His feet are pointed and his black wings, which are like leather and silk at the same time, spread wide around him. I can see that he's warring with himself whether to follow me or not. Finally, he floats to the ground beside me.

"Don't get me wrong," he says. "I still think this is a bad idea."

"Well, why are you coming, then?"

He doesn't reply and folds his arms.

"It's because you know I'm right," I crow.

He shakes his head. "Let's just get this over and done with."

I shrug and lead the way down the driveway. Tall, ancient oak trees loom over the path and owls hoot from somewhere high in their branches. Slowly, Ashbury Academy emerges from the darkness. A blob of shadow at first, and then slowly growing larger until it eclipses everything else.

Finally, we stop outside the school. Tall lamps cut through the shadows with their yellow light, illuminating the darkness.

Emir and I stare.

Wildsmoor is an old house, and maybe even once grand, but nothing like this. Whereas Wildsmoor is ancient and falling down and forgotten, Ashbury is pristine. The lawn leading up to the house is perfectly cut and perfectly green. The driveway is smooth black tarmac. To one side, a bus is parked in the shadows, the same one that brings Clementine and her classmates to Wildsmoor. I can just about make out the gold lettering that loops and swirls across the side.

The building itself is at least three times the size of Wildsmoor, and it reminds me of a castle, with mini turrets and steeples and glass gleaming in the darkness. I reach beyond the glass, and I can feel the sleeping minds of the Ashbury students, flickers of color and movement buried deep somewhere within the school. I want to get closer.

I fly up into the air, and Emir follows me. Without speaking we glide over the building and land on the other side. There is a garden here and we walk through it, stepping stealthily past bushes bursting with roses and bushes cut into spirals and different shapes.

We pass tennis courts and an enormous field, and then more gardens with tinkling fountains and twisting pathways. As we approach the school, neither of us speaks, and I guess by Emir's wide-eyed expression that he is as amazed as I am. Until finally we pass through an arched entrance and into a paved area with a large hole carved into it. A swimming pool.

"This is a school?" whispers Emir. His voice is quiet, quieter than a whisper, but still I can hear the disbelief there. His face is no longer wide-eyed with amazement; instead, it's pinched and dark with anger.

I look at the pool, large and kidney shaped. Although it is currently empty of water, no doubt because it's December, I can imagine the Ashbury girls here in summer, swimming and playing games on a hot day, or relaxing in the shade cast by the old trees that surround the school and its grounds.

"Makes me sick," says Emir.

I nod, because I understand what he's trying to say, in his own over-the-top Emir sort of way. We are locked up with just a few old videos and books for company. We aren't allowed outside apart from drills and once a week to run laps around the scrubby track or to work in the garden. Meanwhile, just down the road the Ashbury girls play tennis and swim in the pool and sniff roses in their beautiful gardens.

"I need to get inside," I say.

Emir shakes his head. "Too dangerous. Can't you just pull her out of her dreams? Like you do with me?"

"I could. But I want to go inside," I say. "I want to see how the Ashbury girls live. Aren't you curious?" I glance sideways at Emir. His arms are folded and his legs are planted and his face is rigid with stubbornness. "Fine, I'll try," I say.

I close my eyes and feel with my senses throughout the school, feeling for the buzz of dreamers that I could sense all the way from here. Immediately, I am overwhelmed by sound and color and movement. Their dreams aren't like the Wildsmoor students'; they are vivid and noisy and completely overwhelming. I pull away again and shake my head. "It's too much," I say. "I would never be able to pick one of them out."

"But you can with me?"

"It's easy at Wildsmoor; the drugs stop everyone else from dreaming properly. You and the rest of the Cure stick out."

"If we go in, we could get caught. They've probably got guards and all sorts."

But I shake my head. I remember Clementine's reaction to the guardians and the security at Wildsmoor—she was shocked. *It's not normal*, she had said. At the time I'd been surprised, and then curious, wondering what a school was like without Matron and her rules, and without guardians and their guns. "They don't have guards and stuff like that," I say. "Come on."

I rise into the air, not bothering with wings, and after a moment, Emir joins me. We stop by a window on the third story. It's been left ever so slightly ajar, a tiny crack just about wide enough to fit my fingers. I try to peer in but can't see anything but darkness.

"What if there's people in there," hisses Emir.

I close my eyes and feel with my mind, but no. All the dreamers are on the other side of the school. "There isn't anyone close," I say to him. "Their dorms must be on the other side."

I fit my fingers into the crack and slide the window open.

"Emily," hisses Emir.

But I ignore him and clamber inside. I conjure up silver orbs of light and find that we are standing in a large room. There is artwork on the walls and old wooden desks covered in stains. Endless pots of pencils and paint and brushes crowd the many shelves.

"An art room?" asks Emir.

I nod my head and walk over to the nearest wall. One of my light orbs follows me, shining a light above my head like my own personal moon. A painting is displayed—a landscape of the village at sunset, with golden motes and gleaming roofs. It's good. Really good.

Something bites deep inside me. Envy.

I would like to paint something like this, something so beautiful and colorful. But at Wildsmoor this wouldn't be possible. Sure, we have our "art therapy" classes and they give us the basics—pencil, eraser, paper, and a tin of watercolors. But the pencils break, and the brushes are old with bristles that stick out in odd directions, and the paper is too thin for watercolors so you always end up with holes.

I examine the painting more closely, the shine and the texture of the paint. I don't know what they used, but it definitely wasn't the watercolors we're used to.

I pace around the walls, looking at the rest of the art. There are self-portraits and more landscapes, a few photographs, and paintings that don't seem to be of anything, just blocks and swirls of color.

"What's that?" says Emir, peering at one such painting.

"I read about it once," I reply. The word comes to me: "Abstract. Abstract art is what it's called."

"I don't get it," says Emir, shaking his head. "What's it supposed to be?"

"I don't know," I admit after a moment. "Maybe it's not supposed to be anything."

"Well, what's the point, then?"

I shrug. There is something beautiful about the looping lines and shapes; I can't take my eyes off it. "Does there need to be a point?" I ask. "Perhaps it just is what it is."

But Emir rolls his eyes and shakes his head. "Stupid."

I turn and look at the door. It's been left open, and beyond that I can see the darkness of a corridor. "I want to go in further," I say.

Emir shakes his head. "Too dangerous."

"Well, I'm going," I respond.

Emir raises an eyebrow at me. "You've changed, you know."

I think about this for a second, and then I nod, because he's right, I *have* changed.

I'm not sure what's left of the old Emily, if anything at all, but there is a new one growing in her place. And she might not be *good*, but she's not *bad* either. And if nothing else, she's definitely less afraid.

We creep through the school. Down corridors and up staircases, through doors and under archways. Everything is old-looking, but also somehow clean and fresh at the same time. Classrooms with stone walls have lines of computers, sleek and expensive. Hallways have stained glass windows, polished to a perfect shine. We pass through an enormous hall, ten times the size of our Wildsmoor one, with red velvet chairs set into lines and a chandelier hanging from the ceiling.

Finally, we move into a different section of the building that I know immediately is where the dormitories are. My bare feet sink into thick carpet and the corridor is lined with doors. There are decorated nameplates on each one, two to each room.

But this isn't how I know that these are their dorm rooms. It's because I can feel them. Dreams flash behind each door, interrupting the stillness of the rest of the school. I stop and stand completely still as I let their unconscious thoughts wash over me.

"What are you doing?" asks Emir.

"Feeling their dreams," I reply. "They're just . . ." I trail off and shake my head. *Overwhelming?* That's the only word that comes to mind.

Their sleeping minds are so different from the sleeping minds of Wildsmoor students. Wildsmoor dreams are gray and cloudy and like moving through fog, whereas the Ashbury students' dreams remind me of the abstract painting we looked at earlier, full of vivacity and movement. They flower behind the closed doors, like colored ink blooming in the darkness. Faces of friends and lovers and family members. Beautiful places and beautiful things. Laughs and smiles.

But just as vivid as their good dreams are their bad dreams. Monsters with red eyes and feathers and wings and snarls and teeth. Dark, faceless things that are always around the corner but no matter how much the dreamer tries to run, they can never run fast enough.

And then there are nightmares of a different sort. One dreams about a boy with eyes like liquid gold and a perfect smile; he takes the dreamer's hand and looks into her eyes, and then he tells her he doesn't love her anymore. Another dreams about a group of girls surrounding her; they laugh and say mean things. Another cries on her knees in front of a grave.

These dreams are worse than the monster ones; their despair clutches at me as I skim past them.

I try to fix as many of them as I can. The teasing girls become ducks that fly away. I turn the golden boy's eyes dull and give him warts and crooked yellow teeth. I can't think how to make the grave one better, or even if I should, so I leave her to her grief.

A thumping noise interrupts me. I open my eyes. I turn to Emir, and he looks back at me, eyes wide.

"What was that?" I breathe in the tiniest whisper possible.

He puts his finger to his lips and points toward the end of the corridor. I hear another thump. And then, a giggle.

"Somebody is coming."

We turn at the same time, an unspoken agreement to leave, but it's already too late.

A girl shrieks, and a moment later, another voice sounds through the darkness. "Emily?"

I can't help myself. I turn around. There is a group of girls standing there. They shrink back, all of them apart from one. A girl in her dressing gown with her hair in a messy knot and eyes so wide with surprise that they look like they might burst from her skull.

"Clementine?" I ask.

"Emily . . ." she says again. Her voice trails off, her eyes flicker from me to Emir and back again. I realize what we must look like to her—glowing and with wings.

Then one of the girls screams, tearing through the stillness of the night. She turns on her heel and runs. The other girls follow, yelling and shrieking.

"You need to get out of here," says Clementine. "Those idiots will scream the whole school down."

Doors begin to open along the corridor. Heads poke out. They gasp when they see us. The sound of footsteps running up a staircase grows louder. And then, an alarm goes off.

Figures appear at both ends of the corridor. One of them marches toward us. "Who are you?" she shouts. An adult's voice, one of the teachers perhaps. "I've called the police."

"Emily, we need to wake up now," says Emir.

But I don't wake us up. I'm frozen, staring at the figure barreling toward us. Whoever it is stops and turns. "Girls, grab a coat and make your way to the assembly point," she shouts above the alarm. "Now!"

"*Now*, Emily," Emir says.

I force my eyes shut and reach for the tethers that tie us to our real bodies back at Wildsmoor. I sever them and a moment later I'm back in my bed. The rough blanket is tangled around my legs. One of my arms has fallen asleep, numb from where I've lain on it too long.

I push myself onto my back and stare up at the ceiling. I wiggle my fingers, trying to get the blood flow going again. Pins and needles travel down my arms and into my hand. Clementine saw me. She said my name.

The doubts I'd felt earlier creep back in. What if he's right? What if she can't be trusted? What if none of them can?

I lie there for a long time, half expecting guardians to come barging into the room. But they don't.

CHAPTER 𝔖ixteen

There's a knock on my door the following morning, just after the wake-up music sounds through the building. I prepare myself. I imagine Matron busting down my door after hearing the news of the break-in. She would drag me back to isolation and never let me out.

Instead, Doctor Sylvie enters. "Hello, Emily," she smiles. She comes to sit on the chair by my bed and I feel an urge to recoil. There is something about Doctor Sylvie now with her smiles and perfect clothes and perfect fingernails that makes me dislike her. I wonder how much money she makes from feeding us poison.

But I resist the urge to pull away and instead I give her the same bland smile as always.

"Is it all right with you if I run a few tests and ask some questions?"

I nod and Doctor Sylvie pulls several instruments out of the black bag she always carries. Blood pressure first, and I roll up my sleeve without making a fuss. Doctor Sylvie straps on the cuff and I feel the familiar pressure as it tightens around my arm. She nods, makes a note, and then unstraps me. After that she listens to my breathing, takes my heart rate, and shines a flashlight into each of my eyes.

Finally, she looks up from her folder and smiles at me. "Perfect," she says. "I was worried how your new dose might affect your functioning but it seems like you're better than ever."

She closes the folder and puts it back in her bag. Her movement sends a waft of air in my direction and I smell her sugary perfume.

I used to like it, but now it just smells overly sweet and cloying, like flowers left to rot.

"How's your sleep been?" she asks.

"Good," I reply automatically.

"Any nasty little disturbing thoughts or feelings?"

"No."

"Any unusual dreams?"

I shake my head. Each day Doctor Sylvie asks me the same questions and my lies are smooth with repetition.

"Well, I'm pleased to say that it looks as if the treatment has taken effect and I'm going to authorize your return to the main school." She beams at me.

Relief floods my body. I smile back at her, almost genuine.

"I thought that might make you happy."

I nod my head. "That's good news, Doctor Sylvie," I reply.

"And we can put all this nasty episode business behind us."

"Of course." I pause before forcing myself to add, "Thank you, Doctor Sylvie."

Doctor Sylvie's cheeks grow faintly pink. "You're welcome." She stands up and turns to go, but then she stops. She turns back around. "There is one last thing perhaps we should talk about. Well, more of a question really."

I nod my head. I notice that Doctor Sylvie is no longer smiling and instead there is a little wrinkled frown marring her perfect forehead.

"There was a disturbance last night, in the village. Ashbury School suffered a break-in, and they are adamant that the intrusion was related to Wildsmoor students in some way."

My heart flutters in my chest and I force myself not to break eye contact.

"Would you know anything about that?" continues Doctor Sylvie.

I shake my head.

"Because Ashbury reported an older girl, and a boy too, both caught trespassing inside the school. Of course this could have been a break-in related to theft, or some other crime; it's not unknown for kidnappers to target the offspring of wealthy or important people . . ." She trails off and shakes her head. "Anyway. They didn't get a good look at the trespassers, but there were strange attributes to their appearance that made them believe it was more likely to be one of the students here . . ."

I shrug and shake my head. "Sorry," I say, trying my best to appear confused.

"It was only that your symptoms appear to manifest at night . . ." Doctor Sylvie shakes her head and smiles. "Sorry, I know it couldn't be you, of course, but just thought I would ask in case you knew anything. We've questioned all the other students too, but it seems that it's a mystery."

"Sorry, I don't know anything about it," I say, swallowing the lump in my throat. I force myself to smile back at her. "I've been here all week."

"Of course you have." Doctor Sylvie sighs. "Between you and me I think it's more likely down to a little bit of teenage hysteria. One girl thinks she saw something, and then the rest start imagining and fabricating the story. It's not uncommon, you know."

I nod. "Sounds like it could be that."

Doctor Sylvie sighs. "But the school is insisting otherwise . . .

Well, nothing for you to worry about anyway. Have a good day, Emily."

—

The next day, I am let out of my treatment room and escorted to class by two guardians. Being back in the main school is disorienting, and as I walk to class, I feel like my eyeballs are being scrubbed with sand. The lights are too bright and there are people everywhere. Students walking the corridors. House staff hurrying past. Guardians standing by every doorway.

Is it just me or are there more guardians than usual? And ones I don't recognize too. They seem to be everywhere, glaring at each student as they pass.

I am dropped off outside Miss Rabbit's classroom. By the doorway, two guardians are standing on duty. One of them I recognize, the young one with a white scar marking one side of his face. But the other one is unfamiliar to me. I stare at him curiously. He has a red slab-of-meat type face, made even more unfortunate by deep acne scars and a squashed nose that I guess must've been broken at some point. His muscles bulge under his uniform and his gun is drawn.

"What are you looking at?" he asks as our eyes meet.

Immediately, I look down at the floor. "Sorry, sir," I say in the demurest voice I can possibly muster.

He makes a short snorting sound through his nose, like a bull. "I can see why you needed help over here," he says. "At my last facility the inmates wouldn't dare look at us like that."

I notice his use of words: *inmates*, not *students*.

"Uh, yeah," says the younger guardian.

The squashed-nose man prods me with the handle of his gun,

jabbing me in the ribs. "Well, what are you waiting for? Are you going inside or not?"

I nod my head and escape through the doorway. I am ever so slightly early and I take my usual seat in the still-empty classroom. I watch as the other kids start to arrive. I'm not the only one who manages to provoke the new guardian's displeasure. Walking too slow, too fast, looking where they shouldn't . . . seems it doesn't take a lot to get his back up.

The other Cure members come into the room in dribs and drabs. Gabriel first, who purposefully meanders past my desk on the way to his own. He smiles his sunshine smile at me and murmurs as he drifts past, "Good to have you back." Margie is next, winking at me before disappearing to her desk at the back of the room. Then Isaiah and Adanya, one in front of the other. Isaiah gives me a brief but tiny smile before sitting at his desk nearest the door, but Adanya does nothing but glare from the second she steps into the room until when she sits down. She looks even angrier than usual, and I wonder what I've done to annoy her this time.

Finally, Emir comes into the room. I'm not used to seeing him in the flesh. His skin is darker in real life, lacking the moonlike shine that our dream bodies have, and the brown of his eyes has more depth. He's wearing his gloves.

He looks up and our eyes meet, and for some reason anxiety catches in my chest. I'm excited to see him, I realize. I expect him to smile, or nod, or even glare at me, something to acknowledge my presence. But instead he looks immediately away again. His mouth grows into a thin, tight line.

Finally, Miss Rabbit hurries through the door. She looks

188

flustered. Her ponytail is lumpy and strands are flying here, there, and everywhere.

"Right. So," says Miss Rabbit, standing behind her desk and looking up at us all.

Miss Rabbit trails off as the two guardians follow her into the room and take positions on either side of her desk, facing us. "It's all right," says Miss Rabbit with a smile to the squash-nosed man. "Guardians don't usually stay for the lesson."

He shakes his head and folds his arms, not looking back at Miss Rabbit and instead gazing around at us all. "New protocol."

She looks at him and for a tiny moment I think I see her nose wrinkle up ever so slightly before she nods and smiles again. "Right." She turns back to us and holds her hands out. "I'm afraid that Ashbury students won't be joining us today, so instead we will practice our skill of the week on each other . . ."

"Where are they?" I blurt out.

Miss Rabbit startles and stares at me wide-eyed.

"Sorry, Miss Rabbit," I say hurriedly, "I didn't mean to call out."

"Yes, well . . ."

"I was just wondering why the Ashbury students aren't coming today."

Miss Rabbit's eyes flicker to the guardians and then back to me. She shakes her head. "It's nothing for you to worry about, Emily, but we're going to be having socialization alone for a little while. No doubt everything will go back to normal soon enough."

The squash-nosed guardian snorts and rolls his eyes. Miss Rabbit looks at him again, and for a tiny second, I think I see a flash of something like anger on her face. I wonder for a moment if she's going to say something, but then she turns back to the whiteboard. She pulls out a pen and writes a word in big, bold letters. "Let's read this all together, shall we."

"Courtesy," the class drones all together, elongating each vowel sound. *Cuuurteeeesieee.*

"Excellent. Now, courtesy isn't so tricky once you get your head around . . ." Miss Rabbit continues with her explanation, but I'm not paying attention. As her words drift over me, I wonder again what's happening. No Ashbury students? I've never known them not to come before.

Miss Rabbit claps and asks us to organize ourselves into pairs. I twist in my seat and spot Margie at the back of the room. I make a beeline for her, tripping over my own chair in my haste. The legs clatter against the floor and everyone looks at me, including the new guardian. "Sorry," I mutter, pushing my chair back in.

I slide into the seat next to Margie, watching as Miss Rabbit darts around, pairing up those students who look lost or are wandering around aimlessly.

Finally, everyone is ready. "Okay, begin." She smiles at us.

The class ever so slowly begins to talk, their stilted attempts at conversation filling up the room with a soft hum. The noise level is a tenth of what it is when the Ashbury students are here. Miss Rabbit would usually sit at her desk, but today she is going around the room and helping each pair with their exercises. I can hear her squeaking out encouragement, trying to chivy the other students into having conversations like normal human beings. *Good luck.*

"So they let you out, then?" says Margie.

I turn to her. "Never mind that." I nod my head ever so slightly in the direction of squashed-nose man. "What's with all the new guardians?" I ask.

Margie raises an eyebrow at me. "You don't know?"

I shake my head.

"There was a break-in over at Ashbury. Kids, apparently. And they made it all the way into the girls' dormitories before they were discovered. But apparently they had *wings*. And then just as soon as everyone saw them, they disappeared, just gone. Poof. Into thin air." She cocks her head. "A girl and a boy apparently, and get this, they were *glowing*." Margie raises an eyebrow at me. "Now I wonder who that reminds me of."

My heart sinks. I suspected it might've been because of my and Emir's break-in, but hearing it confirmed from Margie's lips fills me with trepidation. No wonder Adanya looks like she extra hates me this morning. I look down at my desk.

"Thought so," whispers Margie. "It was you, wasn't it." She shakes her head. "So Ashbury School has said that they don't want anything more to do with us disgusting grimmers over here. So that's that."

"It's not my fault. There have been more and more grimmer breakouts. Emir says you've all been talking about how it was only a matter of time before security amped up. And how do you know all this anyway?"

"My sister goes to Ashbury, remember?"

I nod my head, because of course I remember. In fact, that's the exact reason why I wanted to talk to Margie in the first place.

"I have a favor to ask you," I say to Margie.

Margie does her little bird tilt of the head again, looking at me with keen eyes. "What is it?"

For a moment I hesitate, my eyes flicking over to the new guardian again. He's still looking around the room at us all with an expression I can only describe as proprietorial, like he owns us from the hair on our heads down to our little toenails.

Should I be doing this? Breaking more rules, causing more trouble when already the facility seems to be on high alert?

But then I gaze around at the other kids. Their conversation is starting to die off. Some of them are staring into space, or down at the ground. Their faces are blank and emotionless, completely alone in their heads. They just stare and stare and stare. All of them completely alone.

As I watch them, a deep-down anger begins to form somewhere inside me.

How dare they.

How dare they do this to us.

I take a breath and look at Margie. "Can you get a message to Ashbury?" I ask.

A tiny smile creeps onto her face. "Piece of cake," she says.

"Today?"

"Who do you take me for?"

I nod and look back around at all the kids, registering each blank face.

"And to the Cure too . . . I want to call a meeting."

"You want to call a meeting?" Margie's voice is quiet but tinged with disbelief. Her eyes search my face for a moment. "You've changed your tune."

I nod my head, suddenly feeling impatient. "Tonight," I say. "I want to meet tonight."

CHAPTER Seventeen

That night I consider sneaking out as my dream self but decide at the last minute not to. If I was to get caught, it would be a whole lot worse if I was also using my abilities. And after the Ashbury debacle, it's too soon to run the risk.

So I ignore the pulsing of the dream world, calling to me through the invisible tether, and instead I lie awake in the darkness. Finally, the clock strikes twelve, and a moment later, Adanya emerges from her bed. I watch silently as she creeps from the room. I could go with her, but I don't. It's clear she doesn't like me, and I'm not sure that going into the woods alone with her would be a good idea . . . I'd probably never come back out again. At least not in one piece.

She pulls the door shut behind her and I swing out of bed. I pick up my shoes in one hand and take my school coat from the peg by the door. I try to be quiet, but I don't worry too much. Dreams buzz softly around me, letting me know that the others are asleep. Soft shapes and half-formed images that disperse nearly as quickly as they're formed.

After spending so much time in my dream body the last week, that part of me is getting stronger. Even awake, I can sense the dreams of those unconscious around me, and from farther away too. Beyond the village and Ashbury School there are other pockets of dreamers. One of them I think might be a town, or a city. Their unconscious minds blend together, so many and so vivid it makes my head reel.

Like before I take a moment and try to feel for Amelia. I imagine her face, her smile, the feel of her personality, hoping this might take me to her. It takes me the space of a few seconds to realize that it's pointless. Trying to pick out Amelia's sleeping mind would be like trying to pick out a pixel in a photograph. Besides, I don't really know if the town I can feel is the same one I grew up in, or even if my family still lives there.

A noise interrupts my searching and I wrench my eyes open. A door opens and closes and a guardian appears. He yawns and rubs his forehead as he walks toward me. He hasn't seen me, but it would only be a matter of seconds. I hardly think about what I'm doing and I reach out. His mind is foggy with suppressed sleep. I push his mind further toward unconsciousness. He takes two more steps before he falls to the ground.

For a moment I just stand there, shocked. Then I tiptoe over to him. I nudge him with my foot but he's out cold. I take another second to silently gloat over his unconscious body before continuing to tiptoe my way through the school. Like usual, the front door is unlocked and I step out into the night air. A fist grabs the collar of my coat. They pull, hard, and I stumble back against the wall. My head hits something soft. Before I can scream a hand covers my mouth. I look up and a masked face looks down at me. A long beak and black glass eyes. Gabriel.

He puts his finger to his lips.

The unmistakable sound of footsteps on gravel emerges from the darkness. A moment later and a figure comes into view. A guardian. He's whistling and holding a flashlight. He shines the light aimlessly, catching on bushes and patches of driveway and empty night sky.

194

Gabriel pulls me backward until I am pressed up tightly against him. I can feel his heart thumping and the soft in and out of his breath.

The guardian walks past us and then around the corner of the house, disappearing from view. Gabriel lets go of me and I stumble away. "That was close," he murmurs.

"I saw another one, in the school. I sent him to sleep."

Gabriel looks at me. "How?"

I shake my head. "I don't know, but it was easy."

Gabriel cocks his head. "Useful," he says, and under his mask I imagine his keen blue-eyed stare.

I shrug. "Well, it's my fault that they're here."

"I have something for you," says Gabriel, ignoring my admission of guilt. He reaches under his coat and pulls something out. A mask is gripped between his fingers.

I take it from him and turn it around. I smile. It's a bird mask, but not long beaked or scary-looking like Gabriel's; instead, it's clearly an owl. Snowy feathers emerge from circle eyes, and a beak juts out over where my nose will go.

"To go with your wings," he murmurs, and winks at me.

I feel myself flush, realizing that like Margie, Gabriel has also figured out that the Ashbury break-in was my fault.

"Thank you," I say, ignoring his pointed comment and taking the mask from him. "Where did you get it?"

"There's an old costume cupboard. I don't know why, maybe they used to do plays or something, but it's full of masks and cloaks and stuff like that. Here," says Gabriel. He takes the mask back from me and gestures for me to turn around. I do and he gently ties the mask around my head. The world is changed through the owl's gaze, growing dark around the edges and pinpointing my vision.

"Thank you," I say, turning back around.

"Shall we?" says Gabriel. He bows and sweeps an arm toward the woods.

With him leading the way, we begin to make our way around the school toward the overgrown gate that leads to the woods. The mist from the day still hasn't lifted and everything is wet and pitch-black.

I open the gate and we step through. As we move deeper into the woods, the darkness grows thicker and thicker around us. I can't see a thing. My feet keep catching on roots, and wet leaves and branches brush and snag against my skin and clothes.

Finally, we make it to the clearing. The others are already there, crowded around the fire and holding out their hands for warmth. The flames spit in the wetness and thick smoke fills the air. It stings my eyes and fills my nostrils with its pungent stink. Concealed faces turn around and watch as Gabriel and I emerge from the darkness. They lapse into silence. I note them one by one. Adanya's fox face. Isaiah as a clown. Emir, his face hidden behind white porcelain. Arthur is there. He has also been gifted a mask, a simple black slip with holes in it that reminds me of a cartoon burglar.

I feel their eyes on me as we walk and join them around the fire. Despite the smoke, I am grateful for the warmth, as the mist has sunk through my skin and right into my bones. I am shivering.

"Is this some kind of sick joke?" asks Adanya after a moment of silence. Her eyes glare at me through the holes of her mask.

Gabriel chuckles. "Is there a problem, Adanya?"

"Yes, there's a problem. What is *she* doing here?"

Gabriel shrugs and says in a mild voice, "She's the one who called the meeting, so maybe you should ask her."

Adanya stands up, pulls off her mask, and rounds on me. "What? Why?"

I lift my chin. "I wanted to talk to you all."

"You've got no right, not after what you did."

Suddenly, I'm grateful for my own mask. But I refuse to feel guilty.

"What are you talking about, Adanya?" asks Gabriel.

"She, *and him*"—she turns to glare at Emir—"decided to break into Ashbury School, and obviously they got found out, which means now the school is crawling with guardians. I nearly got caught on my way out here, do you know that? It's not safe for us anymore. We're never going to get out of here now." The air begins to buzz around us and a strange prickling feeling brushes against my skin. Then she turns to Emir and her words are laden with so much red-hot rage that I'm surprised he doesn't just evaporate on the spot. "And *you*. I expect it of her, she doesn't have two brain cells to rub together, but *you* should've known better. You've affected us all with your stupid decisions, and for what? For *her*. Staring after her all the time like a lovesick puppy. It's pathetic."

Emir stands up. "You know nothing about me," he says in a quiet voice. "Don't pretend that you do."

Adanya snorts. "Oh yeah, the mysterious Emir. Nobody understands him . . ." She laughs, high and fake and full of derision. "Let me break it to you, you're really not that special, or mysterious, or anything at all really. You're just selfish."

"Jealousy doesn't suit you, you know."

Adanya's head ever so slightly jerks backward, as if Emir's words have physical form and have punched her in the face. Her eyes go wide. She's clenching her mask in both hands, bending it to the point that I think it might snap.

The others look away or at the ground, clearly uncomfortable. I frown, replaying their words.

I think about what I saw in Adanya's dream—she was kissing somebody. Was that Emir? The thought makes something twist in my stomach.

"This has nothing to do with me and you or *her*. I'm merely questioning why the hell you would put us all in danger like that. The school is overrun with guardians now . . . What were you thinking?" Adanya's voice rises at the end and takes on a high buzzing note that isn't remotely human sounding. Again I feel the prickling sensation brushing my skin, like a thousand little needles stroking up my arms.

"Don't . . ." says Isaiah. He stands, pushing himself upward with his stick and taking a step toward Adanya. Arthur also stands up but instead of heading toward Adanya, he stumbles away from her, taking shelter between the trees.

Her mouth opens and she shrieks. I clap my hands to my ears, trying to drown out her wail.

Emir shouts out loud. His whole body goes rigid. Bolts of light spit and crackle as they zigzag across his mist-soaked skin.

"Stop, Adanya," says Isaiah, closing the distance between them and putting a hand on her shoulder. "You know he can't control it."

Adanya shakes off Isaiah's hand and I think for a moment that she's going to keep going, but then the shrieking stops and Emir's body relaxes again. The bolts of light sputter out. He pulls off his mask and throws it at the ground.

"I could have killed you," snaps Emir. He clenches his gloved hands and electricity shoots up his arms.

Adanya laughs. "You could have killed me? You don't even know what I'm capable of. You think that was pain? That's a hundredth of what I could do if I wanted to."

For a moment there is silence. Emir and Adanya glare at each other, and we watch, all of us holding our breath.

I step forward. "It was my idea," I admit. "Not Emir's. He didn't want to go into Ashbury but I insisted."

"Well, you were caught. And now we're all screwed," says Adanya. "So tell us, was it worth it?"

"Am I interrupting something?" sounds a voice from the trees. We all turn together as three figures step into the firelight.

Margie is at the front, the jewels of her mask glinting in the firelight. Behind her follow two more figures. Unlike all of us, in our school coats and pajamas, they are dressed in jeans and boots and thick coats with hoods.

The other members of the Cure stare warily. "Who's this?" asks Gabriel.

"This is my sister, Sarah," says Margie, gesturing toward the first figure. The girl pulls down her hood and immediately I recognize her from socialization. It's Clementine's friend, the one with dyed blue hair and thick charcoal eyeliner. I realize that behind the eyeliner and dyed hair, Sarah has the same delicate face and big eyes of her sister. They look so much alike that I can't believe I didn't notice the similarities before.

"And I'm Clementine," says the second figure, also pulling down her hood. She stares around at us all, taking in the fire and the trees and all of us in our masks. Her eyes finally come to rest on me. "Emily," she exclaims. "You're all right." She rushes forward and bundles me up in a hug.

The contact takes me by surprise, but unlike the first time Clementine hugged me, this time I remember to hug her back. "You made it," I say.

"I was worried about you. I asked that ridiculous teacher of yours, Miss Rabbit, where you were, but she wouldn't tell me, and now they've stopped our visits altogether, but of course you know that." She pulls away and smirks at me. "I know it was you last night. Just so you know, the whole school had an absolute freak-out afterward, we all got interviewed and the place was crawling with cops . . ." She pats me on the arm. "But don't worry. I didn't tell anyone I knew you or who you are or anything."

I shake my head, aware that everyone else is watching us and still feeling the electric tension in the air.

It takes me a tiny moment to catch up with the sudden influx of information. "Thank you," I say eventually. And I mean it. I was hoping she was someone I could really trust, and now I know that she is.

"Is that part of having the Grimm? Whatever that was last night?"

I nod. "Sort of."

"Wow," replies Clementine, looking at me in awe. "That's incredible. I'm so jealous."

It takes a moment for the words to sink in. Clementine . . . jealous of me. I remember how envious I was of Clementine, seeing her with her friends, her clothes, the makeup, her freedom. Yet for some reason she wants what I have. The notion is so ridiculous that I want to laugh out loud.

"And the rest of you. Can you do cool stuff too?" She turns and looks at them all and they stare back at her. In typical Clementine style, she doesn't appear intimidated at all. "Awesome masks, by the way."

"It doesn't work like that," I reply. "The Grimm is different in each of us."

Clementine's eyes light up even more. "Can I see?" she asks.

Emir steps forward. He folds his arms toward Clementine and Sarah. "Why are you here?" he asks, his voice tight with anger. I suddenly remember his open dislike for the Ashbury girls.

"We were invited," says Clementine.

"Sorry, who invited you?"

"I did," I say.

Everyone turns to look at me and Adanya shakes her head. "This night just gets better and better," she mutters.

Emir also looks angry, his thunderstorm look clear on his face. And even Isaiah is eyeing me warily, his eyes flicking between us all.

"Just listen for a moment," I say, my voice sounding smaller than I would like.

"No," interrupts Adanya, looking around at everyone. "I'm not listening to anything that *she* has to say. Anyone who can put us at risk like this can't be trusted." She looks around at the others, who are silent and listening.

My stomach turns over, and suddenly I realize that I hadn't really considered that the Cure might not want my help, that they would reject me. But now I'm here, I realize that this can't happen. There are things I want. I want freedom. I want to be able to live a life outside these walls. I want that for all of us. I want the world outside to know that we can't be contained. It's our world too.

But I can't do these things alone. I need the Cure.

"Wait," I breathe. Everyone turns to look at me. Suddenly, I am glad for my mask. I feel stronger behind it. Braver. "Yes, last night at Ashbury might've been the catalyst for the tightened security, but it was going to happen anyway and you know it. The continued breakouts . . . it was only a matter of time before things got worse." Everyone is silent, just watching me. I see Gabriel and Margie nodding their heads. "But what it's really made me realize is that they're not going to stop. The more breakouts and the more uprisings, the worse they're going to come down on us. They'll keep us locked up and away from their world forever unless we find a way out. All of us."

"All of us?" repeats Adanya. "Surely you don't mean every kid at the facility."

I nod my head, suddenly sure of myself again. "Everyone."

Adanya laughs. "Are you crazy? There's what? Sixty? Seventy of us at the moment at Wildsmoor? What are you going to do? Break everyone out and then what . . . You can't hide seventy unstable children in the woods, you know."

I nod my head. "I know. We need outside help, it's the only way." I look at Clementine. I remember the manager at the store in town and how he stuck up for us. "And that's where Clementine and Sarah come in. There are people in this world that we can trust. If we're going to survive out there, we're going to have to learn how to pick them out . . ." I trail off, suddenly realizing that what I'm asking of Clementine and Sarah is huge. I turn to them. "I know what I'm asking of you is ridiculously big, so if you don't want to help us, then I understand."

But Clementine shakes her head, her eyes shining in the firelight. "Are you kidding? This is the most exciting thing that's ever happened to me. You'll help too, won't you, Sarah?" She turns to her friend and gives her an encouraging nod, but Sarah just looks stunned. She ignores Clementine and looks toward Margie. For a long moment the two sisters communicate with nothing but their eyes, then Sarah turns back to us and nods. "If it helps Margie, then I'll do it."

"Thank you," I say, breathing an internal sigh of relief.

"Let's get this straight," says Adanya. "This is all completely irrelevant because you're not even a member of the Cure. You can't make these sorts of decisions for us." Adanya turns to the others. "We should at least have a vote on her first . . . It's only fair."

"We didn't vote on anyone else," points out Margie.

"She really doesn't like you, does she . . ." murmurs Clementine in my ear.

I nod my head. "No. She doesn't."

"You know," says Clementine, "that Emily is right. All facilities are upping their security."

"Because of the increased breakouts?" Gabriel asks.

"Yes, and since the stuff with Professor Grimm has come out, shit is really hitting the fan."

"Stuff with Professor Grimm?" Gabriel's full attention is on Clementine, and I imagine his hungry gaze under his mask.

"You really don't know?"

Gabriel shakes his head.

"Wow. Well . . . The prime minister gave an address last night." She fumbles in her pocket and pulls out her phone. "Here, let me show you."

We crowd around Clementine and her phone, peering over her shoulder. The screen flickers to life under her thumbs. She clicks and types, and a moment later, a static box appears on the screen with a face in it. At the bottom of the screen is a banner with the words *breaking news*. She presses a play button at the bottom and the screen unfreezes. The face begins to talk and I realize that it's a news anchor, like I used to see on the television when I was a kid.

"A series of continued breakouts has occurred over the prior seventy-two hours at facilities up and down the country. Belle Vue, Biddick Hall, and Lord Blyton's are the most recent locations to be struck by violent unrest and mysterious disappearances. It is now thought that over a hundred fugitives are on the run from authorities and the prime minister has made it clear that anyone with any information on their whereabouts is legally obliged to come forward." The news anchor's face disappears and a photo of a man appears on screen. He has thick eyebrows and wrinkles that swallow his face, and I immediately recognize him as Professor Grimm from the newspaper article that Doctor Sylvie showed me.

"In a sudden twist of events, there is new information that would indicate they are being aided by none other than Professor Grimm, the well-known neuroscientist famous for discovering the Grimm-Cross affliction . . ."

I look up then. My eyes meet Emir's. It's the first time he's looked at me all day and I hold his gaze in mine until the intensity of his stare becomes too much.

The broadcast continues.

". . . nobody seems to know why Professor Grimm is aiding these escapees, but it's believed he's been suffering with poor mental health for some time, and this might be a factor in his involvement. Now over to our reporter Rebecca, who is currently outside Biddick Hall with all the latest information . . ."

Eventually, the news briefing comes to an end and we all just sit there stunned. There is nothing but the hiss and spit of the fire and the deep silence of the woods.

"Whoa," says Gabriel eventually in an awe-inspired voice. "This is really it, then."

I am equally taken aback. Sometimes it's hard to remember that Wildsmoor isn't the only facility, that we're not the only ones suffering, that there's a whole other world out there. I take a moment to think, letting all the pieces of my plan fit together like a puzzle.

"That's who we need," I say.

Gabriel looks up at me. "Who?"

"Professor Grimm. If anyone has the answers, and if anyone can help us, then it's him. We gather everyone together, we contact Professor Grimm, we escape with Clementine and Sarah's help, and then we'll all be safe . . ."

". . . and we all live happily ever after?" breaks in Adanya. "You expect him to hide everyone? All of us living out our days in hiding thanks to the man responsible for putting us here?" Adanya looks around at everyone. "Let's keep it simple, and put it up to a vote. If you think we should carry out this stupid plan and recruit everyone, raise your right hand, and if you think we should keep focus on getting ourselves out, *on our own*, raise your left." Immediately, she puts her left hand in the air . . . And after a long moment, so does Emir. I stare at him but he doesn't look back at me.

Anger bubbles in my belly.

Gabriel puts his right hand in the air and so does Margie.

"I think I'll stay out of this," pipes up Arthur, holding up his hands.

Adanya ignores him and her eyes settle on Isaiah. "I know you agree with me," she says. "She's too much of a risk."

Isaiah says nothing. He's staring down at his hands, as if he can't decide. Then he looks up at me. After a long moment, he speaks. "Sorry, Adanya. Everything we do carries risk. Look at us right now"—he gestures around to us all—"the only difference between us and them is that they got caught. Besides, we've been going around in circles for months . . ." Isaiah takes his mask off and turns to look at me. His expression is thoughtful and there is something in his eyes that for some reason makes me feel seen, but not just the old me, the new me too. "Perhaps Emily is who we need to lead us out of here." Then he raises his right hand in the air.

I let out a breath. Three against two.

Adanya lets her hand fall. Her eyes well up slightly, shiny in the light. "Fine. You're all idiots. I can't wait to tell you all I told you so when we're caught and locked up for the rest of our lives. You're living in a dream world if you think you can pull this off."

I nod, and suddenly I smile, because Adanya's right, I am living in a dream world, but luckily dreams are just what I happen to be best at.

CHAPTER eighteen

I sit at dinner, my tray in front of me. I am exhausted, and tiredness fogs up my brain to the point where I almost feel like I'm drugged again. We stayed in the woods until the early hours of the morning, watching and reading everything we could on Clementine's phone about the breakouts, and then arguing and talking about everything obsessively.

I look across the table at Emir. His eyes look vacant and there are bags under his eyes. Clearly, he didn't get much sleep either. He looks up and catches my eye, but then quickly looks away. I grit my teeth together as I realize that I've been waiting for his attention, craving his eyes on mine.

I look back down at my dinner tray. Two sausages, mashed potato, and three bits of limp broccoli—the same meal we are served every Wednesday. I resist the urge to look back up at Emir. We've not spoken at all since what happened at Ashbury, as if our dream adventures never happened. Part of me wonders if I pushed him too far the other night while the other part of me knows that it shouldn't matter. He should be the least of my worries.

I look around the hall and count the guardians. Two by the door, two by the teachers' table, and four more stationed at different points around the room. I turn my gaze to the barred windows. The winter sun set behind the hill a few hours ago, but still I can see more guardians circling. I count their flashlights. One, two, three in the driveway. And then at least two more in the distance, circling the fence.

And who knows how many more of them are around the house. And this is in comparison to how many kids? Sixty? Seventy? If our plan is going to work, if we are going to actually escape Wildsmoor, then this is going to make it so much harder. It's going to take all of us.

Us against them.

And all we have to do now is recruit the whole school to join the Cure while watched by what feels like a thousand armed guardians.

So should be easy, then . . .

I am grateful to escape the throngs of guardians and find the quiet of the library. As soon as I walk through the old crumbling archway and into the quiet, stuffy room, I immediately relax, the musty smell of decaying paper greeting me like an old friend. I trace the rows of books as I walk through. Old bound leather and wrinkled paperbacks under my fingertips.

I make my way to the back corner of the room and sink into my usual chair. I remember the last time I sat here, the first time I spoke to Emir. That was only a few weeks ago now, but it feels like a lifetime.

A noise interrupts the stillness and I peer through the gloom. A door opens at the very back of the room and Mr. Caddy emerges from the doorway. He turns, pulls a key from his pocket, and closes and locks the door behind him. Next to the door is his book trolley. He lifts a stack of paperbacks off the top and places the key down, before putting the books back over the top.

His eyes widen slightly when he realizes I'm watching and our eyes meet. Immediately, I look back down on the book on my lap, keeping my face still and pretending to be engrossed in the text.

Footsteps sound across the floor, getting closer. I can't help but look up. Mr. Caddy pauses in front of me. His eyes are watery with age, but behind that there is a keenness to them that scrutinizes me sharply. It is the same way he looked at me and Emir that day. At the time I had assumed he was suspicious of us, that somehow he knew I had stopped taking my medication, but now I recognize the expression for what it is. Kindness.

"Good evening, Mr. Caddy," I say in the most monotone voice I can muster.

"What are you doing back here?" he asks.

"Reading, Mr. Caddy."

"There's more comfortable seats by the entrance, you know." He gestures with one wrinkled hand back toward the front of the library.

I shrug and look at him blankly.

He looks around and then back at me. "It is quiet back here though, I have to admit."

I nod. "Yes."

After another long moment, his eyes begin to drift away from me, and I can tell I have lost his interest. "Have a good evening," he says.

"You too, Mr. Caddy," I murmur.

I watch out of the corner of my eye as he slowly makes his way down the nearest aisle of books and back toward the front of the library.

I wait a minute, then another minute to be safe, before closing the book on my lap and standing up. I look around for a moment, checking to make sure I am completely alone, before treading over to the door I saw him emerge from.

I turn to the book trolley, still sitting next to the door. I rummage between the paperbacks for a moment before my hand falls on something smooth and cold and metal. It's an old key, bronze colored and the metal scratched and nicked with long years of use. I pull it out and stare at it.

I try it on the door Mr. Caddy came from. It goes in smoothly, as if it's been used often. I push the door open, step inside, and close the door behind me. I'm enveloped by a blackness so dense that I can't see my hand in front of my face. I feel around the walls, my hands patting over crumbling, damp stone. Eventually, I find what I'm looking for, a smooth square set into the wall. I press the switch and lights flicker on. I'm standing at the end of a short corridor, beyond which there is nothing but a flight of stairs, descending steeply downward.

Slowly, I make my way to the end of the corridor and head down into the gloom. There is a smell hanging in the air that grows stronger and stronger with every step, musty and also sweet somehow.

At the bottom, I find myself in a large room. The dust is overwhelming. It covers everything—the wooden floor, the beams above—a thick white layer that tells me how long it's been since this room has been used.

Strewn across the floor are piles of books, towering up toward the ceiling. Pathways have been trodden through the dust, twisting around the teetering stacks of books. I follow one and the trail leads me to a haphazard pile of paperbacks that rises and falls like a mountain range. My eyes trace the spines. Some are colorful, some are black. Many of them have titles written in gold or silver. I reach out and pick the first one off the top. I wipe dust off a silver-winged monster that's been etched on the front.

I pull a few more out of the pile. One has an image of a strange half-human, half-animal creature on the front, another one a gold compass type thing surrounded by stars, another a figure wearing a pointed hat and a long cloak.

I choose one at random and spend a few minutes flicking through, skimming over different passages. It's a storybook, a children's story, I'm guessing by the prose. But it's not like any book I ever read as a child. There are kids in the book like us, and although they don't say out loud that they have the Grimm, it's clear as day. They can do things, impossible things. Only they don't call it the Grimm or "abilities" like the Cure sometimes do. They call it magic.

I remember what Emir had said about the government banning any books with made-up things in them, anything that could encourage children with the Grimm. I frown, looking around. These ones weren't destroyed. Mr. Caddy has kept these a secret.

I slap the book closed and shove it into the waistband of my skirt. Emir has to see this.

I hurry back up the stairs, leaving the smell of must and mold behind me. I close the door and step back out into the library. I turn and lock the door behind me, stashing the key back into the trolley.

—

I check the reading cubicles at the front of the library first, followed by the aisles of books closest to the entrance. Most of the other

older kids are here. Gabriel and Isaiah are sitting on chairs opposite each other. Isaiah is engrossed in whatever he is reading, but
Gabriel is flicking aimlessly through the pages, his eyes staring
off into space. Adanya is also nearby. She's not even pretending to
read; instead, she's slouched back on her chair, inspecting her
fingernails.

Finally, I find him in a far corner, browsing through an aisle of
dusty books.

"Emir," I say, treading carefully over to him.

He turns to me and flinches, as if I'm something he should be
afraid of. My stomach gives a little lurch. "I've found something you
have to see," I say in a rush.

Emir turns back to the shelf of books and shakes his head. "I
don't think so," he murmurs in reply.

"I promise you, you're going to want to see this," I try again. "I
found a locked room full of books. I think like the ones you told me
about, that were banned when they discovered the Grimm."

For a tiny second his head tilts back toward me and his eyes
widen. But then he turns back to the shelf and a slow frown creeps
onto his forehead. "In a locked room?"

I nod. "Look." I show him the book that I took.

He looks down at it and his frown grows deeper. "You just love
breaking into places, don't you?"

I blush. "It wasn't like that. Mr. Caddy just left his cart right
there with the key on it. Almost as if he wanted me to find it."

Emir's jaw clenches and he shakes his head. "Adanya is right.
You're too impulsive to be trusted."

I clench my fists. "How does it feel to be so afraid all the time?"

He stares at the books, pretending to look for something that isn't there, as if I don't exist.

"I think it must be pretty lonely," I continue, but he continues to ignore me.

Finally, annoyance spurs me to grab one of his hands, to try to force him to look at me, but instead of feeling his gloves under my fingers, my hand closes over his bare wrist.

Our bare skin touches. My skin reacts, a surge of heat that is concentrated hottest where my fingers grasp his wrist.

Emir gasps and his head whips toward me. I hear an almost imperceptible crackling noise and see a tiny flicker of light weave down his hand and between his fingers. With his free hand, he reaches out and shoves me away. I stumble backward and fall to the floor. My ankle twists beneath me and I cry out in pain.

Emir stands over me. His face is twisted and pale, like a skeleton, devoid of color. He looks from his bare wrist back to me. "Emily," he says. "I didn't mean . . ." He trails off and looks down at me for a long moment, rubbing his wrist where my fingers were, as if I've burned him with my touch.

His face regains some of its color before hardening again. He yanks his sleeve back down over his bare skin. "You shouldn't touch me. Don't touch me ever again. Stay away from me, Emily." Then he turns on his heel and walks away.

I lie there for a moment, stunned. My ankle throbs, but worse than that, humiliation fills the space that he's left, an emotion so physical it makes me feel sick.

A moment later, music sounds softly through the room. The evening bell.

I push myself to my feet and limp my way out of the library, straight to my dorm room. I go inside and am relieved to find it is empty. For several minutes I just sit on the end of my bed, feeling a swell of emotions that compete for space inside me. Humiliation and anger and something else that I don't have the words to describe but makes my chest hurt. I want to go and find Emir and push him back, and stand over him and see how he feels, small and stupid and insignificant on the floor.

The door opens and Adanya comes into the room. She looks at me and she looks away again. But then she stops and looks at me again. She sighs. "Has something happened?"

I shake my head.

"Really? Because you're obviously blubbing about something."

It's only then that I realize she's right, I am crying. I reach up with angry fists and scrub away the tears.

Adanya surveys me for a long moment. Finally, she rolls her eyes. "It's Emir, isn't it."

"No," I say, but it comes out too quickly and too loud and it's obvious that I'm lying.

She comes and perches on the end of my bed. "We're not friends, but I'm telling you now, you would be best off just forgetting about him."

"I don't know what you're talking about."

Adanya glares at me. "I've been there"—she gestures at me—"in your exact same position."

I stare at Adanya in surprise. Although it's obvious now I take the time to think about it. Her warnings about him, the tension between them, the way Emir accused her of being jealous.

"Is that why you hate me?"

Adanya snorts and shakes her head. "I don't hate you. I just don't trust you."

I nod at her words—there is that all-important word again, *trust*.

"You know," I say eventually. "There's nothing going on between me and Emir. We've barely spoken, really." Which in some ways is the truth. The only time that we've ever had a conversation that didn't end in one of us storming off is when we're in one of my dreams.

Adanya rolls her eyes. "Don't be stupid. We all see the pathetic way he looks at you. And the way he's always trying to protect you?"

I stare, confused. "He doesn't try to protect me and I don't need him to."

"Do you not remember his reaction in the Ashbury shop, with that woman and the guardian?"

I shake my head. "He was just pulling me back, stopping me from exposing you all."

"How about when he went after you that time in the woods, then? Or when he got all uptight about me using my ability on you?" She shakes her head. "If you can't see it, then you're even more clueless than I thought."

I say nothing and just look down at my hands. I frown and shake my head. "This isn't what any of us should be focusing on," I say, and it's the truth. I shouldn't take such pleasure in the fact that he'd dreamed of me. I shouldn't look forward to the depth and darkness of his eyes on mine. I shouldn't have enjoyed the surge of his electricity through my skin as much as I did. It shouldn't be pos- sible to hate someone as much as you want them to want you. I'm not equipped to deal with a situation like this, especially when there are far more important things happening.

"Look . . . Emir is . . ." Adanya shakes her head. ". . . aloof. No, that's not the word. Damaged, or something. He's got walls around him, and nobody can get past those."

"Don't we all?"

"Worse than any of us though. He's so wrapped up in his own pain that he can hardly see anything else. He's selfish."

I nod. That much at least seems to be true. I reach down to rub my sore ankle. I pull down my sock to inspect it. It's starting to swell. Adanya frowns down at my ankle, and when she speaks again, it's in a gentle tone of voice that reminds me of her dreams and the surprising softness there. "He's incapable of love. Or anything remotely close to it."

I look up, suddenly curious. I want to ask Adanya about what happened between her and Emir, but at that moment the doors open and the other girls walk in—Jessica followed by the two others. They walk robotically to their bunks and start to undress. They don't notice me and Adanya, even though I am still puffy eyed and disheveled, and even though Adanya is sitting on the edge of my bed—something that is forbidden at Wildsmoor.

I take a deep breath. If we're going to do this, then I might as well start now. "Hello," I say to the other girls.

They ignore me and continue to undress.

"Hello," I say to them again, in a louder voice this time. "I'm Emily. And you're Jessica . . ." I point to the girl nearest to me, the one who also sits next to me at mealtimes. "What are your names?" I ask the other two girls.

The two girls look at me for a moment. Frowns and confusion briefly cloud their expressions before melting away again.

"Monika and Isla, right?" says Adanya, pointing to each of them in turn. Monika is tall, with poker-straight blonde hair. Isla is mousy-looking and delicate, with a little upturned nose.

"Talking is forbidden," says Monika in a surprisingly deep voice. She turns back to pulling on her pajamas and Isla follows her lead.

Only Jessica is still looking at us. She looks afraid, eyes wide and frozen, half-undressed. "We do not talk in our dormitories. Those are the rules," she says. Then she turns back to folding her school skirt.

Adanya and I watch as the three other girls finish changing into their nightwear and get into bed.

"Tomorrow night," Adanya whispers to me as the others lie there and watch the ceiling, just waiting for the lights to go out. "We bring them."

CHAPTER nineteen

It's cold tonight. Freezing, even. The other members of the Cure are still arriving, feet crunching on frost and breath coming out in plumes as they take their places around the fire.

With them they bring others, kids I recognize from classes and mealtimes. They sit with the others on scavenged branches and logs, but maskless, looking around the clearing with pale, stricken faces.

Jessica from our dorm is one of them, dragged here by Adanya. Then there is a pair of identical twins, Angel and Destiny. They sit close to the fire, holding hands. Gabriel has brought a boy I recognize from art therapy, Jakab. He sits next to him, his arms wrapped around his middle, nodding along to Gabriel's chatter.

Isaiah comes and stands next to me. His clown mask is fixed into its usual disconcerting smile, but underneath his eyes are full of soft warmth. I'm glad to see him. Isaiah's gentleness has a calming effect on me. He smiles before turning back to the fire and holding his hands out next to mine. "There will be snow soon," he says.

I nod my head. Isaiah's right. Autumn has well and truly left us and winter is taking hold. I am not looking forward to it. We are so high on the moorland here that winter is usually a mix of freezing wind, rain, snow, and frost. And it's endless. We shiver our way through classes and wear thick sweaters in bed all the way until May.

"Well, it is December," I reply.

Isaiah nods. "Christmastime . . . something to celebrate at least."

I snort and smile, but I do not laugh. Christmas at Wildsmoor is a dreary time, marked only by the forced horrible performance we put on for the few families that visit and a soggy attempt at Christmas dinner, complete with cheap crackers with bad jokes inside and colorful paper hats that we're forced to wear. At that moment Margie walks into the clearing, accompanied by Clementine and Sarah. Clementine grins at me and gives me a wave before taking a seat with the others across the fire.

Suddenly, I realize everyone is falling quiet. Isaiah goes and sits down, leaving me standing alone by the fire. The Cure members watch me from under their masks and, following their lead, so do the new arrivals.

I stare back at them all. What are they waiting for?

Gabriel lifts his mask and makes a face at me as if to say, *Go on, then.* Margie nods at me. And even Adanya is quiet, just watching me with folded arms and her fox eyes glaring. The only person who isn't looking in my direction is Emir. He sits and stares at the ground, his hands jammed into his pockets. I look back at everyone, realizing the horrible truth. Somebody has to step up and lead, and somehow that person seems to be me. I look at Gabriel again hopefully; after all, he seemed to be the Cure's unofficial leader at some point. But he just smiles and leans back, watching with all the others.

For a moment I think I might crumble under their stares, and maybe the Emily from a few weeks ago would have, but that's not who I am anymore. I plant my feet farther apart. I take a deep breath and lift my chin. "Thank you for coming," I say, looking at each of our new members in turn. "I understand this must be very strange and confusing for you all, but I promise that you'll understand more in time." I pause for a moment, wondering where on earth I should start. I think back to my first time properly meeting the Cure, my eyes flickering to Gabriel and then around to all the newcomers.

"For those of you joining us for the first time, you can consider this another class on your schedule. The most important one. Now, what do you think you know about the Grimm?"

—

I sit alone and watch as the original members of the Cure support the new kids with discovering what they're capable of. Chatter rises into the air, accompanied by steaming plumes of breath. There is even the odd shout of laughter, bursting out into the winter air.

The new members, still under the influence of their medication, are struggling.

I watch Jessica and Emir across the clearing. Jessica says that before she came to Wildsmoor she was able to influence the wind, but so far she hasn't been able to produce even the tiniest gust. I imagined Emir to be a terrible teacher, but in fact he's gentle and reassuring. He nods in encouragement at Jessica as she finally manages to produce a tiny breath of wind that rustles the leaves behind their heads.

Destiny and Angel, the twins, are having slightly more luck. One can create fire and one can create ice. They sit with Adanya, who is cajoling them in turns, first Destiny to create fire, and then Angel to put it out again. Tiny flames flicker between Destiny's fingers before Angel makes frost creep up from the ground and smother them until they sputter out.

Arthur also isn't doing too badly. He floats above our heads, taking strides through the air as if walking some invisible ground the rest of us can't see.

The last new kid, Jakab, is an anomaly as he says he can't remember how the Grimm manifests in him. We had all been shocked when he told us that he had arrived at Wildsmoor the day after his fifth birthday. He's sitting with Gabriel, and the two of them are talking and laughing. Well, Gabriel is at least; Jakab looks more just shell-shocked, although every now and again I see a smile creep onto his face.

Gabriel at that moment looks up and catches my eye. He grins his liquid sunlight smile and pushes himself to his feet, coming over and sitting down beside me.

He sighs and waves a hand around the clearing. "Isn't it beautiful?" he says.

"What?"

"Oh, you know, just a handful of messed-up kids in the woods, committing felonies and planning on taking down an entire government."

"That's not the plan and you know it."

"That's not the plan . . ." He turns and grins at me. "Yet."

I look at him severely. "This is just a precaution," I say, waving a hand at the other kids practicing. "Just in case. If we can get everyone out without a fight, then that's the best way."

"Just one teeny-tiny fight?"

"No."

Gabriel sighs, long and loud and as dramatic as always. "Always so sensible," he says.

"I'm not," I snap, defensive about being called sensible, although I'm not sure why. Sensible is careful. Sensible will keep us all safe.

But Gabriel just laughs and turns his blue-eyed stare on me. "I like you exactly as you are," he says. "Our sensible leader."

For some reason I flush at his words and I'm glad of my mask. I sigh and shake my head, turning back toward the others.

"What is it?" he asks.

"It's taken us two weeks to just find five new people willing to listen to us. It's taking too long. We need a quicker way."

"What are you going to do, then?"

"I have an idea," I say. "But I'm just not sure that it'll work." I look at Emir for a moment. Perhaps Jessica will be the next girl he decides to confuse with his conflicting signals. I turn to Gabriel. "Come with me?" I ask.

—

The noise of the others practicing their abilities diminishes as Gabriel and I walk out of the clearing and into the darkness of the trees. The world falls quiet again. The silence of the woods helps, my senses somehow amplified in the quietness. I close my eyes and focus on Wildsmoor. I can't see the school, but this doesn't matter; I can feel it. Dreams. Lots and lots of dreams floating up into the air, calling out to me.

My dream senses extend from me like phantom arms and fingers that I use to touch each unconscious mind, feeling the flavor of each. I drift over them, most of them nothing more than half-formed images and blurred figures moving among the grayness.

One particular mind stands out, brighter and more fully formed than the others. Curious, I stop for a moment, entering the dreamer's unconscious. A girl crouches. She is afraid and skinny and hiding in a cupboard, her knees tucked under her chin and her neck bent sideways in the small space. Shouts and screams and crashes sound from elsewhere in the house.

"Anita!" screams a voice. *"Anita!"*

The cupboard door wrenches open and a sudden bright light floods the space where the little girl is hiding. She's dragged out and begins to wail. A woman has her by the wrist. The woman is tall and angular with pinched lips.

She drags her through the house and points at a potted plant that's fallen from a shelf. Dirt is strewn across the floor.

"Did you do this?" The woman takes her arm and thrusts her toward the fallen plant pot.

"It was an accident."

"And I suppose you didn't think to clean it up . . ."

"I couldn't find the brush," the girl says in a tiny voice.

"This is my house and you will be careful and clean," the woman says. *"Those are the rules."* Then the woman pulls back a hand and slaps the little girl across the face. She lifts a hand to slap the girl again, but before she can, I recoil, whipping away my phantom senses before I can see anything else.

"What is it?" asks Gabriel.

I open my eyes, suddenly remembering that he's there. "You don't want to know," I mutter, still stunned by what I've seen. I know that the little girl is Matron; I could see it in the shape and color of her eyes. I wonder who the woman was . . . her mother, perhaps? If so, then this would go a little way toward explaining why Matron is how she is.

I push it from my mind. *No.* I need to focus. Lots of people have horrible upbringings. It doesn't give them a right to go around torturing other kids in turn.

I close my eyes and reach out with my dream senses again. It's tricky, deciphering one person's dreams from another's, but finally I find the person I'm looking for. Her dreams are hardly dreams at all really. Just a soft buzzing of blurred shapes. But it doesn't matter, I don't need to see her dreams, I just need her.

I take a deep breath, then I yank her with my dream arms. Suddenly, she is standing in front of me. "It worked," I whisper to myself.

Of course I'd pulled Emir from his dreams before, but that was always when I was asleep too, never when I was awake. I'm learning more and more just how much I'm capable of.

Meera, the oldest girl at Wildsmoor, who hands out the medication, stands in front of me. Transparent and blurred at the edges, her body shimmers in the darkness. She looks down at herself, at her hands, which glow, and then back up. Her mouth opens and closes. Her eyes are wide, a mixture of shock and horror. "Where am I?" she whispers.

CHAPTER twenty

It's just after midnight. I drift down the corridors just as I've done for the last two weeks. My mask clings to my face and my stockinged feet pad noiselessly on the wooden floors. There are more guardians than ever now but this doesn't matter. I am as silent as a breath of wind and they never see or hear me coming.

I peer around the corner and see the dark figure of one at the end of the corridor, one of the few female guards standing watch in her usual place. I pad closer, and closer, then when I am only a few paces away, I reach into her mind and tug her into the world of sleep. She slumps down the side of the wall.

I stand in front of her for a moment and watch her sleeping face, ponytail now disheveled and mouth ajar. I never used to think much about the guardians, but recently I've been thinking about them more and more. I wonder what this one's life is like outside Wildsmoor.

"You are terrifying," whispers a voice in my ear.

I turn and see Gabriel standing there in his mask. Beneath us, the guardian stirs slightly, and I put a finger to my lips. I beckon Gabriel onward and together we make our way through the school. I see two more guardians on our way, and each time I do the same thing, sending them to sleep before they even notice us.

Terrifying, Gabriel called me. It could be perceived as an insult, but actually there is something I like about that word, and something I like about the way he said it. It sums up somehow who I am becoming, or who I want to become at least. Powerful. Intimidating. Strong.

We reach the library and Gabriel pushes one of the doors open. He holds it and bows at me, gesturing with a hand for me to go through. I slide through the doorway and the door swings shut behind us.

I relax, knowing that the guardians don't keep watch in here.

"That never gets old," says Gabriel.

"It's necessary," I reply. And it is necessary. Now that the guardians are knocked out, the other kids can sneak out without being caught.

We make our way through the library to the back of the room where the door leading to the hidden basement is. I find the key in its usual place in the trolley and unlock the door. I open the door, switch on the light, and lead the way down into the dusty cellar.

We come out into the basement room to our new, alternate meeting spot, with its towers of books and thick layers of dust. Unlike Emir, Gabriel was fascinated with the idea of a hidden library. It makes us more unpredictable, and the books have surprisingly turned out to be a huge help in getting the new kids to understand that the Grimm isn't necessarily bad. The books are full of kids like us, but they're the heroes in their stories, not the villains.

Gabriel pulls off his mask and begins to meander through the piles of books. I follow him aimlessly, trailing my fingers over the covers as we pass. For a while we don't speak, a comfortable silence between us. I've found myself gravitating toward Gabriel more and more over the last couple of weeks. It's refreshing, being around someone who actually seems to like me.

"What do you think old Caddy does with all these?" he asks.

"Reads them?" I suggest.

"But they're all kids' books," he protests. "And he hates us. Why would he read books with kids like us in them?"

"Does he hate us?" I respond. Like with the guardians, I've been thinking more about the other adults in our lives recently. I always assumed that they all hated us, that they were all just an extension of Matron's evilness. I'd never really thought of them as people in their own right.

But now I'm not so sure. I remember the guardian earlier slumped down against the wall. She'd looked vulnerable and human and for all I know, maybe she just thought she was doing what was best. Or maybe this is just a job for her, a way to provide for her family.

"He sure acts as if he hates us."

I shrug. "I just mean that maybe it's not really about us at all. Maybe these books mean something to him that we don't know about. He would have read them as a kid himself, most likely."

Gabriel strolls back over to me. "That's what I like best about you, you know."

I pull back slightly. "What?"

Gabriel still hasn't put his mask back on and his piercing gaze holds my own for a long moment. "You think about things," he says. "You're smart." He reaches out and taps the side of my forehead. "And powerful," he adds, his eyes taking on his hungry look. His hand lingers there, then with one finger traces down the side of my face. The skin is sensitive there and every nerve ending feels like it's come alive.

My face flushes hot and I pull away. Gabriel drops his hand. He grins at me as if he knows what I'm feeling inside. It's not like when Emir touched me, which was pure electricity. This is more like a deep ache that I want to somehow fill.

For a moment we just stand and look at each other. I think about stepping forward. I think about touching his cheek in return. I think about pressing my lips against his. I may have never experienced it in real life, but I know enough from old books and the few films we are allowed to watch.

But in real life, it doesn't seem to be as simple or as clear as that. I know everything but also nothing at all. Closing that physical gap between us just seems somehow impossible.

At that moment, the door opens and Emir walks in. He looks at me and Gabriel, standing too close together. His eyes take in the scene for a moment, and I expect him to scowl or glare for some reason, but he doesn't. Instead, he just looks away again, his face completely unreadable. He walks over to the far side of the room where our meetings usually start. With his back toward us, he sits on one of the book stacks and puts his chin in his hand.

Gabriel looks at me and winks, then strolls in Emir's direction. "Well, hello to you too," he says as he walks. Emir ignores him, not sparing him a nod or a wave, or even a look.

I don't move, taking a moment to press my hands against my hot cheeks. I feel embarrassed that Emir, of all people, saw us so obviously close. But there's another part of me that is glad.

The door opens again and Adanya and Isaiah walk through, followed slowly by the rest of the Cure members. I drift over to the side of the room where everyone is gathering. Isaiah smiles and says hello and so does Margie. I walk over to where Meera is chatting with Jessica.

"Hi," I say.

Jessica holds up a hand in greeting and Meera fixes me with a serious stare and nod. "How's it all been?" I ask, directing my question at Meera, who has become the most vital member of the Cure since her arrival, helping us by slowly decreasing the amount of medication being handed out to the students who agree to it, day after day.

"Everything is fine," says Meera, in her same serious voice. "Nobody suspects anything."

"That's good," I say.

"Although a boy had an episode during math yesterday . . ."

"And I saw another one on the way to lunch," jumps in Jessica.

I nod and sigh. That is the one massive side effect to having half the school withdrawing from their medication. The episodes.

"I suggest that we slow down the withdrawals," says Meera. "Reduce the dose even more slowly."

I nod. "That's a good idea. Think you can arrange that?"

Meera nods. "Easy enough."

"Thank you." I smile at her but she doesn't smile back and nods at me instead. At first I thought that Meera was just struggling with withdrawal or perhaps unhappy with me, but I'm starting to realize that actually this is just her nature. She's tall, beautiful, serious, and also dignified in a way that I couldn't ever dream of emulating.

The other kids have arranged themselves into a rough sort of circle. Since the first newcomers joined us three weeks ago, everyone has started to relax. They talk and laugh softly among themselves.

Not all of them, however. There are a few who still sit silent and pale faced, one of them a tiny girl who looks impossibly young. I go and sit next to her. She is shivering and shaking but her face looks shiny with sweat.

"What's your name?" I ask.

"Keira," the girl replies, looking up at me. Her eyes are ever so slightly glazed.

"How old are you?" I ask

"Ten," she replies. "Just. I had my birthday last week."

I frown at that. We've mostly been concentrating on recruiting the older kids so far, but slowly we're getting younger and younger. Keira, with her skinny arms wrapped around her waist, looks so tiny that I think she might snap.

"It gets easier," I say to her. "Give it a few days and you won't miss your medicine at all."

She nods doubtfully and looks at me sideways. "Are you really going to get us all out of here?"

Maybe. Hopefully. But I don't say these things; instead, I say, "Of course."

I see a spark of hope in her eyes behind the feverishness. "Then it's worth it," she says, her voice suddenly taking on a note of determination that wasn't there before.

"Wait here," I say to her. I go and fetch a book from one of the stacks that I flicked through the night before. A kids' book, about children who travel into a fantastical world and meet strange creatures who have abilities like us. Only once again, they call it magic and spells and enchantments, not the Grimm. It's a happy book though, and one where, like many of the books in the room, the kids are brave and fight for justice. I sit back next to Keira. "Here," I say. "You should read this book. Only you need to hide it away. Think you can do that?"

Keira takes it from me and nods.

I stand up and wait for everyone to fall quiet. My heart thumps in my throat as their eyes turn to me. "Uh, hi," I say, holding up a hand in greeting. Although I have somehow taken on this leader role, it does not come naturally to me. Gabriel would be better suited for this, with his bright smile and natural eloquence, but he's insisted that it has to be me.

I put my hands behind my back so nobody can see my fingers twisting together. "I'll make this quick so that we have more time to practice. I'm sure we're all aware of the rise in episodes recently and the only way for us to combat this is to gain control over our abilities. The more control we have, the less likely we are to have any future outbursts."

"Plus the more powerful we are, the more advantage we will have in a fight," pipes up Arthur.

I turn to him and shake my head. "I'm not sure where you heard that, but a fight isn't part of the plan."

His eyes flicker to Gabriel and then back to me, and I resist the urge to roll my eyes. Of course he's been talking to Gabriel. Gabriel has been telling anyone who will listen that we should incite a riot to aid our escape. He says it will be "fun" to get some revenge and would also reduce the risk of anyone following us.

But he's not in charge. I am. And Arthur is younger than him by

231

several years. He shouldn't be exercising his influence like that. I give Gabriel an annoyed look and he just shrugs and smiles back at me, as if he has no idea what I could possibly be vexed about.

"If it comes to it," Arthur says, standing up and looking around at everyone, "I'd rather fight than retreat like a scared little mouse. There's enough of us now that if it came to it, we could win."

"And at what price?" I ask. "People would die."

"That's a price I'm willing to pay," he says.

Out of the corner of my eye, I can see other people nodding.

I push my fingers to my forehead, thinking. I shake my head. "It's irrelevant anyway. We'll practice our abilities, and we'll continue with planning a coordinated and quiet escape like before. If there's no other option, then fine, we fight, but *only* as a last resort. All right?"

I look at Arthur and he looks back at me. His arms are folded and despite his age, there's a defiant glint in his eyes, but after a moment he nods and sits back down.

"All right, let's pair up and start practicing."

The room slowly stirs before coming alive with movement as people find pairs and start to practice. I do not pair with anyone, and for a while I just watch. I am intrigued by the new members' abilities, which after a week or two of coercing are starting to emerge and grow from strength to strength.

Jessica's wind has progressed beyond a gentle breeze and turned into full-on gusts. She sends powerful whirlwinds through the room, making the book pages ruffle and her partner stumble. The twins' fire and ice powers are also gaining strength. Angel brings frosts that coat the room in crystals and make us all shiver, before Destiny burns it all away again, controlling huge circles of fire that erupt from under her sweeping hands.

Arthur has moved on from making himself float to levitating other objects too. He launches himself into the air and waves his arms. The old pages that litter the floor fly up and swirl in the air, a snowstorm of paper. He laughs above us, throwing back his head in glee as his paper tornado whips through the room.

Jakab, the boy who can't remember why he was sent to Wildsmoor, has also slowly started to explore his abilities, although it's still a mystery what he can really do. Sometimes when he concentrates hard, his body parts seem to swell before deflating back to their usual size. Or his face will suddenly coat itself with hair. Strangest of all was when his skin broke out with large pustules that covered him from head to toe. But even these small feats take up a lot of his effort, and I have a feeling that we're not really seeing what he's capable of yet.

Possibly one of the strangest manifestations of the Grimm is in Aisling, who can animate dead things. Turns out that the forest is full of dead critters and bigger animals too, and she brings them to her, making their rotting bodies perform for us. She seems to take enjoyment from this, smiling and swaying as she whispers to their jerky bodies. I don't mind Aisling, although she is nearly as odd as her ability, but the other kids avoid her, and I don't blame them.

There are more abilities, each one unique to the holder. One older boy sees visions in water, whether dreamed up or visions of the future, nobody knows. Another can sow fear in anyone who looks into their eyes. And then there's Tom, who it seems can travel into the past, disappearing for minutes at a time before reappearing with a dazed look in his eyes.

All too soon the two hours are over. Slowly, the room empties, kids making their way in ones and twos back to their dormitories. I hang back, waiting for everyone to leave. Isaiah and Adanya are the last to go. They give me a brief wave before slipping through the door and leaving me with nothing but the dust and silence, and books.

I meander through the stacks, picking books out at random. I look at covers and read the little blurbs on the back. Finally, I choose one and settle down in a corner of the room. For a little while, I just read, letting myself be absorbed into the writer's world.

It takes a while for my brain to focus on the words, but slowly but surely pictures emerge from the pages. The children attend a school in the book and go to classes, but not like classes I know—math, English, socialization, art therapy—instead, they learn magic and spells and mythical creatures.

Things happen in the story. They make friends and enemies. They do exciting things. I skip to the end of the book, and I find out that there is a happy ending. They save their school from an evil power and restore peace to their little world.

I gently close the book and think about us. About me, Emir, Gabriel, Isaiah, Adanya, and everyone else. There is an evil power at our school too, although it's not so obvious. The evil power is more complicated than just one man who wants to kill everyone. Our evil power is in our government and our parents and our teachers and doctors, and even us. It's the thoughts that we carry around with us, and the things that happen because of these thoughts. It's in the lives we live and the air we breathe.

The Grimm is sickness. The Grimm is bad. The Grimm is evil.

Gabriel and Arthur want to fight, but do they really even know what they're fighting? How can you get away from something that is merely a thought? How can you defeat it?

I sigh and push myself to my feet. I should go to bed, before it gets any later. I weave around the towers of books and back up the stairs that lead to the main library. I close and lock the door behind me, before replacing the key back in its usual place in the trolley.

It's only then that I realize I'm not alone. Somebody is lounging against the wall next to the doorway. I freeze for a moment, startled and body suddenly full of adrenaline, like an animal that senses a predator nearby.

It takes a moment for my brain to register who it is. I half expected a guardian, or worse, Matron, but instead it's Emir. He's watching me sideways. His face is blank but he's fiddling with the sleeves of his dressing gown.

I consider asking him what he's doing there, but then I decide that I don't really care, that he doesn't even deserve that tiny bit of my attention. I spin on one heel and walk off.

"Wait," he says. I hear his footsteps behind me, hurrying to catch up. I speed up my pace. "I have something to say. Something important."

I ignore him and carry on walking. I turn right at the old chair I usually sit in and toward the front of the library. I head down the wide corridor that separates the aisles of books.

"So you're not speaking to me now? Is that it?" Emir is suddenly in front of me, his hands spread wide.

His words make the irritation I'm feeling turn to anger. I stop, suddenly furious. "You told me to leave you alone. To stay away from you. Well, that's exactly what I'm trying to do."

"This is important," says Emir. "It's about . . . everything."

"Find somebody else to tell, then." I turn on one heel and escape into one of the aisles of books. It's darker here, the low lights of the library unable to reach us. I hurry along, feeling an urgent need to get away from Emir.

"It's about Gabriel."

I keep walking but I can feel my face flushing with heat.

"You should stay away from him," says Emir.

I stop walking again and spin to face him. I'm glad of the gloom, as I can feel myself losing control. My hair is falling down around my burning face, wisps flying in and out with my breath. I don't know how to express what I'm feeling, so instead, I laugh. I'm proud of the way the laugh sounds, loaded with so much derision and anger that it would rival any of Adanya's. "So I should stay away from you. And I should stay away from Gabriel. Is there anyone else you think I should stay away from? Do you just not want me to speak to anyone, is that it?"

"You don't understand. I've known Gabriel a lot longer than you, and he's selfish through and through. He collects people who he thinks could be useful to him. He collected all of us, after all. You need to understand, it's your power he wants, not you."

My face grows even hotter. "Because I'm so repulsive that nobody could ever want me?"

Emir shakes his head. "Of course not. But Gabriel is different. All he cares about is the fight, and winning, and he'll do anything to get that to happen. Our abilities in a way are a reflection of ourselves, an extension of our personalities. Gabriel can replicate himself a hundred times over, and his personality is just as duplicitous. Who knows which Gabriel is the real one."

I'm quiet for a tiny moment, digesting his words. I'd never thought about our abilities as being a part of us in that way before, but now that he says it, it's obvious. Emir is all storm clouds and sudden light, Adanya expresses the pain she carries inside, Margie's gifts with animals reflects her kinship with them, and so on, and so on.

"Why do you think he's letting you lead the Cure?" says Emir. "He gets what he wants but without any of the risk."

I think about this a moment more, my head hurting with it all, but then I decide that it really doesn't matter. Gabriel might be *duplicitous*. He might be out for his own gain, and have his own agenda, but don't we all? And does it matter if he's just interested in me because of my abilities? He's never pretended otherwise, I realize; in fact, he's been perfectly open about it.

"He may not be a perfect person," I say, looking at Emir straight in the eyes. "But he's never made me feel bad about myself the way you have."

Emir's head startles back and his eyes widen a fraction, but I really don't care. It's the truth.

Emir would like me to be exactly who he wants me to be, but I am not defined by how others perceive me, including Gabriel or Emir or anyone else. I may still not really know exactly who I am yet, but this is something I want to discover for myself.

I walk off, and this time, Emir doesn't follow.

That night I dream walk, feeling restless. I call my she-wolf to me. She growls and pushes her head into my hand, and I realize that, like the others with their abilities, the wolf is also a manifestation of who I am becoming. Or at least, who I want to become. Fierce and strong and a leader of the pack. For a while we do nothing but roam the woods, sometimes running together and sometimes me riding on her back, and despite everything, I feel free.

CHAPTER twenty-one

In art therapy, the blank piece of paper stares at me, taunting with its emptiness. I usually enjoy a picture emerging from where there was nothing, but today my mind is elsewhere.

With every day that passes, my anxiety grows. More kids join the Cure every day and with that, the risk of being found out is growing. But all that will be for nothing if we can't find a way to reach Professor Grimm and keep ourselves a secret in the process. I feel like I'm walking a tightrope high up in the sky, and one false step means I could plummet to the ground at any moment. Everything we're dreaming of crushed and gone.

I sigh and reach for my paintbrush. Music surrounds me, gentle and lilting. A piano piece that builds slowly and should be calming but instead just fills me with a growing feeling of apprehension. Time is running out.

"Emily," hisses a voice next to me.

"What?" I look up at Adanya.

"You've been staring at that piece of paper for half an hour now . . ." She looks up at the front of the room where the art therapy teacher, Mrs. Ball, is starting to circulate, looking at each kid's work. Then she looks meaningfully at the side of the room, where three guardians stand in a line. Three. All of them with guns holstered at their waists.

"I'm getting there," I mutter back. I dip my paintbrush in the water and then into my watercolor tray, not bothering to check which color I've chosen. I make a broad stroke across the paper. It's red, scarlet red, like a sunset. Or like blood.

I go with it and paint in the rest of the sky around it. Orange and reds and a blue so dark it's almost black where the night sky creeps down to meet the burning horizon.

I am absorbed in my painting when a shriek tears through the gentle silence of the classroom. A girl stands up, her chair clattering backward. She points at the boy next to her. "Your fingers . . ."

It's Jakab. He stands up. He stares down in horror at his hands. His fingers are swelling up, like fat pale sausages. His arms lengthen and grow hairy, followed by his legs. He grows broader and there is a ripping noise as the seams of his school shirt tear open. His body begins to shake. "Help me," he cries out, looking around. But nobody moves.

"Oh shit," hisses Adanya next to me.

His body erupts, suddenly swelling to meet the ceiling. He roars, a sound that drowns out everything else and sends everyone closest to him scrambling to get away. His face is bulging and full of teeth. He roars again. He is terrifying, but I can see in his eyes that he's afraid. I want to go to him, to try to calm him.

The guardians are moving now. They pull their guns and advance across the classroom.

"Everybody out," yells Mrs. Ball, pointing toward the door. The other kids scramble out of their chairs and half run, half stumble out of the room.

The guardians point their guns at Jakab. He's frantic now, twisting and stamping and sending desks and chairs flying around the room.

"Wait, don't shoot," I shout. "Don't shoot." I take a step toward Jakab, but then Adanya's hand is on my arm. She tugs me in the opposite direction and we run from the room along with everyone else. The last thing we hear is gunshots.

———

"It's going to happen," whispers Adanya in front of me. The medication line stretches in front of us, neat heads staring forward and hands behind backs. Every ten seconds or so we take one step forward, closer to where Meera is handing out the nighttime medication from the little hatch in Matron's office.

"They *shot* him, Adanya. Actually shot him." I can't stop my hands from shaking.

"You don't know that."

I give a tiny shake of my head. "I don't know if I can do this anymore."

We take a step forward. I can see Meera's face now, her expression blank as she hands out little cups and handfuls of pills. She's been trying to reduce the other kids' medication slowly, and only with their permission, and this does seem to have reduced the number of episodes. As well as the other Cure members slowly learning to control the Grimm.

But apparently this still isn't enough. I never thought that somebody would die because of the decisions I'm making.

"You don't have a choice," hisses Adanya.

"Unsupervised conversations are forbidden," says a deep voice behind us.

We turn to see Monika, the tall girl from our dorm, staring at us with a severe expression.

"What's it to do with you?" hisses Adanya, giving her a filthy stare. "Besides, you're talking too."

"I'm a prefect now." She points at her school blazer. On it is a red capital *P*, pinned just below the Wildsmoor crest.

"Prefect?" scoffs Adanya. "We don't have prefects."

"We do now," says Monika. She steps out of line and walks up to one of the guardians. It's the big one with the squashed nose. She says something quiet to him and suddenly he's coming toward us. He grabs Adanya by her ponytail and yanks back her head. "You think the rules don't apply to you?"

Everyone freezes and turns to watch.

Monika steps smoothly back into line and focuses her eyes back on the hatch up ahead.

Adanya says nothing but her face contorts into a scowl.

"Don't look at me like that," he says.

"Like what?" retorts Adanya.

It happens so fast that I barely see his arm move. But then his gun is drawn and he holds it to Adanya's head. "Apologize," he says.

For a second Adanya says nothing. Her eyes blaze with obvious rage, but then she looks down at the floor. Her face relaxes into an expression of submission. "Sorry," she says. Her voice is meek.

He lifts his gun and strikes her around the head with it. Adanya collapses to the floor. She lies there limp for a moment, blinking. She lifts a hand to her head and when she pulls it away again, it's covered with blood.

"Get your meds and get to your room, and perhaps that'll teach you to learn some respect." He steps back and holsters his gun like nothing has happened.

This is the other side effect of our planned escape. With episodes increasing, and the outside world panicking about Professor Grimm and the escaped facility students, more and more guardians have been arriving at the school. They watch our every move. A wrong step can be enough to earn yourself a beating.

I resist the urge to help Adanya up and instead watch blankly with everyone else as she pulls herself to her feet. She accepts her pills from Meera, puts them under her tongue, and leaves the room.

It's my turn. I snatch my pills from Meera's hand and throw them back under my tongue as quickly as possible.

I hurry after Adanya. Back in our dorm room, Jessica is already there, picking up her washbag. She turns to look at us as we come into the room.

"What happened?" she asks, her eyes fixed on Adanya's bleeding forehead.

"Guardians, that's what," growls Adanya. "And Monika too. What was all that about?"

A flash of red catches my attention. I point to Jessica's blazer, where a little red *P* is also pinned. "What's that?" I ask.

Jessica looks at where I'm pointing and her cheeks tinge red. "Matron is giving them out," she says. "I didn't ask for it, but"—she looks up at us pleadingly—"I couldn't say no."

"Yeah, but what does it mean?" I persist.

"It means I'm a prefect. We're going to get special privileges in exchange for . . . information."

"Information about what?"

"If anyone breaks any rules . . . stuff like that."

Adanya and I stare at her.

"But I'm not going to say anything, obviously, it's just she told me I was going to be a prefect and I had to say yes."

Adanya rolls her eyes and picks up her towel. She lifts it to her head and presses it against her wound, stanching the still-trickling blood. "Well, good," she says.

I turn to her and frown. "What do you mean good?"

"Jessica can keep an eye on them all, can't you?"

Jessica nods her head, looking relieved. "Yes . . . Yes, I was going to suggest the same thing."

At that moment the door opens. Monika and Isla walk into the room. Isla doesn't look at us and blankly makes her way to her bed, where she begins to undress. But Monika pauses in the doorway. She looks around at us all, and suddenly her blank face stretches into a smile. Her eyes are empty but her lips are fixed in a way that reminds me of Isaiah's clown mask. Chills run down my spine. "Shouldn't you all be in your pajamas by now?"

The three of us turn back to our clothing. As I shrug off my blazer, I look sideways at Adanya and our eyes meet. And although we don't say anything, I can tell that for once we are on the same wavelength. How is the Cure going to meet now that they have eyes on the inside?

This is bad.

How bad? I guess only time will tell.

Out the window, snow begins to fall.

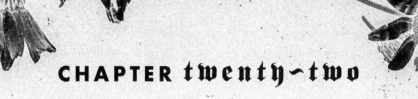

CHAPTER twenty-two

Snow clings to every branch and the ground is a carpet that creaks underfoot. In the middle of the clearing, fire blazes into the sky. The softly falling snow hisses and spits as it meets the flames. There are at least twenty kids here in person, and twenty more attending as dream incarnations, pulled from their unconsciousness. They mingle with the others, shimmering apparitions shining among solid flesh.

It's something that I'd been thinking of attempting since the night when I first pulled Meera to us here in the woods. If I can pull kids from their dreams rather than us all sneaking out at night, then this reduces the risk of our being found out. And if we were to be discovered, or something else was to happen, I could cut the tethers to their dream bodies and minimize the number of kids being caught.

It takes an enormous amount of energy for me to hold them all here, but it seems to be working, and slowly we're all getting used to the sight of the ghostlike apparitions dotted around the clearing.

I watch as the others practice, learning mastery over their abilities. Ice and fire flicker and crackle from fingertips. Objects fly around, moved only with the power of thought. Illusions flicker and electricity dances through the night sky.

A howling noise. Wind blows into the clearing. I stumble and fall, as does everyone else. I look up to see Jessica standing tall among the crumpled figures, like the one still-unfelled tree in a forest. Her eyes and mouth gape open. "Was that me?" she asks.

Some of the kids laugh.

Her partner, Aisling, pushes herself to her feet and claps her on the back. "You're getting stronger."

"I guess I am."

The other kids surround Jessica, patting her on the back and giving her friendly punches on the arm. She blushes and smiles at the attention.

At that moment, three more figures sidle into the clearing, Margie followed by her sister, Sarah, and Clementine. All three of them are bundled up, coats heavy with clumps of snow. Clementine spots me and grins, walking over.

"Move over," she says, bumping me with her hip and squeezing in to get closer to the fire. Despite her long, puffy coat, I can see her cheeks are red with cold and feel her body shivering up against mine.

"Are you all right?" I ask.

"Apart from being a human ice cream cone, yes." She leans forward and holds her hands out to the flames.

"I thought you might not come," I say.

Clementine shakes her head. "Tempting, considering the weather." She peers at me through the fur of her hood. Flames reflect and dance in her bright eyes. "But we finally have news."

I look back at her, suddenly feeling wide awake despite my fatigue. "You've found Professor Grimm?"

"Not exactly, but we've found somebody who says they can get a message to him. A friend whose brother escaped from a facility down south somewhere. Apparently, Professor Grimm helped them and found them somewhere safe to stay."

"Where?"

"We don't know exactly."

I frown. "Have you told him about us?"

Clementine pulls off her gloves and stuffs them into her pocket. She holds her now-bare hands out to the fire and wiggles her fingers. "We didn't tell him exactly which facility, but we had to give him a bit of information so that he would trust us. He's already passed on the message, asking Professor Grimm for help."

I think Clementine can see the doubt in my eyes as she puts a reassuring hand on my shoulder. "We can trust him," she says. "He feels the same. That what we're doing to you all, keeping anyone with the Grimm locked up, is wrong. There are a lot of people on the outside who want to find a way to help and he's one of them."

I nod. "Thanks, Clementine," I say, but worry still nags at my belly. "Matron's got spies on us now. She's made prefects out of some of the grimmers. The Cure is learning to control themselves more and more, but it's slow and there are eyes everywhere . . ." My chest suddenly feels tight and my breath catches in my throat. "A boy died the other day because he had an episode. They shot him in broad daylight. I just don't know how much longer we can wait . . ."

Clementine puts a hand on my shoulder. "You can rely on the others. You can rely on me and Sarah. We're working on it nonstop. You don't have to do it all."

I nod and let her words soothe me. "You're right, of course . . ."

"Emily," says a voice. I look up to see Meera standing in front of me. She looks down at me with her big, serious eyes. "Sorry to interrupt, but Keira is upset," she says, pointing to a little huddled figure on the other side of the fire.

"Uh . . ." I reply, eyeing Keira's hunched-over frame and wondering what she wants me to do about it.

"Don't you think you should talk to her?" asks Meera.

"I can," I say, standing up. "If you think that would help . . ."

Meera nods. "Yes. I do."

I walk over to Keira slowly, feeling uncomfortable in the face of someone else's emotions. Holding her knees, Keira rocks, back and forth, back and forth. She looks up at me. Her eyes are full of fear and red with tears.

Forcing myself to put my own feelings aside, I crouch down next to her. I hesitate, before reaching out and putting a hand on her shoulder. "Are you okay?" I ask.

Kiera shakes her head. "I'm scared," she whispers.

I nod. *Me too*, I want to say. But I don't say that; instead, I say, "You need to try to be brave."

She shakes her head. "Even if we escape, where will we go? Back to our families?"

"Do you wish you could be back with your family?"

"No," she says immediately.

"Me neither. So we won't." As soon as I say it, I feel guilty, Amelia's face flashing briefly in my mind.

"And brave people aren't like me," Keira says. "I'm scared. You can't be brave when you're scared."

I rack my brain for something to say. "You're wrong," I say

finally. "Being brave is being afraid but doing it anyway. That's what real bravery is. Like the book I gave you. You think those kids weren't scared? Of course they were, but they didn't let it beat them."

Kiera seems to consider my words for a moment. She wipes her eyes with her fists. I think about what Emir said, about how the Grimm is an extension of our personalities. Keira has a strange ability to make other people feel joy. It's so harmless that I wonder how anyone could ever justify locking her up in a facility. Is spreading joy really something that needs to be cured?

"Besides," I say softly. "Look around. Do you really think Matron and her guardians are a match for *us*?"

Keira's eyes flicker around the clearing where the other kids are still practicing their abilities. As if on cue the ground begins to rumble and an enormous boulder breaks through the earth. Arthur swings his arms upward and the rock, at least double his size, rises up into the sky. He sends it careering back down again, where it lands with an enormous thump and cracks in two.

"See?" I say to Keira. "Just imagine that coming down on top of Matron and squashing her flat."

Keira gives a little giggle and I pat her shoulder and smile back at her.

"Want to practice with me?" asks Meera over my shoulder.

Keira nods and pushes herself to her feet.

"Thank you," I mouth at Meera. She nods back at me, the same serious expression on her face as always.

"That was well done," says a voice behind me. Emir's voice, I realize, and my heart fast-forwards for a moment, suddenly skittish as an animal. Immediately, I feel annoyed at myself. "Can you please not do that?" I snap.

"Do what?"

"Sneak up on me. And I don't need your praise." I walk off, back toward the fire.

I hear footsteps on frost and I can feel him behind me again. "I think we should talk," says Emir.

I scrunch up my face. Is he joking? I turn to face him and immediately regret it. He's not wearing his mask and our eyes meet. He is absurdly good-looking in a way that's almost annoying. My stomach twists.

"I don't want to talk to you," I say. Anger burns, not so much at him but at myself. My body's reaction to his presence is infuriating, the way my heart beats faster and my stomach squeezes. It seems that for some reason, despite how I'm changing, Emir can still get under my skin. "I hate you," I add, and immediately feel annoyed at myself again as I realize how childish and vulnerable that little phrase makes me sound. Hating someone just makes it clear that you still think about them.

Emir slowly nods. "I get it. You hate me, and after the way I've treated you, I deserve that. But I need to at least try to explain some things to you."

I shake my head.

"Please, Emily." His face, which seems to be fixed into a permanently wooden expression recently, suddenly animates. His eyes turn soft and brows tilt up. His hands half reach out toward me.

I am taken aback. Is Emir really pleading with me? I look at him properly. He looks almost miserable.

I bite my lip. I know I should say no. I know that Adanya is right; Emir is incapable of trust or love or being even remotely close to another human. But I've never seen Emir look vulnerable like this before, and apart from anything else, I'm curious. Curious to learn something about this boy, who seems to have walls of steel and spikes surrounding his head and his heart.

Fine. I'll listen to him, but that doesn't mean I have to be nice about it. "You get one minute of my time, and not a second more," I say. I fold my arms and curl my lip, mimicking Emir's own look—the same one that made me feel so small when I first met him.

"Fair enough," he says, then he spins on one foot and turns and walks away from the fire. He disappears into the shadows of the trees at the edge of the clearing. I follow him and we face each other. Ready to talk, or fight, I'm not sure which.

I tilt my chin, unapologetic. "Okay, one minute," I say. "Go."

"I just wanted to say . . ." He looks pained for a moment. "That I'm sorry."

I wait, but he doesn't elaborate. "Is that it? Is that really all you have to say?"

"No," he says.

"What are you even sorry for?"

He lets out a long breath and his lungs deflate. He looks vulnerable again, somehow smaller and more frail than usual. "For everything. I'm sorry for everything. I acted like an asshole when I first met you. And then again after what happened at Ashbury and what happened in the library. You said yesterday that I made you feel bad about yourself. That was never my intention, and I can't begin to tell you how much those words have tortured me. Because the truth is that I would never want you to feel bad, not about your-self, and not about anything else," he says.

"Why?"

"Are you really going to make me say it out loud?"

I don't reply, I just look at him, as cold and blank as he's been to me.

"Fine. You asked me once why I hate you, but the truth is that I don't hate you at all. Actually, it's the total opposite."

"The opposite of what?"

"I like you, Emily," Emir says, pushing his hair back and looking exasperated. "Isn't it obvious?"

My stomach twists again. Even though Adanya said as much, I am still shocked by his admission. *I like you, Emily.* I forget my cold look and instead my mouth gapes open.

"Don't look so surprised," he says, a faint smile tilting his lips.

"No," I say eventually. "It's not obvious. You're either glaring at me like you despise me or smirking at me and making me feel stu-pid. You barely speak to me. You push me away. You voted against me joining the Cure and tried to turn everyone else against me. Is that how you show somebody you like them?"

He nods. "I know, and like I said before, I am sorry for all that. But all that stuff, I was just trying to protect you."

Gabriel's words after he'd watched me put one guardian to sleep after another ring in my head. *You are terrifying.* I shake my head and laugh. "From what? What could you possibly be protecting me from?"

"From us. From this." He nods back toward the flickering

clearing, still alive with the others' chatter and sounds of them practicing their abilities. He looks down at the ground. "From me, mostly." He pauses for a long moment, takes a deep breath, and releases it in a slow exhale. "It's only that I could never be with you like that, not in a way that's more than just friends, not now and not ever."

I shake my head. "So you like me but you can't ever be with me?"

Emir puts his head in his hands. "You don't understand."

"You're right. I don't."

"I will never be able to be a normal person in that way and it wouldn't be fair to you. I can't touch anyone . . . you, or anyone else."

"We've touched before," I point out.

He gives me a faint smile and shakes his head. "Only in your dreams, Emily."

"Not just in our dreams," I say. I still remember the surge of heat that cascaded through me when I touched his wrist in the library. It was electric, but not in a bad way.

He shakes his head. "I can't. I can't trust myself."

"You can." I point back to the clearing. "Isn't everyone else proof of that?"

He pulls off his gloves and throws them to the ground. He looks angry now. His eyes are black and shadowed and his whole body is tense. "You don't understand." As his hands start to crackle, he takes several steps back, farther into the trees. "Stay there," he warns. Electricity runs up his arms, over his shoulders, and then over his whole body.

"Emir, what are you doing?"

He reaches out and touches a tree. Bolts of light leave his

fingers and lick around the trunk. There is a noise that splits my head in two, and the tree splinters and cracks. And a moment later, flames. Flames of white and blue that lick up, up into the night.

We watch as it burns. Until eventually, there is nothing left. Just a black husk and the odd charred branch lying on the ground. The smell of charred wood stings the back of my throat.

Emir walks out from the trees until he's standing in front of me once more. "That's why, Emily. That's why you can't touch me. I'm dangerous, and the people who get close to me, they die."

"What do you mean they die?"

"I told you before that I hurt somebody, but I didn't tell you the whole story." Emir shakes his head as if he's trying to rid himself of the memory. "My older brother was walking me home from school. I was much younger than him and he always used to make me hold his hand when we crossed the road. A car came out of nowhere." Emir pauses. The muscles in his jaw clench.

"Did it hit you?"

Emir shakes his head. "No. But it didn't matter. The fear I felt watching as the car came toward me . . . The sound of the brakes— and the horn was so loud." He pauses and visibly swallows. "The Grimm burst out of me. I'd been trying to hide it, you see, and I'd bottled it up and bottled it up some more until finally it just came out. All it took was a little bit of fear."

I nod slowly. I feel sick looking at the expression on Emir's face. I know what he's going to say next.

"I was holding my brother's hand. He didn't survive the jolt of electricity." Emir looks down at his hands, his eyes wide. I also look down and see shadows there, pooling in his palms like blood. "I killed him," he says. "I killed him."

All I want to do is reach out to him then. I want to take his hands and tell him it wasn't his fault, but I can't.

No wonder he can't touch anyone. No wonder he can't be close to someone. No wonder he doesn't trust anyone when he can't even trust himself.

Emir killed his own brother, and I don't even know if it's possible to move on from something like that. I feel helpless to my bones. Emir is always telling us that we're not dangerous, but he doesn't believe the same about himself. And besides, if his past is anything to go by, perhaps he's right. Amelia ended up with a broken arm, but what about the next time something like that happened? Would it have gone further? Would she have died like Emir's brother? I think about Isaiah, who blew up his parents' house, and how many more kids like us have the same sad stories. I have to admit that on some level the rest of the world is right . . . we are dangerous.

A little voice speaks in the back of my head. *But so are they.*

"It wasn't your fault," I say. "Just because we aren't taught how to control our abilities doesn't mean we're a threat. The government should guide and help children like us, not lock us up and treat us like criminals. And what we've been doing over the last few weeks proves it. They're scared of us. Too scared to face us and let us into the world we all share. The world is changing, and they refuse to accept it. They're cowards."

I watch his dark eyes absorb my words. There's a glint in his eye that I haven't seen before.

Hope.

—

Back in the clearing, everyone has now grown tired of exploring their abilities and instead stand huddled in groups around the fire. They chat and laugh. They tease each other. They almost look happy.

I don't join in and instead I sit to one side, near enough to the fire to not be cold, but far away enough from everyone that they don't talk to me. I'm exhausted. Pulling people from their dreams and holding them here takes energy. Energy that I barely have at the moment.

My eyes sneak to Emir. He stands with Jessica and Aisling and Tom, the boy who can travel through time.

Emir is laughing with them, but I can tell by his folded arms and the way his eyes flit around that he's not really listening.

I sigh and stare at the fire. The flames are hypnotic, and I start to see pictures hidden in the coals, castles with flickering turrets and lions with manes of red and hands with burning fingers. I yawn and everyone's dream bodies flicker. I can feel their actual bodies calling them back, tugging on my consciousness.

I stand up, about to call for everyone's attention and put an end to the night. But before I can so much as open my mouth, Tom runs into the clearing. Or I should say, future Tom, as his present self is still standing by the fire. He's dressed in nothing but a medical gown that swings around his ankles and his eyes are wild. "You need . . . to run!" he yells, barely getting his words out around his heavy breathing. "They're coming," he says, then he disappears.

I jump to my feet. Immediately, I let go of those I've summoned in their dreams. Their bodies flicker for a split second before disappearing. I feel them travel along the tethers I've created and back to their real bodies, still asleep in their dorms.

"Into the woods," yells Emir.

But before we can go anywhere, figures emerge from the shadows. Guardians. There are at least thirty of them and we're surrounded from all angles. In their hands are guns, and they're pointed right at us.

I see out of the corner of my eye Margie taking hold of Clementine's and Sarah's arms and pulling them into the trees. One of the guardians shouts and shoots his gun at the now-empty space. He makes a move to follow them but Adanya runs toward him. She rips off her mask, throws back her head, and shrieks. We clap our hands to our ears as her banshee scream fills the night.

The guardian who shot at Margie and the others falls to his knees first, followed by the other guardians nearest to her, who collapse on the ground. Their faces twist in pain and their screams join Adanya's. I've never seen fully what Adanya could do before, and it's terrifying, but also incredible. She is a mistress of pain.

"Her first!" yells somebody.

A guardian walks over and hits her in the stomach with the butt of his gun. She falls to the ground, suddenly hunched over on her hands and knees. "Stop whatever you're doing before I show you what real pain is," he says, stamping on her hand with his big boot and grinding it into the ground.

Adanya's wail chokes in her throat, becoming a moan, and a second later the guardians stop screaming. Whimpering, they pull themselves back to their feet. They retrain their guns, eyes wide and hands shaking.

I consider our options for a moment, and quickly realize that we have none. There are less than twenty of us left and we're heavily outnumbered. I can hear the fear in the guardians' voices and see their fingers closing on the triggers. It wouldn't take much for them to shoot, just like with Jakab. And if we choose to fight and flee, we'll have no place to run to. "Don't retaliate," I say, putting my hands slowly into the air and looking around at everyone. They look back at me and I nod at them, trying to make my face as reassuring as possible. "Everything's fine," I add, even though, clearly, it's not.

"Move out of the way," snaps a voice.

The guardians part and Matron strides into the firelight. At her heels follows Monika from my dorm. She's pinned her prefect badge to the front of her coat. The red *P* gleams in the firelight, as if it's burning.

"Are these the ones?" asks Matron.

Monika nods. "This is them. Just like Jessica said."

Just like Jessica said. The words sink in.

I turn and look at Jessica. We all do. She looks at the ground miserably for a moment. Then she walks ever so slowly across the clearing. She comes to a halt next to Monika, her eyes fixed resolutely on the ground.

"Thank you, girls," says Matron. "You will be rewarded for your hard work."

"Traitor," hisses Aisling.

"You'll pay for this," says somebody else.

"Shut your mouths, you filthy grimmers, or we'll shoot you all on the spot," says one of the guardians.

"You're going to shoot all of us?" a voice shouts out.

"Quiet!" yells Matron. She scowls around at us all, training her eyes on each one of us in turn. Fury contorts her face. "How dare you all," she says, in little more than a whisper. "Your punishment for this will exceed everything you've ever known. You will be screaming in pain by the time I've finished with you. Round them up."

They round us up and strip us of our coats and boots, checking them for weapons before throwing them in a pile. Her eyes gleam in the lights from the house, and I get the strangest feeling that she's enjoying herself.

"Now," she says. "Where are the ringleaders of your little gang? Step forward now and perhaps we'll let the rest go."

Nobody moves or speaks.

Matron gives a slow smile and I get the feeling she was hoping we wouldn't say anything. "Fine. Who shall we punish first, then?" Her eyes travel down the line until they find Keira. She stands out, partly because of how tiny she is and partly because of the sobs that are racking her body.

"That one," says Matron, pointing.

Guardians step forward and pull Keira out of line. She tilts her chin up, and I can see defiance there, despite her tears.

"Fingers first," says Matron with a smile.

I step forward, but it's already too late. The guardian reaches out and with one quick twist, breaks the pinkie finger of her left hand. That tiny snap of bone is the loudest thing I've ever heard. Keira screams.

"Me," I say. "I'm the leader."

A split second later and Emir steps forward. "And me," he says.

I look at Gabriel, half expecting him to come forward as well, but he doesn't. Instead, he winks and gives me a sly smile. His body shimmers. Figures appear from nowhere, Gabriel's blond head and skinny frame and sly smile replicated over and over again.

The fake Gabriels swarm the guardian holding him, like ants submerging a crumb. We can't see him but we hear a shout followed by gunshots. A moment later and all the Gabriels are running, scattering into the woods.

"Don't just stand there, shoot them!" yells Matron.

The guardians, who up until that point had just been staring, their faces a mixture of horror and confusion, snap into action. They turn their guns and shoot at the Gabriels as they disappear into the woods. But it's already too late, and the last thing we hear is the sound of all the Gabriels laughing, chuckles echoing eerily through the woods.

The gunshots stop and for a moment all of us stand there, stunned, guardians and kids alike.

Matron throws up her hands. "Useless! What were you all waiting for? A written invitation?" She glares at the guardian who had hold of Gabriel.

"I tried to get him . . ."

"Forget it," says Matron, cutting him off and dismissing him with a turn of the shoulder. "Take these ones back and put them all into isolation," she says, gesturing around at everyone. Then she points to me and Emir. "Except these two. These ones I have special plans for."

Then they bind our hands and feet and all but drag us back into the woods. We stumble and shiver on the long walk back. The snow seeps through my socks, icy and painful at first, before turning my feet completely numb.

As we are herded back inside, snow begins to fall again. It settles on our shoulders and our hair and on our faces. It lands on my lips, winter's chilled kiss.

A cold like nothing I've ever felt before settles into my bones.

CHAPTER twenty-three

We are ushered, pushed, and prodded back into Wildsmoor. The guardians lead the other kids out of the entrance hall until eventually it's just me and Emir left. We are held tightly, two guardians each. Their fingers pinch under my arms, so tight I know there will be bruises.

Matron stands in front of us. She comes closer until she's near enough to touch and she stares at me with her ice eyes. I stare right back, refusing to give her the satisfaction of looking away.

"Such insolence. Such bravery. But don't worry, there's an isolation cell with your name on it. I could leave you in there to starve and nobody would notice."

I think about those blank four walls and feel a flash of panic, followed by anger. I'm so sick of being afraid. I try to struggle out of the guardians' grip but they hold on tightly. I feel moisture in my mouth and I spit. Saliva flies from my numb lips and lands on Matron's face.

The red patches on Matron's cheeks spread, covering her neck and forehead. She reaches out and grips me by the collar of my shirt. "You'll pay for that." She turns to one of the guardians. "She's out of control. Use the Taser, as high as it will go."

"No," says Emir. "She's not out of control."

"Do it," says Matron.

I look at the guardian and realize that it's the one I always think of as "the young one." His face is pale and his arms by his sides. "But she's detained," he says eventually, eyes flicking to the other guardians and back to Matron.

"Get out of the way, lad," says one of the others, pushing him to the side. "You're so green it's embarrassing." Then he pulls his Taser from his belt and points it in my direction.

"Don't!" shouts Emir.

There is a little pop and then it hits me. Every limb and muscle in my body seizes up. Bees swarm under my skin. Then comes the pain, like being hit with a sledgehammer. I want to scream but my jaw is locked up just as tight as the rest of me.

I'm on the floor. I see the toe of Matron's shoe, shiny and polished. She kicks me in my gut, once, twice, three times, too quick for me to take a breath. For a moment I am completely incapacitated, body curled up, no air, no control over my limbs.

Finally, I manage to take a tiny breath.

"I hope that was worth it," says Matron, looking down at me.

I remember what it felt like to be spat on. Humiliation and embarrassment and the feeling of being small, and if Matron feels even a fraction of that, then yes. Yes, it was worth it. I look up and try to say as much, but my words come out as nothing more than moans. This seems to please Matron and she smiles again, mistaking my defiance for compliance.

"Take them downstairs," says Matron. "I'll work out what to do with them tomorrow."

Arms yank me up from the floor. My head feels heavy and my chin lolls to my chest. I can feel wetness on my face. Maybe tears. Maybe drool.

We are taken through the school and down a narrow flight of

stairs I've never noticed before. At the bottom there is nothing but a dirty metal door. The guardian unlocks it, revealing a short flight of stairs that ends in nothing but darkness. He unlocks my handcuffs, then pushes me through. I stumble on the top step, legs collapsing underneath me, before tumbling down the rest of the stairs. My already hurting body screams even louder, each step that I roll over pounding at the inside of my skull.

Emir is thrown in beside me and is immediately on his feet again. "Hey!" he shouts. "You can't . . ."

But then the door is slammed shut and we are left in nothing but the pitch-black. I just lie where I am on the concrete floor, too tired and too cold to think beyond anything else. I hear Emir moving around the room. His footsteps walk from one side to the other, then around and around and around.

Eventually, my eyes adjust and I realize that we're not in total darkness after all. Tiny slivers of light escape from around the door frame, allowing in just enough light to see by. Just.

I pull myself into a sitting position and tug my knees to my chest for warmth. I look around, squinting through the gloom. We are in what I can only guess is an old basement. Other than Emir and me, the room is empty, nothing but stone walls and stone floor and silence.

I watch as Emir circles the perimeter of the room, running his hand over the walls.

"What are you doing?" I ask eventually.

"Looking for a way out," he replies.

"And?"

He shakes his head. "There's nothing here. The only way out is back through the door."

I nod, unsurprised. He comes over and crouches down beside me. "You're cold," he says.

I shake my head. "I'm fine," I say, shivering.

Emir pulls off his school blazer. "Here," he says, draping it around me.

"But then you'll get cold," I say.

Emir shakes his head. "I don't get cold, never have. Something to do with the electricity in my body, perhaps."

It's true that I can feel warmth radiating off him. "Useful," I say, pulling the blazer tight around me.

He says nothing and stands up again.

"What do we do now?" I ask.

Emir walks over to one of the walls and slides down until he's also sitting in a hunched position. He puts his head in his hands. "I guess we wait."

—

I hunch into a ball on the floor. I am exhausted, but despite this, I don't sleep. I grow colder, my wet clothing stealing any remaining warmth from my body. The night replays in my head, strange and jerky. I hear the snap of Keira's little finger. I feel the toe of Matron's boot. I see Margie and Clementine and Sarah disappear again and wonder what happened to them. I hope that they got to safety.

After a while, these thoughts begin to jumble and blur, the events distorting and rearranging themselves. Faces grow monsterlike teeth and hands grow claws. I hear Gabriel's laugh, over and over again.

I see Matron, but as a little girl. *Those are the rules*, she says, but in a child's voice, petulant and playful. I wonder what path her life must've taken to end up here, to take enjoyment from another person's pain, and I imagine what she's got in store for us tomorrow. For some reason, I start to laugh, soft giggles at first, before turning into a coarse, hacking laugh that sounds like a crow's cawing.

"What is it?" asks Emir, looking up from his hands.

My laughs turn into a weak, involuntary cough. Suddenly, the world seems fuzzy. I'm in a room with Emir, just me and him. "How did we get here?" I try to ask, but instead my words come out slurred and barely audible around my clacking teeth.

Emir stands up again and comes over to me. He crouches down and peers at me.

"You're not looking so good," he says.

The world blurs and his face twists for a moment in the darkness, sharp toothed and sneering. "Neither are you," I try to say. But again my words are barely decipherable, just a stuttering mess of syllables.

Emir ever so slowly pulls off his glove. Then he reaches out and touches my bare hand with his. I stare, surprised. He pulls his hand away again. "You're ice-cold," he says. "And clearly confused. How's your breathing?"

I think about this for a moment, registering the shallow rasp of my breath. I cough again. "Hard," I manage to say.

I watch as he takes off his school sweater, rolls it up, and puts it on the floor next to us. Then he gently pushes me back down so my head is cushioned by the sweater and I'm facing away from him. He lies down, his body curving around my own.

"What are you doing?" I ask.

"Getting you warm."

"But you can't touch anyone."

"If I don't, you'll die anyway. Hypothermia is serious."

After a minute or so, I start to feel the soft warmth of Emir's body penetrating through my clothes. It's only then that I start to realize just how cold I am. Bone cold. So cold that it's all I am. My body starts to shake, convulsions that rattle me from head to toe.

"You need to take your wet clothes off," Emir says. "I won't look."

I nod and sit up. I try to take off my clothes, but my hands are shaking too much and my fingers are still numb. Eventually, Emir has to help me. He pulls off my blazer and my wet socks. I wiggle my way out of my thermals until I'm wearing nothing but my old night shirt and Emir turns away. I would usually be embarrassed to be showing so much skin, but I'm so cold that I don't care. He hands me back his blazer and I wrap it around myself before lying back down on his sweater, him curved around me again. He's still being careful; although his body is pressed up against my own, he keeps his arms to himself. Again his warmth radiates off him.

I wiggle around to face him, desperate for more. I press my hands against his body, feeling the heat of his skin under his shirt. He hesitates for a moment, but then he pulls me to him. One of his arms slides under my neck and the other curves around my back and pulls me close.

For a long time we lie like this, our bodies clasped tight together. Finally, the shaking fits become less frequent and milder. My head clears and my breathing eases up. My toes and fingers feel stiff and painful. I clench and unclench them, grateful for the pain, which means blood is now traveling through my extremities again.

Suddenly, I am all too aware of how close we are. My head has settled into the crook of his arm. I could pull away, but I don't.

And nor does Emir. He lies perfectly still, his embrace still tight around me. The only movement is the rise and fall of his chest, tiny inhales and exhales.

"Why do you think she did it?" I ask eventually.

For a long moment Emir doesn't reply and I assume he's fallen asleep. My eyes are closing as well when he says, "Who?"

"Jessica."

Again he doesn't speak for a long moment. "Fear, most likely," he says eventually.

I scowl at his response. "We're all afraid. That's no excuse."

"You asked me why."

"You were right about Gabriel too," I say.

"Does it matter anymore who is right?"

"But you were," I murmur. "He planned this perfectly, the little snake. Taking a back seat so when the time came he could disappear and I would take the fall."

"Maybe," says Emir. "Who knows with Gabriel, really."

I think about how he encouraged me to take the lead. His encouraging looks and fake words. *You're amazing, Emily.* "He knew it would happen eventually. He used me."

Emir sighs. "Perhaps. But to be fair to him, I think he did like you, for what it's worth, in his own way."

"He liked my abilities, nothing more."

"Then he's a fool. There's so much more to you than the Grimm."

"Like what?" I ask.

"Are you fishing for compliments?"

I smile. "Perhaps. But I think you owe me them."

"When I first met you, you came into my dreams. You were beautiful and mysterious and like nobody I had ever met before."

"But that's not really me," I say.

"Let me finish. It *is* a part of you, and I can't help but admire that part, but you're right, you're also more than that. You're interesting and brave and you're always thinking of other people, like tonight with Keira. And sometimes you're even fun."

I snort with laughter. "Sometimes?"

He laughs too. "All right, maybe having fun is something we both need to work on a bit."

We both fall quiet for a moment. "What do you think they'll do to us?" Emir asks.

I shake my head. "I don't want to think about it."

"We have to. We should prepare ourselves."

"No," I say. "We don't have to."

"The morning will come, Emily, no matter what we do."

"I know, but for now, I just want to forget."

I have an idea. Slowly, I pull up his shirt and slide my hands onto his bare skin. He gasps but doesn't pull away. Our skin is touching. Like before, my skin reacts to his. Gentle shivers still travel through my body but now so does his electric heat, my nerves on fire where our skin is touching.

"How will this make us forget?" asks Emir.

"Like this," I say.

Then I tilt my head up, and he tilts his head down, and turns out I was wrong—kissing someone isn't difficult at all; instead, it's the easiest thing in the world. Our lips gently press and somehow my whole body comes alive. My head swims and my heart beat, beat, beats, sending my blood rushing through my body. He pulls me closer. His hands are in my hair. One of them grips into a fist and gently pulls and where he tugs every nerve ending comes alive. A pit of longing opens up in my stomach and grows and grows until I am nothing but need.

My hands are unbuttoning his shirt and his are unbuttoning mine, and now our bare torsos are pressed together. The heat from his bare skin floods through me. I feel a soft crackle of electricity and smile. "There's that control."

"I thought you hated me," he says, his lips moving softly against mine. I can hear laughter there and feel his lips curving into a smile.

I blush in the darkness, remembering how stupid I sounded. "Shut up," I reply. Then I kiss him again and run my hands down over his chest. He groans and kisses me back harder and now I'm the one smiling, enjoying this new sense of power.

I wanted to forget and for a while we do. Tomorrow, we will remember to feel pain and despair, but for now there is nothing but me and Emir and the heat between us. We have nothing else to lose, after all.

CHAPTER twenty-four

Although my body is getting some much-needed sleep, my consciousness is not. I sit by the door in my dream body, my back pressed up against the stone wall. My wolf is by my side. She snarls and I reach out a hand and bury my fingers in her long, wiry fur.

A Wildsmoor student always tells the truth.

A Wildsmoor student is seen and not heard.

A Wildsmoor student is always obedient.

With nothing else to do, I recount the Wildsmoor school rules over and over again. I don't know why, but it helps me focus. These laws have shaped my whole life since I was eight years old. But as Clementine says, *Rules are made to be broken.*

I just need to figure out which ones I need to break to get us out of here.

I run through options in my head. As far as I know, neither of us has lock picking skills or an ability to walk through walls. Even if I set out in my dream body, my real body and Emir would still be stuck here, not to mention the rest of the Cure in isolation. I can't think how Emir's electricity would work either.

I hear a noise at the door. The slide of a key in the lock. My wolf growls under my hand and I put a warning finger to my lips. A silhouetted figure comes down the steps.

"Hello?" whoever it is whispers. They're holding something. A weapon perhaps.

I wait until they're on the final step before swinging into action.

My wolf pounces, knocking whoever it is to the floor and pinning his chest to the ground with her enormous paws.

"Help!" he shouts.

"Shut up," I hiss. I walk quickly over to him. It's a guardian, the young one with the scar.

"Don't hurt me," he says. "I was only trying to help you." The thing he was carrying lies discarded on the floor. A thick school blanket, on top of which lie two energy bars and two bottles of water.

"You were bringing us blankets?" I ask. "And food?"

He nods.

"Why?"

He shakes his head. "I don't know. It's freezing down here. I just wanted to help."

I stare at him for a long moment, trying to figure out what his real agenda is. "I don't believe you," I say, but my eyes flicker to the discarded blanket again.

"What's happening?" Emir scrambles to his feet.

"He says he was bringing us supplies." I point to the scattered food and blankets.

"Why?"

"No idea."

"I didn't want you to die of cold down here," says the guardian. "I don't want to be responsible for that." He lifts a hand and rubs his scar, and once again I wonder how he got it. I realize that although his life has been free of the Grimm, it hasn't been free from pain.

Emir blows out a sharp breath between pursed lips. "Whatever. I see you brought your gun too." Emir points and I realize he's right. As well as the blankets and food and water, a gun also lies on the floor next to him. My wolf reacts, snarling in the guardian's face.

"Thanks for this," says Emir, reaching down to pick up the gun. He examines it for a moment, turning it this way and that. "It's heavier than I thought it would be." He points it at the guardian still pinned to the floor.

"Please," says the guardian, his words now quick with panic. "Please don't. I really was just planning on helping you. I have a family, a girlfriend . . ."

"Stop groveling. I'm not going to shoot you," cuts in Emir, disgust clear in his voice. "Although I'll probably regret not."

"Just give us the key," I say, nodding toward the door. I look at Emir. "We can just lock him in here. That'll give us a little while at least."

"I'll give you the key . . ." The guardian looks toward the door. "But just let me go first. If they find me here, they'll know I was trying to help you. I'll lose my job . . ."

"Do you really think I care if you *lose your job?*" Emir cuts him off.

"I could end up in prison. It's happened before to other guardians who've gone soft. It's against our code of conduct, you don't know what it's like for us . . . and my girlfriend, she's pregnant—"

"Key," I say again, holding out my hand. For some reason finding out about his pregnant girlfriend annoys me, the fact that he's been allowed to have a normal life, go to school, grow up, get a job, a girlfriend . . . "We didn't ask for your life story."

He falls silent for a moment. The light from the still-open door filters onto his face and there is nothing but pure misery etched across his features. He puts a hand in his pocket and pulls out a small ring, bursting with keys. He starts to unhook one.

"We'll take all of them," I say.

He nods and holds them out. Emir reaches down and takes them from him.

"Thanks," I say. Then I close my eyes, follow the tether to my real body, and wake up. I open my eyes again, resisting the urge to moan in pain as the injuries from the night flood back through my mind. Frostbitten toes. Stiff muscles and joints. Bruises on my arms and thighs. Grazes down my back.

I scramble to my feet. "Let's go," I say.

We go up the stairs, Emir still pointing the gun in the guardian's direction. "Please . . ." is the last thing I hear the guardian say.

I think of Jakab, and the red-faced one hitting Adanya, and how they tried to shoot Clementine and Margie and Gabriel. I don't want to feel bad for him. This man, or boy, or whatever he is, may not be the one pulling the trigger, but he still watches silently while the others do. How could the gesture of a simple blanket be enough to know whether someone is capable of being on the right side of things?

Emir is about to close and lock the door behind us when I stop it with my foot, leaving it ajar.

"If you really have any intent of helping us, you'll stay here for one hour. And my wolf will have no issue sniffing you out if you decide to run early."

The guardian nods gratefully.

We manage to somehow make it through the school and into the library without seeing a single guardian. "Where are they all?" I ask Emir.

"I don't know," says Emir, shaking his head. "Maybe with all the other kids, over in isolation."

"Maybe."

We make our way to the back of the room and down into the hidden book room. The familiar smell of old books and mold soothes me and I take a seat on the floor with my back against the wall.

"What now?" asks Emir, perching on a stack of hardbacks.

"We need to escape, tonight."

"You and me?"

I shake my head. "Everyone, same as before."

Emir looks at me and raises his eyebrows. "How?"

I shake my head. My mouth goes into a thin line.

A Wildsmoor student is obedient. A Wildsmoor student always tells the truth. A Wildsmoor student strives to get better.

"By breaking all the rules."

—

I put myself to sleep and then Emir. Emir is trickier to force into the realm of sleep, far harder than the on-duty guardians. They are already halfway there, the late nights and silence and sense of safety already pulling them over into unconsciousness.

Emir, on the other hand, is pumped full of adrenaline, his mind wired with the knowledge of what's to come. "You need to relax," I hiss at him.

"I'm trying," he snaps.

"You could just stay here, you know."

"No."

Eventually, I find a tight knot of something like exhaustion, buried deep in his mind. I unfurl the knot, letting the weariness take grip. Finally, Emir yawns. He slumps down to the floor, his head dropping onto his chest. I guide him to the ground, giving him a final nudge into sleep. After this, I summon his subconscious out of his body and finally he stands in front of me, lit with the same silvery glow as me. "Finally," I say. I give us both wings, mine furred and owl-like again, contrasting with Emir's leathery spiked ones.

Emir looks at his wings, bringing them around his body. He grins. "I missed these."

I roll my eyes. "Come on, we have work to do."

We squeeze through the tiny basement window and jump to the ground below. Above us, the night sky is covered with low-hanging clouds, lit gray by the lights that surround the facility. Thankfully, it's stopped snowing and there is only a thin coating of soft white on the ground. But we're not planning on walking anyway, too slow.

We fly over the woods, skimming above the snow-covered treetops. I expected the woods to be silent and empty, but they're not. Groups of guardians move among the trees, flashlights swinging left and right.

"What are they all doing?" Emir asks.

"Search party," I say grimly. "Looking for Gabriel and Margie, no doubt."

"Let's hope they don't find them before us."

"They won't," I reply. I feel again for the little flicker of dreams that I felt before. I alter my direction slightly, heading toward it.

We land on the very edge of the woods, just within the tree line. On the other side of the trees I can see a road, also coated in a thin layer of snow and only made clear by the tufts of grass poking through on either side. In the distance I can see a patch of glimmering lights that I guess must be Ashbury village. Somewhere not too far away I can hear the guardians, still bashing their way through the woods.

Emir looks around. "They're here?"

I nod.

I lead Emir through the woods until three fallen trees block our path, thick trunks crossing over one another.

"Look," says Emir, pointing to where two bicycles lie half-concealed in the undergrowth.

I nod. "Wait here," I say. I bend down and crawl my way under the trunks, following a roughly dug tunnel until I reach a tiny den, cocooned by the fallen trunks and branches and partly dug into the earth.

"There you are," I say.

Margie's pale and scared face stares back at me. She lets out a long breath, then puts her head in her hands. "Thank god," she says.

On one side of her are Clementine and Sarah. They sit with their backs pressed up against a trunk, dozing against each other and holding hands. On the other side of her is a fox. The fox hisses at me, a rasping vicious noise that warns me to stay away.

"Sorry, Mama," says Margie, reaching out and gently stroking the fox's back. "We'll leave you in peace with your babies soon."

It's only then that I realize the fox is curled around tiny, squirming bodies. The fox gives me one last hiss and turns back around. She licks each of her babies in turn, making them squeak.

"Only a few hours old. But mama fox was still kind enough to share her den with us."

Clementine's eyes open. "You're here," she says. "See," she says to Margie. "I knew she would find us."

Sarah also wakes up. She lifts her head off Clementine's shoulder and yawns. She looks at me and then around at the den. Finally, she sighs. "I was hoping this was all just a bad dream, but no such luck."

Clementine looks at her. "Just imagine how *they* feel," she says, irritation making her words snap.

Sarah holds up her hands. "Calm down. I understand. Margie is *my* sister, remember? You're always so testy when you're tired."

"Am not," grumbles Clementine. But then she flashes Sarah a smile and pecks her on the lips. I stare, realizing how stupid I was not to see it before, but they're clearly together in a way that's not just friendship. I realize that Clementine's motive for helping us might be as much for Sarah to liberate her sister as it is for me.

Clementine sees me staring and winks.

"What are you all doing here anyway?" I ask. "The woods are crawling with guardians, you know."

"We were waiting for you," says Clementine, turning to me.

"How did you know we'd even be able to break out? Let alone find you?"

Clementine shrugs. "I just did. I knew that you would find us and sort all this mess out."

"No pressure, I guess." I shake my head and can't help but laugh, hardly understanding the amount of belief they had in me. Although they're not wrong. I did find them.

"So what is the plan, then?" asks Margie, looking at me.

"We leave tonight. It's now or never."

Margie nods, looking completely unsurprised. "Where will we go?" she asks.

"For now we'll take Gabriel's advice. We'll head to the coast and try to figure it out from there. After that, we can split into smaller groups. Some of us can—"

"Oh god," says Clementine, cutting me off and putting her head in her hands.

We all turn to look at her.

"What is it?" asks Sarah.

"If my dad ever finds out he is going to kill me." She sighs and looks up. "I have somewhere we can go. It's not ideal, but it'll be a hell of a lot better than just some cave in the cliffs somewhere."

My heart does a little hopeful jump. Margie and I exchange a look, then turn back to Clementine. She's gnawing her lip as she looks back at me and there is a pained expression around her eyes that I've never seen before. I shake my head. "You don't have to . . ."

"I do," she says.

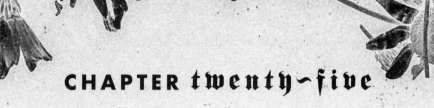

CHAPTER twenty-five

We don't bother flying back over the woods; instead, I just wake us both up, cutting the stretched tethers of our consciousness. As I wake, I am reminded once again of my injuries, my bones stiff and sore and flesh bruised like fruit. I stretch, moving my neck this way and that.

Next to me, Emir does the same, slowly standing upright and stretching his arms way above his head. "Here," he says, reaching out a gloved hand to me.

I look at his hand and feel an immediate reflex to refuse his help, even for something so small as this.

But why? something else in me asks. At some point, I am going to have to learn how to trust, how to rely on other people, and right now seems as good a time as any. Even if it is just an outstretched hand.

I reach out and accept Emir's hand and he pulls me up to my feet. For a moment, neither of us moves. The room is so quiet you could hear a pin drop. Our only spectators are stacks of books, watching on in a circle and filling the air with their woody scent.

Our eyes lock and I am suddenly thinking about what happened between us only a few hours before. We are standing so close that it would be easy to press my lips to his, only one step to close the gap between us.

But then Emir takes a step back and a moment later, so do I. My cheeks are hot and I resist the urge to press my hand against them.

Something is different now. I wonder if he regrets getting so close to me.

"Let's go," says Emir. "The last thing we need is Clementine and Sarah getting back before us."

I nod and take a deep breath, in and out. For a moment my head fills with a hundred different possibilities and outcomes, all of them bad. Things that could go wrong. Terrible stuff that could happen. Capture. Violence. Death, even.

"Are you ready?" asks Emir.

Finally, I nod. I parcel up all my negative thoughts and put them in a corner of my brain. "Ready."

Emir picks up the gun lying on the floor. He turns it over in his hands, examining the shiny black metal. He strokes a hand over the barrel, looking almost in awe.

"Do you even know how to use that?" I ask.

Emir shrugs. "Point and pull the trigger. How hard can it be?"

I nod, not convinced. "You should use the Grimm, if you need to. The gun is a last resort."

Emir frowns. Tiny lightning bolts weave around his fingers. Where they touch the metal of the gun, they crackle and spit. "I know," he says. He pockets the gun, turns, and walks off. I follow.

Together, we make our way out of the basement, back through the library, and into the main school. We move carefully, sneaking as quietly as possible through the shadows. Luckily, most of the guardians still seem to be out searching the woods and we don't see a single one until we reach the corridor where the isolation rooms are.

I pause outside a closed door. Through the frosted glass, I can see the outline of a head. Using my dream senses is easier when I'm asleep, but still I close my eyes and reach out. Immediately, I feel the overwhelming tiredness radiating from the guardian standing on the other side. A gray fog of sleep is already weaving through his thoughts, making him groggy. I smile and give him a tiny mental shove. He slumps to the ground, disappearing from view. Then his back pushes against the door and it swings open. He collapses in front of us, mouth already open and eyes shut.

"He's completely out," says Emir, staring down at him wide-eyed. "How long will he sleep like that for?"

I shrug. "It varies, but he was already exhausted, so I'm predicting a nice long while."

We step over him and onto the corridor. The corridor is more barren than any other at Wildsmoor. Instead of old carpet or wood, the floor is hard linoleum, and the walls have been stripped of any decor and painted a stark red. Blue lights shine at intervals, revealing metal doors with barred windows and numbers painted on each.

From my pocket I pull out the keys that we took from the young guardian. Again, as I look down at them I wonder why he decided to help us, and whether I was right in deciding to trust him.

"You keep a lookout?" I say to Emir. He nods, his face tense in the blue light. From his pocket, he reaches for the gun, but I shake my head. "If they see you with that, they'll just shoot you first, and unlike you, they have practice."

Emir frowns and for a moment I think he's going to argue with me, but then he nods and takes his hand back out of his pocket.

Luckily, the keys are clearly labeled and numbered. Isolation one. Isolation two. Isolation three. Room by room, I unlock each door, stuffed with three to four kids each. One by one, they look up when I open the door, faces full of fear at first, then surprise, then a flood of relief.

We all huddle together around the end of the corridor. Adanya's hand is bloody where the guardian stepped on it. Keira clutches her pinkie that someone has braced to her uninjured ring finger with a makeshift wrap. Meera. Aisling. Arthur. Isaiah. They all stare at me, waiting for orders. I give the Cure a garbled rundown of what's happening, leaving them to make their own choice if they want to come or not.

We're going to attempt to escape, tonight.

It won't be easy. It might all go wrong.

But it's up to you. If you want to come with us, then come; if not, stay.

Some of them linger in thought for longer than I would like. But eventually their heads nod in unison.

I am about to give instructions for our next step when it happens. Footsteps pound on the stairs, echoing down the corridor. The far door bursts open. All of us turn.

Guardians press into the hallway, guns raised. I look and realize that the guardian I sent to sleep is no longer on the floor. He must've raised the alarm.

"Stop!" yells one of them. "Don't move and hands in the air!"

The guardians hold their fire momentarily, as they take long strides toward us, approaching in a sure, measured way with their guns expertly pointed in our direction.

Emir softly pushes me toward the entrance with one hand while reaching for the gun from his pocket with the other. "Lead them out," he says.

"Don't be stupid," I hiss. "They'll shoot—"

I don't get to finish my sentence as at that moment a noise like thunder roars up the stairwell. The guardians halt their creeping approach. The door bursts open and laughter fills the air. Not just one person laughing, but many, hundreds of cackles bouncing off the walls and joining together to make one long, loud, hideous noise.

Through the open doors, Gabriel after Gabriel floods into the corridor, all of them laughing and their eyes lit with glee.

"What are you doing?" I yell at one of them.

"Saving your sorry behinds is what," he replies.

Emir shoves the group of us against the tide of figures and into the stairwell. The last thing I hear is gunshots, followed by more echoing laughter. Alarms begin to sound through the building. Not the usual fire alarm, but a long repetitive wailing that lets me know there's no going quietly anymore.

We come out onto the lower corridors where the dorms are. Doors open like a wave and children tumble out still in their night-clothes. Some of them Cure members and some of them not, but it doesn't matter; they all run alongside us as we leave the building.

As we burst out of the double doors and onto the gravel at the front of the school, I can see that the other members of the Cure are already fighting a small knot of guardians. Light and bangs and shouts fill the driveway. There is no sign of Clementine and Sarah, which means one thing: We are going to have to fight our way out.

CHAPTER twenty-six

We race over to where the fighting is happening, the remaining Cure members close on our heels. A deafening bang sounds from behind. We all turn just in time to see the windows of the dining hall explode. Shards of glass spray into the night sky, gleaming under the floodlights. We cover our heads as the fragments pitter-patter down around us like falling stars.

The Gabriel replicas clamber through the now-gaping windows, spilling out onto the driveway. There is a smaller figure among them—Arthur. They run toward us.

Arthur stops in front of us. Shards of glass cover his hair and clothes. Blood speckles his hands and face. "Where's Clementine?" he shouts.

I shake my head. "Not here yet," I reply.

"Well, *do something*! There's about a hundred guardians on our tail!"

But already it's too late, and a moment later, guardians are everywhere. They come from the broken windows and the doorways and from the grounds. They come at us without mercy. Ruthless. Efficient. They shoot their guns into the night.

I half expect the Cure to give up and surrender. To run or retreat. But they don't. Instead, they stand their ground.

The guardians have guns, but that's all they have, and we have something that they can only dream about, or at least have nightmares about. *The Grimm.* Our abilities.

Our *magic*.

We are not sick. We are not diseased. We are a powerful force to be reckoned with. And more than that, we're *desperate*.

The Cure members group together, then swarm outward again, choosing their targets. They scatter across the driveway, each of them engaging in their own fights. We fight like dogs who have been beaten their whole lives and have nothing else to lose. It's terrifying, but amazing.

Destiny and Angel, the fire and ice twins, send billows of flame and frost through the night. Arthur floats up into the sky and lands on the roof. He rips up slates and sends them peppering down on the guardians below. The Gabriel replicas dart in and around the fighting, causing confusion and blocking the guardians' view.

A whirlwind of screams and light steals my attention. Adanya and Emir, fighting side by side. Despite their differences, they are somehow seamless together. Adanya makes the guardians scream and fall to the ground and Emir comes in with his electricity, shocking them into unconsciousness. The night is alive with his crackling heat and spidering bolts of light.

I reach out to the guardians' minds, with an idea to try to send them to sleep. But I quickly realize that their minds are too awake, wired and full of adrenaline. I try again but the guardians don't so much as slow down.

"Get out of the way!" A hand tugs on my arm and I turn to see Isaiah. "You're no good standing there like a sitting duck." I let him pull me away from the fighting and back into the shadows of the house. The other kids, the younger ones and the ones who aren't members of the Cure, are also hanging back in the shadows. They crowd close to the entrance, looking on with wide, fearful eyes. Some of the younger ones are crying, shoulders shaking.

I can see teachers and other members of staff among them. They stand, open-mouthed, staring at the battle that's unfolding in front of the school. Mr. Peters is there, wearing nothing but a tartan dressing gown, as are Mrs. Ball, Mr. Caddy, and Miss Rabbit, also in their pajamas and gowns. But no Doctor Sylvie or Matron. I feel a bit disappointed. I *want* them to see. I want them to understand that everything they have created at Wildsmoor has come undone.

"No," says Isaiah. He takes a tiny step forward. I turn and follow his eyeline and my breath sticks in my throat. A guardian is advancing on Keira. She looks absurdly small next to his hulking frame. Suddenly, a smile spreads across his face. He looks confused for a moment, looking down at his hands. Then, still smiling, he lifts his gun.

"No!" I shout, taking a step forward.

A figure breaks away from the knot of watching children hanging by the entrance—Jessica, her braided hair flying behind her. She sprints toward them, holding out her hands and shouting something wordless. Wind sweeps into the clearing, howling and swirling, before gathering and focusing on Keira.

The guardian shoots his gun. Keira is blown from her feet, her body pirouetting in the air before slamming into the ground like an invisible fist slamming her to the floor. The guardian is also knocked off his feet, the gun flying from his hand.

I run over just as Keira pushes herself to her feet. I scan her tiny body. No blood. No obvious bullet wounds. The guardian missed. Relief floods through me.

Jessica reaches us at the same time. "Are you hurt?" she asks, her voice frantic and eyes fixed on Keira.

Keira shakes her head. "I'm fine."

I glare at Jessica. "Traitor," I hiss. I wave a hand around at the fighting. "This is your fault, you know."

"You don't understand. I had to give you up," she garbles back at me, her head twisting left and right, looking for other threats as the symphony of battle erupts around us.

I consider for the tiniest of seconds. There are so many things I want to say to her, but right now isn't the time. "Fight with us, then," I say. "You owe us that at least."

Jessica nods. She turns and holds her hands out and makes a long sweeping motion. Wind howls from all directions, across through the woods and over the rooftops and through the fence. I feel it bluster past as it seeks its targets. Then, just like before with Keira, all the guardians crash to the ground, as if slammed by some mighty hand.

"Good," I say.

The Cure members advance on the fallen guardians, making use of their sudden advantage.

A noise sounds from the woods at the back of the house. Margie bursts through the trees, finally back through the woods. But she's not alone. She runs toward us, accompanied by hundreds of animals. Birds javelin above her head. Mice and badgers and foxes swarm alongside her. There are even dogs and cats, hissing and barking alongside the rest.

The animals throw themselves into the fight. Buzzards swoop, snapping with their hooked beaks. The smaller birds flap around the guardians' heads, causing confusion. Animals bite their ankles and swipe with their paws.

I hear a gunshot and turn to see a guardian advancing on me. I freeze for a moment, panic flooding my body with an ice-cold feeling. Then Emir is there, electricity dancing from his fingertips. He turns to me and glares, furious. "Get back!" he yells.

I am embarrassed and annoyed, but I also realize he's right. I'm nothing but a hazard standing there, and the frustrating truth is that awake, I have nothing of real use to offer to the fight. I run back to where Isaiah is still looking on, hanging back in the shadows.

We watch silently for a while, for what feels like forever, although in reality only a minute or two could've passed. The fighting begins to slow, like a storm petering out. I look around, frowning. Something is wrong.

"It's not enough," says Isaiah. And with a horrible wrench in my gut, I realize he's right.

The Cure and the other kids are clearly growing tired. Adanya's banshee shriek is more of a wail. Emir's electricity is becoming flickers, rather than bolts. Arthur is still on the roof, but he's no longer sending boulders and slates around; instead, he's on his knees, his head drooping. Most of the Gabriel replicas have disappeared, leaving only a few darting in and among the fighting. The guardians have returned to their feet.

Realization slams into my heart like a fist. We're losing.

Adrenaline and desperation made us fierce, but now it becomes clear that in some ways we are still outmatched. The guardians are organized and trained in combat, whereas we are chaotic and amateurish, and it's obvious. Some of the bullets find their targets and kids drop to the ground.

Again I try to reach out with my dream senses, but it's no use. Adrenaline is still pumping through the guardians' bodies and they're about as far from sleep as a human mind could possibly be. Frustration stabs at me, little needles of pain that feel almost physical. I am helpless.

I turn to Isaiah. "What about . . ."

He shakes his head. "No," he cuts me off. "I couldn't. Nobody would survive if I was to give in to the Grimm."

Panic begins to sow its seed and some of the Cure members turn and try to run. Others raise their hands in submission and the guardians use Tasers to stun them before they're handcuffed and dragged to the side.

"No. No, no, no," I say out loud. I turn to Isaiah. "We're going to lose," I choke out.

He nods, his face contorted with grief.

The rest of the Cure are raising their hands. The gunshots stop. The animals that Margie had summoned run back into the night. An eerie quiet begins to fall.

A figure strides into view, emerging from the entrance. A fat, bustling figure.

Matron.

I choke on a sob that rises from my chest.

At Matron's command, the guardians are forcing the kids to their knees, telling them to put their hands on their heads. She drifts around, looking down at them all. She seems dissatisfied for some reason, as if looking for something that she can't find.

Then she looks up. She looks around, eyes skirting left and right. Somehow, I know she's looking for me. Our eyes meet and finally, she smiles.

She's striding across the gravel toward me. My eyes blur and all I can hear is the crunch of her boots.

She stops in front of me. "Emily Emerson, what are you doing hiding in the shadows? I guess you didn't fancy getting your hands dirty, did you? Standing here pulling the strings of your puppets," she says. "Although I already know you're a coward, I still remember all your screaming the night your father handed you over to us . . ."

My skin flashes hot. Finally, I look up and meet her eyes. There isn't a single remnant of the child she once was there; instead, there is nothing but an endless cold, and in the gleaming reflection of her pupils, I get a glimpse of the future. The unspeakable cruelties she would be permitted to commit now that we have stepped so far over the line. Fear explodes through my skull as if I've been struck with an ax. I don't even think about what I'm doing as I reach out through my dream senses and do the only thing I know how to do.

CHAPTER twenty-seven

Nightmares, that's what I'm looking for.

I close my eyes and sense the buzz of sleeping minds in the nearby village. Children asleep in their family homes, and all the girls at Ashbury in their dorms, unconscious minds drifting.

I find their bad dreams and without even thinking about what I'm doing, I pull. And I pull and I pull and I pull.

Terrifying manifestations of their deepest fears fill the driveway, stolen from sleeping heads. Hulking bodies loom up into the night. Slimy skin and spikes and bulbous faces with glowing eyes. Teeth and claws and growls.

And then there are the nightmares that don't have physical form, the ones that are somehow all the more scary for their subtlety. Feelings of unexplained terror. Shadows that hunt you through molasses. Noises that embody fear itself, a hundred times worse than nails being dragged across a blackboard.

I go farther. Past the village and to what I guess must be a nearby town. The sleepers of the town spread out like flowers in a field. I pluck their nightmares from their heads and bring them to me.

Part of me is shocked to find out that my abilities are far bigger and vaster than I could ever have guessed. But another part of me accepts that this makes sense, as if this other part of me knew what I was capable of all along. After all, I've been pulling humans from their dreams for weeks. Why shouldn't I be able to take control of what they dream about too?

By the time I've finished I've created what can only be described as an army. An army of nightmares.

And then, like well-trained dogs, I turn them all on Matron and her guardians.

They have no physical form, but the guardians don't know this. They stamp and roar and swipe at my instruction. They seed fear into their hearts and addle their minds with panic. The guardians scatter outward. Matron's rosy cheeks drain of their color, and for the first time ever, I see something like fear enter her eyes.

"Go on, then! Fight!" yells a voice. I turn to see Mr. Caddy hobble into the fray, dodging around the monsters that stamp across the gravel. It takes me a moment to realize that he's not talking to the guardians but to the kids. "On your feet!" he shouts.

The other members of the Cure do as he says and pick themselves up. Light and noise fills the driveway once more. Mr. Caddy continues to yell his encouragement, pulling the last kids to their feet.

Aisling puts her ability into action, animating the bodies of the dead guardians and forcing them to fight by her side. Their bodies jerk like puppets on strings despite their lifeless faces. The guardians' fear turns to terror. They begin to retreat.

"No," shrieks Matron, striding toward them. "Hold your ground."

I follow her across the driveway. It's time to finish what we started.

"Hey! Anita!" I yell.

Matron turns and looks at me. Her eyes narrow with fury. "Get her," she yells, pointing a stout finger in my direction. "She's their leader."

Guns turn on me and the few remaining guardians rally and try to come in my direction. I pull my nightmares to me, blocking their way.

Matron snatches a discarded gun from the ground and strides toward me until we're nose to nose and I can see the burst blood vessels in her red eyes. "Emily Emerson. You are nothing. You are nothing but a disgusting Grimm-ridden worm. You are nothing but a sick, stupid child. Stop all this now and maybe I'll let you live."

I breathe in her antiseptic scent and my skin flashes hot again. My breath hitches in my throat. I can't breathe. I suddenly feel the strain of the dreams. They want to return to their owners' heads. The monsters begin to flicker and fade.

But then Emir is by my side. "Emily," he says. "Don't listen to her. You're not sick or stupid. What a load of shit."

Matron raises her gun. She aims, but not at me, at Emir. Her finger closes on the trigger.

"No!" I scream. Anger flares hot and bright in me again. My nightmare monsters grow strong once more. My she-wolf bounds toward me, howling and snarling. Matron turns just in time to be knocked from her feet. My wolf throws back her head and howls.

Emir steps forward. He lifts his bare hands and electricity shoots from his fingers. Matron begins to convulse as the bolts of light make contact with her skin. Her body seizes up and the gun falls from her fingers. She shudders, her mouth fixed open in a silent scream as electricity runs over her body.

"This is for what you did to all of us. Numbed all of us into compliance. Put us in isolation. Tortured us," says Emir.

I watch horrified as she cooks alive. *The smell.* Like burning hair and roasting meat. There is a strange poetry to Matron's dying like this.

But then I look at Emir. His face is contorted, as if he is in pain. "No, don't," I say. "Don't kill her. You're not a killer."

I reach out toward him and the electricity flickers and dies. Matron is unconscious on the ground. Emir looks down at his hands, as if surprised by what he sees there.

The guardians begin to run, fleeing in every direction. The last guardian to run I recognize. It's the squashed-nose man. I watch as Adanya brings him down with her banshee wail. She strides up to him and pulls his own gun from his hand. I turn away and a split second later the last gunshot echoes through the night.

I let my nightmares go, sending them back to their dreamers' heads.

Quiet descends among us. Kids are scattered across the gravel, most of them still standing, but some of them sprawled on the ground. Bodies of guardians, injured or dead, also lie still at intervals. A little knot of younger children and those who didn't fight is still huddled by the gates. All the teachers have disappeared, no doubt wanting to save their own sorry skins.

Only Miss Rabbit remains. The youngest children are huddled up against her. She soothes them with shaking hands and whispered words.

Mr. Caddy is also still here but lying on the ground. I can tell by the splay of his limbs and the pool of blood that surrounds him that he's dead. I feel a strange sense of loss looking at his broken body. I knew nothing about this man, I realize. But I think I understand now why he kept those books all these years.

I see Gabriel standing stunned nearby. I march over to him. "Happy?" I seethe. "Is this what you wanted?" I gesture around at the devastation.

Gabriel looks at me, wide-eyed. Dried blood darkens his hair and flakes from his forehead. "I didn't cause this, Emily."

He's right, of course. But the realities of the fight are almost too much to bear. The screams and flashes and bangs, the toppling of bodies. "You wanted this," I say to him, pointing a shaking finger in his direction. "You wanted *this*."

A hand rests on my shoulder. "It's all right, Emily," says Emir. "It's over now."

A vehicle grumbles in the distance. We all turn to watch as headlights grow closer until the driveway is flooded with light. A bus chokes to a halt outside the facility gates. It's the same bus I used to see parked outside during socialization classes. The same bus Emir and I saw when we broke into Clementine's school all those weeks ago.

Across the side of the bus are looping letters: ASHBURY ACADEMY FOR YOUNG LADIES.

"Arthur," I shout. "The gates!"

He nods and throws out his hands. The gates bend in on themselves. Metal crumples and tears and screeches, before flying several yards into the air. Kids scatter as they land again. The twisted metal bounces on the gravel before falling still. The bus stutters to life again and rolls through the now-gateless driveway. It pulls to a stop in front of us. The bus makes a hissing noise and the door swings open. A moment later a figure jumps down the stairs, before stepping into the glare of the headlights. Clementine. Finally.

Sarah clambers off the bus and Margie rushes forward to hug her sister. I also stride over and wrap my arms tightly around Clementine's shoulders. "Thank you," I manage to choke out.

Clementine pushes me away and looks over at Sarah. "Sorry it took us so long to get here. We had a few . . . motoring difficulties."

Sarah pulls away from her sister, looks over, and frowns. "Give me a break, I've only just passed my test." She looks at the bus. "And that's for a car, not this monster."

I nod and try not to show any doubt on my face, but I know that this really isn't the most ideal getaway. A seventeen-year-old driving a bus full of kids in the snow . . . What could go wrong?

CHAPTER twenty-eight

Clementine and Sarah fall silent as they look around at the devastation. Most of Wildsmoor's windows are smashed and the roof ripped up. Bodies are dotted around in front of the house, crumpled and left in pools of blood. More devastation surrounds them, roof tiles and scorch marks and holes in the ground.

"Are they . . ." Clementine trails off as she looks at where two bodies lie crumpled nearby.

"Dead," I say.

Clementine's face completely drains of color and she puts a hand to her mouth. I hear the screams and gunshots again. I see the terror of the dying. It threatens to overwhelm me. But I can't let it, not yet. We're not safe yet.

The Cure members who are still standing have gathered in front of the headlights. They look toward us with weary eyes, clothing ripped and bloody, exhaustion clear in their slumped shoulders.

"What do we do?" asks Aisling, looking around at the devastation, then back at me. There is anger in her eyes, and I understand; we have all risked our lives tonight, and some people gave them entirely. I can only hope that the price is worth it.

I feel the burden of other people's lives settle heavily on my shoulders, both those who are still hoping to make it out and those who didn't survive. It's so heavy, it's almost crushing. But then Isaiah puts a hand on my shoulder. "We offer the chance for everyone to come with us," he says in his soft, soothing voice. Everyone turns to him and I feel some of the crushing weight lift off me. "They can make the decision if they want to or not."

With the other members of the Cure, we round up all the kids we can find and herd them onto the bus. Some are injured and need to be helped on. The ones that are dead, we leave their bodies where they lie.

The fire and ice twins, Destiny and Angel, are two of them. Their bodies lie next to each other, mirror images, even in death. I choke back a sob as I force myself to look at each of them, committing their faces to memory. I don't want to ever forget the sacrifice they've made for us.

Finally, I go over to the knot of children still huddled by the entrance with Miss Rabbit. Her usually scraped-back hair hangs loose around her shoulders and she's wearing a set of pink pajamas with flowers on them. She looks so *young*. "It's not too late, Emily," she says in a tiny voice that is almost a whisper. "Think about what you're doing."

I shake my head and look around at the other kids. Mostly younger kids, but a few older, many of Matron's prefects included. "We're leaving," I say, making my voice sound sure and in control. "Anyone who wants to join us can. But we're going now, so make your decision quickly."

Most of the kids shrink backward, shaking their heads and remaining mute. I can see horror in their eyes, no doubt from watching the fight that just happened. I sigh, understanding that what they've just seen might not portray us in the best possible light.

"Where are you even going?" Monika asks. She's still wearing her red badge.

"Somewhere safe," I reply, loud enough for them all to hear. But the truth is that I don't know, and it terrifies me.

She considers me for a long moment, and in those few seconds, I think I see something like longing in her eyes, but then she shakes her head. "I don't believe you. There's nowhere safe for people like us."

Jessica hovers nearby, snow collecting on her bare head. Her arms are folded and she's staring at the ground.

"You can still come with us, if you like. They would forgive you in time. It might've all ended in a fight one way or another anyway," I say, feeling suddenly generous. "I know you were probably just afraid . . ."

"That wasn't it," she cuts me off in a low voice.

"Well, why did you do it, then?"

"It was the right thing to do." She looks back at me and all the doubt is gone from her face; instead, she is a picture of defiance, chin lifted and arms folded.

I stare, surprised at her answer. "But you just fought with us?"

She shakes her head. "I tried to stop people from dying, but I didn't fight *with* you."

"I don't understand."

"Don't you see? You all used the Grimm as weapons tonight, and people died because of it. Everyone else is right, we *are* dangerous. You can't deny that."

"It's not that simple."

She nods her head. "It's the truth. I made up my mind after what happened with Jakab. Wherever you go, people will get hurt. You can't escape the Grimm, no matter how far you run."

"Nor do I plan to."

My eyes fall back on Wildsmoor. There is a lone figure watching from one of the upstairs windows. Doctor Sylvie? It's too dark to tell, but its roughly where her office window would be. I wonder what she thinks of all this. I imagine her eyes wide with fear as she watches, and suddenly I smile.

I am the Grimm and the Grimm is me.

We did use the Grimm to kill tonight. We ended the lives of people that really we know nothing about. Just as the guardians used their guns to kill us, ending the lives of grimmers they failed to try to understand. We're all capable of being dangerous. And we're going to need to be dangerous if we're going to survive what lies ahead of us. The world belongs to grimmers too, and everyone else will have to find a way to learn to live among us.

"Coward," I say to Jessica, then I turn away from her, leaving her standing there, snow gathering across her head and shoulders.

In the end, only three come forward. A younger boy with a defiant tilt to his chin, and two older, both of whom I recognize but don't know by name. There is hesitation in their eyes, and fear, but they come and stand next to me regardless.

"No," says Miss Rabbit. "Stay with me. We'll look after you."

I hold up a hand. "Be quiet," I say.

She looks at me. "I just want to help, that's all."

I look at her in disgust. "I have a feeling you've been telling yourself that what you're doing is *helping* for a long time. But I think you know that's not true."

Miss Rabbit's lower lip quivers. "We're not all bad, you know."

I look at her for a long moment. "Maybe you don't mean to be.

But you're definitely not good either." *And nor am I*, I add in my head, but I don't say that out loud.

I lead the three who've decided to come with us over to the bus. Already the others are clambering on board. It's begun to softly snow again, tiny little flakes that drift and swirl under the floodlights.

The original members of the Cure are the last to climb on. Gabriel, then Adanya, and then Margie. Until finally, apart from the huddle of kids staying behind and the bodies that still lie on the ground, the driveway is empty.

It's time to go.

I feel a hand in mine. Emir. I look down and to my surprise I realize that he isn't wearing his gloves. Our bare skin is touching.

"You're not afraid you'll lose control?" I ask in surprise.

He shakes his head and fixes me with a sideways smile. "No. After tonight, I don't think I'm afraid of anything anymore. Besides, some things are worth the risk."

He pulls me gently to one side of the door and suddenly we are steeped in shadow. For a moment, it's just us alone in the darkness. He bends down and his lips ever so softly brush mine.

And despite the fact that we haven't anywhere near escaped or gotten to where we need to go yet, for a tiny second I give myself over to the kiss. It's softer and sweeter than our kisses in the basement, which were born from desperation and the need to forget. Those kisses made my body ache, but this gentle grazing of our lips is better somehow. My head spins and my whole body feels light.

I pull away and our eyes meet and for once everything about

him is entirely open. Somehow, we've learned to trust each other. "We've won," he says.

"Something tells me this is only our first step."

Suddenly, I notice a lone figure still standing in the shadows to one side of the bus. I peer closer. "Isaiah, is that you?"

He walks out of the shadows, eyes fixed on me and Emir. "You need to get out of here," he says. "Before the police arrive."

"After you," I say to him, gesturing at the steps. But Isaiah shakes his head. I stare at him. "What's wrong?"

"I'm not coming with you," he says.

It takes a moment for his words to compute. "What? Why?"

"It's too risky. Without my medication, it's only so long that I can last . . ."

I shrug. "So learn to control it, like the rest of us."

"I can't," cuts in Isaiah, a bitter twist to his mouth.

"Don't be ridiculous . . ." Emir tries, holding his hands out to Isaiah.

"Go," he says. There is an angry edge to his voice that I haven't heard before. "Besides. Somebody should stay and help the others." He gestures toward Wildsmoor, where the remaining kids are retreating inside.

"We need to go, Emily," says Emir, tugging on my arm. "We've run out of time."

I pause for a moment longer, my insides churning. Isaiah lifts his chin and nods at me, his eyes hard with determination. Finally, I let Emir pull me onto the bus.

The bus chokes to life and makes a wide turn before rolling out of the gates.

"Where's Isaiah?" asks Adanya, suddenly behind me.

I shake my head. "He's not coming."

Adanya looks stricken. She stands up, but it's too late. Both of us look back at Wildsmoor out the window. Isaiah stands there, a last lone figure left in the darkness.

———

There aren't enough seats on the bus and the oldest among us sit on the floor. Nobody speaks, other than the odd murmur. Some of the younger kids sleep and I can feel their dreams on the periphery of my mind. But I barely notice the flickering dreams or subdued silence, as the whole drive I feel like I'm suffocating under waves of panic.

Every second I expect us to be stopped again. Every car that passes us makes my heart leap into my mouth. Every flashing light I assume are more guardians sent by the government to stop us.

Soft whimpers and sniffles join the rumble of the bus's engine, no doubt as the horror of what just happened sinks in. Across from me is Adanya, silent tears dribbling down her face. I wonder if she's thinking of Isaiah, left behind to whatever horrors the future has in store for the remaining Wildsmoor kids. I try to feel for my own tears, but my eyes are dry as a bone.

I push myself up off the floor and make my way to the front of the bus, stepping over sleeping bodies. Sarah is driving, her hands white-knuckled around the steering wheel and staring fixedly at the road. Clementine is next to her.

"How much longer?" I ask.

"Not long," replies Clementine. "We're close now."

I nod and look out the front windshield. The sun is just rising, a ball of red that glares over the fields. Turns out I needn't have worried about the snow. As soon as we left the moorland and descended into lower ground, it all but disappeared. There is the odd patch, clinging to the tops of barns or the roadside, but not much.

"How are you holding up?" asks Clementine, turning to look at me. Her face is drawn and serious in a way that I've never seen before, and I feel a flash of guilt that the look on her face is my fault. She thought she was signing up for an exciting adventure, and instead she got a horror movie of death and despair.

"I'm all right," I reply. Because what else can I say?

We turn into a country road and keep going. The road narrows and widens, sometimes big enough for two cars and sometimes only one. Luckily, it's still early, and a Sunday not a weekday, so the roads are quiet. The few cars that we do meet squeeze past us and keep driving, the drivers concerned with going about their own day, and not what a bus full of kids is doing driving through the countryside so early in the morning.

We ascend a steep hill shrouded by trees. Sarah manipulates the gearstick and the bus slows, groaning under its full load as it creeps upward. At the top of the hill the landscape suddenly opens out beneath us.

I gasp as I catch my first glimpse of the ocean. It gleams under the rising sun and it looks so big that I feel like it might swallow us up.

Clementine looks back at me. "Have you never seen the ocean before?" she asks.

I shake my head. "Not since I was a little girl, and I can hardly remember it."

I'm not the only one. The bus wakes up, filling with murmurs and everyone peering out the windows. One of the younger kids shouts, "The sea!" And for the first time since we left Wildsmoor, the panic and despair lift slightly. There is so much innocent glee in that voice, and it reminds me that we're doing all this for a reason.

We continue down the road until we enter a tiny village right on the edge of the water, so small that it's nothing but a couple of cobbled streets, a pub, and a few granite cottages looking out over the water.

The bus falls quiet once more and I can feel the others around me falling into unconsciousness. I walk back up the aisle and sit down on the floor next to Emir who dozes with his head against a seat. I put my head on his shoulder and close my eyes. Finally, I relax.

A strange peacefulness holds us in its grip and with nothing else to distract me, I turn inward, feeling the Grimm stretch and flex inside my body. Since I called all those nightmares to me during the fight, I can feel that my abilities have changed. Freed from the prison of my own doubt and shame, they're like an extra muscle, strong, powerful, and eager to be used, completely in contrast to my broken and beaten body.

An idea strikes me.

I give in to the Grimm, letting my senses unfurl. I ignore the dreams of those nearby and instead reach far, far into the distance. I struggled to go so far before, but now it's easy. I imagine my mind like a lightning bolt, zigzagging through the realm of unconsciousness, letting it find its own way.

Dreams flow past like a river, until finally, I'm there.

I fall into the dream. I'm up high on a mountainside. A blizzard batters the steep terrain, blinding swirls of white. A girl climbs toward me with nothing but her bare hands. Her curled hair is scraped back and cheeks chapped and red. There's a determined look in her eyes.

I calm the blizzard until it's nothing more than soft specks of white falling gently around us. I gentle the terrain until she's no longer climbing upward but walking on a clear path toward me.

The girl pauses. "Hello?" she says.

The snow lies thick around us, but far below the landscape turns to a rolling green, a lush valley where silver water snakes toward the ocean. I wonder if this is somewhere she's already been, or somewhere she wishes to go.

I didn't think it would be possible. But I've done it. Somehow, I've found her. "Amelia," I say.

The girl walks closer. She peers into my face. "Emily?"

I nod my head. "It's me."

"It's really you," she says. And then she closes the gap between us and grips me by my shoulders and smiles. She's older, puppy fat gone, leaving high cheekbones and an oval shaped face in its place. But her freckles are just the same and in her eyes I see the same things that are in mine, disbelief and wonder and hope.

I swallow. "I found you," I say. Then the tears that escaped me on the bus finally come. "We made it," I say. "We're safe. We made it."

ACKNOWLEDGMENTS

First and foremost, I owe thanks to the person who contributed to the story's inception: my sister, Hannah. It was a conversation about superheroes that sparked a cascade of ideas and "what ifs" that eventually borne *A Better Nightmare* into existence. Thank you for the conversation and for schooling me in what *OP* means in the world of superheroes and gaming (it means "OverPowered" for those also wondering).

Thank you to my beta readers, Izzy and Sophie, who were the very first people to read this book and who took the time to give me their thoughts and feedback. You guys are fabulous beta readers and even more fabulous sisters-in-law.

Thank you to my agent, Elizabeth, who read *A Better Nightmare* so quickly and whose enthusiasm for the story and encouragement meant so much. Thank you also to Natalie, Dianne, and everyone else at Northbank Talent for your support.

Thank you to my UK team at Chicken House. Barry and Rachel, thank you for your words of wisdom, enthusiasm, and input—I'm very proud to be a "chicken." Also, thank you to Laura, Rachel H., and everyone else for your input and hard work.

I would like to express my deepest appreciation to my editor across the Atlantic, Sam. Your tireless involvement really has shaped the book into something far better than I could ever have imagined. Thank you for your emails and comments, and for not being even the slightest bit annoyed when I presented you with a swollen, rambling manuscript on our round of second edits. You knew exactly what to do with it and where the story should be focused, so for that, thank you.

Thanks also to my mum, dad, brothers, and other family members for your support. Last of all, thanks to my husband, Aaron, who for years has been asking "where is my book?" and now I can finally say: IT'S HERE.

ABOUT THE AUTHOR

Megan Freeman writes young adult fiction and loves all things magic and mythology. She juggles writing with her day job working for a children's mental health charity, promoting well-being through surf therapy. Megan hails from the far west of Cornwall, and when she's not working or writing, she loves tramping around the moorland and swimming or surfing in the sea.